Wood Co Library
251 N. M ain
Bowling G , OH 43402

04/08/2015

The Thunder of Giants

The Thunder of Giants

JOEL FISHBANE

ST. MARTIN'S PRESS

NEW YORK

This is a work of fiction. All of the characters, organizations, and events portrayed in this novel are either products of the author's imagination or are used fictitiously.

THE THUNDER OF GIANTS. Copyright © 2015 by Joel Fishbane. All rights reserved. Printed in the United States of America. For information, address St. Martin's Press, 175 Fifth Avenue, New York, N.Y. 10010.

www.stmartins.com

The Library of Congress Cataloging-in-Publication Data is available upon request.

ISBN 978-1-250-05084-7 (hardcover)
ISBN 978-1-4668-5180-1 (e-book)

St. Martin's Press books may be purchased for educational, business, or promotional use. For information on bulk purchases, please contact the Macmillan Corporate and Premium Sales Department at 1-800-221-7945, extension 5442, or write to specialmarkets@macmillan.com.

First Edition: April 2015

10 9 8 7 6 5 4 3 2 1

Contents

The Thunder of Giants

The Real Thing

IT WAS RUTHERFORD who discovered her, Rutherford the Thin, Rutherford the Sallow, Rutherford the man whose unhappy face bore the ravages of his life. He was forty-six, had wire-rim glasses, and wore his great failures like a scar. Rutherford Simone, who had been too small to fight in the war. Who had lost the film rights to the Dionne quintuplets to Twentieth Century Fox. Who had never given his wife a child. Rutherford the Unfortunate.

He worked for his wife's brother, a Hollywood producer who had exiled him to the rest of America until he could find the Next Great Thing. He found actors and made screen tests that he jettisoned back to the coast. In church, when he went to church, he prayed that one of these discoveries would be the next Barrymore or Garbo, a prayer that was never realized because Rutherford the Scout had a tremendous eye for opportunity but none for talent.

No man ever forgets a failure, and in the seventh year of the Great Depression this particular man came to Detroit with redemption on his mind. His newest plot was to write a stage play about the Dionne quints and then sell the movie rights to *that*, a clever strategy that would allow him to circumvent the exhaustive clauses in the children's contract and wreck vengeance on his enemies at Fox. But he could not cross the Ambassador Bridge right away. Almost broke, he burrowed into a room at the Wolverine Hotel to await his

Hollywood stipend. By now, this salary was little more than a pension, and he always suffered a terrible agony waiting for it to arrive.

This was his condition when he saw her. Pacing outside Western Union, clenching his butt cheeks to keep the anxious farts at bay, he noticed the grand goliath towering high over the populace.

She's at least eight feet tall, he thought. If not more!

He decided she was a mirage, produced by the same anxiety that had forced his stomach into knots. But the next day, while plugging the holes in his shoes with a clever combination of newspaper and gum, he saw her again. This time, Rutherford sprang to life. She should have been easy to follow, for her head and shoulders swam above the masses. But she was a glacier on the move, and he had to run to keep up. Eventually she came to rest outside a shop window, where she stooped to examine a display of men's shoes. At the exact moment he caught up to her, someone in a nearby music shop played a fanfare on an old trombone, and so it was that Rutherford the Desperate managed to make a dramatic entrance. The temperature at that moment was forty-eight degrees yet he was drenched in sweat, his heart wild, his Clark Gable moustache throbbing from the chase.

"Tell me you're an actress," he panted.

"I'm *definitely* not an actress," she said.

"Then tell me you've dreamed of being seen by the world."

He knew by her face that he was not the first to ask this question.

"I won't be a sideshow freak," she said.

"Good. You're far too unique for a sideshow. But you're perfect for the movies. How would you like me to take you away from Detroit?"

He leapt around her and tried to block her path. This should have had the effect of a weasel trying to stop an elephant. But she paused in midstep. He could not have known this, but inadvertently Rutherford the Lucky had said exactly what she had been waiting to hear.

SHE FOLLOWED HIM into a small café, where he impressed her by paying for two coffees and a pair of doughnuts laced with powdered sugar. He watched her in wonder. Her size had made her ageless, in the way the subjects of great art are immune to the passage of time. Her accent was exotic—a smattering of Spanish blended with a twang of working-class Detroit. At the table, she fought to eat like a lady. She clearly wanted to devour her doughnut. When had her magnificent stomach last known a full meal?

He asked for her name.

"Andorra. Like the country."

"There's a country called Andorra?"

"It's a principality. It's where I was born."

"What's the difference between a principality and a country?"

She rattled off the answer, which she had clearly given many times before. "A principality is a sovereign state officially ruled by a monarch from somewhere else. Andorra sits on the border between Spain and France. My *tata* lived there, and my mama walked halfway across Spain to be with him. Andorra was her salvation."

"I know the feeling." Rutherford Simone drew a small notebook from his shirt pocket. It was as tattered as the rest of him, but the pages were covered with a neat, almost-feminine script.

"I'm really not a performer," she said.

"At least let me tell you the idea."

"I know the *idea*," said Andorra. "I've spent my whole life listening to the sorts of *ideas* you people have."

Rutherford realized she had seen it all before; men just like him had probably been mistaking her for their salvation for years.

Vaudeville, burlesque, sideshows, carnival tours: the whole wide world of show business had almost certainly pursued this behemoth her entire life. He imagined the stream of men as a flood, her very existence unleashing every scout, agent, producer, huckster, con artist, and pitchman in the world. He held his breath. What was there to do but hope? Maybe, at the very least, his dramatic entrance would set him above the rest.

"I want you to star in a movie about Anna Swan," he said.

"Who's Anna Swan?" asked the Principality of Andorra. Having not even finished the first doughnut, she was already eyeing the second. Rutherford motioned toward it as he opened his notebook.

"Anna Bates, née Swan. Born 1846 in Nova Scotia. Height: somewhere around eight feet—it tends to vary depending on the source. She was one of P. T. Barnum's star attractions in the nineteenth century. Married another giant. Traveled across Europe. I think they even dined with royalty."

"And you want to make a movie about her?"

"It isn't me. It's my wife and her brother. They knew her, you see. Anna was very close with their father."

Andorra stirred her coffee, rattling the spoon against the side, making the sound into a short tune. Dat. Dat-dat-dat-dat-dat. Dat. Rutherford recognized the song: it was the first line in "Take Me Out to the Ballgame."

"So why haven't they made their picture yet?" said Andorra.

"They've never had anyone to play the lead. Until now." He grinned, revealing two broken teeth and one missing one. "They'd bring you down to Hollywood. All expenses paid, of course."

"It's impossible," she said. "I told you I'm not an actress."

He waved his hand. "You'd be a giant playing a giant. You're better than an actress; you're the real thing."

"I'd have to think about it."

Rutherford did some calculations in his head. He totaled the amount of spare change and crumpled bills in his pocket and subtracted the cost of survival: hotel, food, a telegram to the West Coast. There was barely enough to last the week.

"Think very fast," he begged.

SHE STAYED TO NURSE her coffee. Nothing of the doughnuts remained; even the powdered sugar had been licked away. Rutherford Simone had been right about a great many things, including the fact that her eighteen-inch stomach had been empty for years. The smells around her were the cheap ones of toast and coffee; they were intoxicating, as dangerous to her inhibitions as a snort of cocaine. She forced herself to escape, hands trembling as she stole the shaker of salt to add to the stockpile at home.

She lumbered back into the street, absently massaging the pain in her lower back. Again she floated across the top of the crowd until she had returned to the shop where Rutherford the Dramatic had made his appearance. He had been right about *that* too: of all the men who had mistaken her for salvation, none—not even her husband—had ever arrived in such an incredible way. Rutherford had appeared like a hero thrust from a storm.

There was a glare on the shop window, and she had to lean in close to see the thing that had caught her eye. The boots were brown and lined with fur. Too expensive for a casual purchase, too expensive even as a gift. Too expensive for anything, really, except for catching the eye. They couldn't possibly be the right size, she thought, only to realize that she didn't remember what the right size *was*. And why would she? Her husband's measurements had never been as memorable as her own. She continued to stare and soon became lost in the illusion: in the joy of buying shoes, in the fantasy of bringing them home, in the great yearning dream of sliding them onto her husband's feet. Her beautiful husband. The husband she had lost. The husband she had killed.

A scream in her back brought her back to the world. Rising to her full, incredible height, the widowed principality made her way to the library so she could read everything she could about the life of Anna Swan.

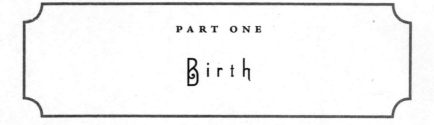

PART ONE

Birth

ONE

The Stone That
Swallowed a Stone

Tatamagouche, 1846

To BEGIN WITH, she was born in a log cabin in New Annan, Nova Scotia, on the shores of the Northumberland Strait. The region was once inhabited by the Micmac Nation, but by the day of her birth—August 6, 1846—the area's name was the only part of the Micmacs to survive. Even this was a corruption. Those Native Canadians had called the region *Takeumegooch*, a word that means "at the place that lies across." Unable to pronounce this word, the Scotch settlers revised it so it sat much easier on the tongue: *Tatamagouche*. This would be Anna Swan's first encounter with revisionist history; much more would come.

Neither of her parents resembled the sort of people who could spawn a baby twenty-eight inches long. Alexander Swan was an average-sized émigré from Dumfries while his wife was a tiny thing whose largest attributes were the dimples on her knees. Their first child's single peculiarity had been his complete disinterest in the world, as if he had known he was destined to live less than fifteen months. He died in the crib, and his grave was still soft when Alexander came to his wife in the middle of the night. "The best cure for grief is hope," he whispered; ten months later, his wife was so swollen with his hope that she found herself restricted to bed.

Ann Swan was so large that Alexander believed they were having twins. *Boys*, he decided, as if his authority was all it took. Two mighty oxen to help with the farm. The theory gained spiritual endorsement from the Reverend Blackwood, the white-haired clergyman who had recently taken residence at the Willow Church. Educated in both medicine and vanity, it was assumed he would be called to oversee the birth—and until that moment, the arthritic reverend had only overseen the births of men. Anna's mother did not believe she was having either boys *or* twins—but no one was listening to her. No one was watching her at all as she lolled in bed: it was expected that she suffer in silence.

"Pregnancy is a blessing," said Alexander. "To complain is to be ungrateful in the eyes of God." So even though Ann Swan knew something was very different about her second baby, she kept it to herself. By April she felt she had swallowed a stone; by May she imagined the *stone* had swallowed a stone. In June she wondered if the baby, like Athena, would spring from her fully grown. In July she became convinced she would never survive the ordeal. She should not have given birth until September, but by the middle of summer she knew she could no longer endure the weight of her husband's hope. On the sixth day of August, while attempting to make herself porridge, her water broke and ran like a river down her leg. The subsequent cramps were so cruel that she fell against the rough timber walls of the cabin. Clawing at the logs for support, she drew jagged splinters that stuck into her palm. Yet even then she remained silent, gripping the pain between her teeth as a horse chews on a bit.

"I'll get the Reverend!" said Alexander, and he raced from the cabin. Ann Swan didn't object. She couldn't. If she opened her mouth, she was certain to scream. On hands and knees, those hard splinters still in her fist, she crawled to the bed on her own even as she listened to the sounds of Alexander riding away. The cramps whipped her insides into a froth. Her jaw began to ache. Her poor teeth, weak from a bad diet, jiggled in her gums. As she wrapped herself in her quilt, her head knocked against the wall. Barely a tap really, but in her torment it felt like a great crash. She lost her stamina. Having locked away her fury for seven months, three weeks, and five days, she finally released a howl that gave voice to the storm.

She was still screaming when the men returned. It curdled the blood. The Reverend hobbled inside, but Anna's father remained with the horse. He would stay outside the rest of the night.

The moment he saw the pregnant woman, the Reverend understood he had come to the moment when God would test his skill. Sprawled on her back, her great belly bubbled. With trembling hands, the Reverend boiled water, sterilized his tools, and poured warm whiskey down the mother's throat. He tried to pray but suspected God wouldn't hear him over the screams.

Ann Swan began to push. For a few moments, it seemed they were in crisis: the baby had crowned, but her shoulders were too wide for the narrow opening of the womb. Then the world fell silent as Ann Swan lost her scream.

She lay unconscious while Anna herself sat halfway into the world. Forceps would be needed to yank the baby free, but the arthritic reverend could barely pick up the tool. With nothing but his bare hands, he grabbed Anna by the head and wrestled with her stubborn womb until, at last, in a miraculous moment, the stone that had swallowed a stone finally shot free. The force knocked the Reverend onto the ground; he was so prepared for twins that he peered into the empty womb, convinced something vital had been lost.

Ann Swan remained in poor health for days. Afraid she might die, Alexander gave her name to their daughter and steeled himself for the widower's life. But he had no talent for prophecy: he had been wrong about having twins, and he was wrong about this. Ann Swan was back on her feet by Thanksgiving; by the following fall, she was swollen with another stone. She would have ten more children, but none would ever make her cry with the same fury as her first daughter, eighteen pounds and twenty-eight inches in length. Ann Swan gave birth to the rest of her children in silence; it could be said she never found her scream.

THE REVEREND BLACKWOOD had lost his unblemished record of male births, but he had gained something of greater worth: the certainty that, in the course of drawing Anna into the world, God had guided his arthritic hands. Or rather his *formerly* arthritic hands: he swore that his arthritis had completely disappeared. It was this that convinced him of divine involvement, and when he spread the word of the birth, he went so far as to suggest that Anna might someday prove to be a saint.

The mere suggestion of this meant that as the months passed the Swans found themselves under attack. Everyone wanted to see the Future Saint, as she was known, and they bought their way inside with gifts of butter, preserves, and jugs of moonshine. People came to the farm and waylaid the family in the streets. Not one person who lived on the shores of the Northumberland Strait thought it strange to pay a visit to a family they had never met. This was a corner of the world where a barn raising was cause for delight; the appearance of a Future Saint inspired apoplectic joy.

Private by nature, Alexander Swan hated the attention, and at the start of Anna's fourth summer, he went down to the gates of the farm with some lumber and paint. There, in the swelter of the June sun, he erected a sign whose message was as short as it was blunt:

ALL PILGRIMS WILL BE SHOT

"Not very charitable," remarked Ann Swan.

"I couldn't agree more," said a voice. While Alexander had been erecting his sign, a witness had appeared on a dappled horse. Elaborately bearded, he was nearly bald everywhere else. "Nope," he decided. "Not very charitable at all."

"I'm giving them fair warning," said Alexander. "You ask me, that's charity enough."

"People are traveling a great distance to see her."

"Only 'cause their heads are muddled. I don't need them tramping through my house."

The stranger leaned in closer. "Maybe you need to put her somewhere else. Give her a proper venue so your house can stay in peace."

Ann Swan examined the man a little more closely. His beard wasn't the only thing that was elaborate. His clothes, while dusty, were finer than any she had seen. Even the horse seemed to have a regal countenance, as if it were used to carrying kings. "You aren't from around here," she declared.

"H. P. Ingalls," said the man. "I'm from New York."

Alexander tapped the sign. "You obey signs in New York?"

"Nobody obeys anything in New York." H. P. Ingalls grinned. "I represent a man who has interest in promoting human curiosities. Word is, that's a good way to describe your daughter." He winked at Ann Swan. "Given that you survived her birth, I'd say it describes you, too."

Ann Swan laughed.

"Get out of here," said Alexander.

"There would be money involved, of course."

Alexander swiped at the New Yorker with his hammer. "Get off my land."

"You write if you ever change your mind," said H. P. Ingalls. Two cards appeared as if by magic in his hand. He gave one to Alexander; perhaps knowing it would be destroyed, he slipped the second to Ann Swan.

Alexander indeed tore up the card. The next day, he changed the sign.

ALL PILGRIMS AND NEW YORKERS
WILL BE SHOT

It was entirely true that the Swans were not rich. Alexander farmed in the warm weather and cut timber when it was cold. It was a humble life, and Anna's appetite—for food, for clothes, for furniture—was growing all the time. Yet Alexander would never take money for something he believed to be a lie. To him, she was a girl, not a miracle. Anna's mother wasn't sure she agreed. She was already looking into the future, down the road toward all the days and years to come. Her daughter would always be the inadvertent flagship of an otherwise average armada. *She's a big boat in a small pond,* thought Ann. *Don't we have a duty to let her set sail?*

It's possible that Ann Swan would have swallowed these thoughts just as she had swallowed the pain of pregnancy. But that Christmas, during a spirit of celebration, Alexander finally cracked open those jugs of moonshine that had been donated after Anna's birth. They had turned to rotgut, and a terrible sickness seized him just as the new year began. Burnt by fever, he was suddenly confined to bed. With him unable to work, the family found themselves spiraling closer to poverty. Now there was no choice; as the March frost clung to the fields, Ann Swan dabbed the sweat from her husband's fevered brow with the complete understanding that the time had come. She may have lost her scream, but that didn't mean she had lost her voice.

"I'm taking Annie to Halifax" she declared.

"Absolutely not!" her husband said.

"I'll bring the Reverend. The pilgrims won't have to come to us. *We* can come to *them.*"

"I forbid it!" spat Alexander.

"Someone has to do something," said his wife. "We're all going to end up sleeping in the rain."

The next morning, Alexander woke to find himself being nursed by a neighbor; his newest daughter was asleep in the crib. As for Anna, Ann Swan, and the Reverend Blackwood, they had already left.

They traveled across the snowy province wrapped in furs and pulled by a team of industrious dogs. Upon arriving in Halifax, the Reverend presented the Future Saint to the press, but the newspapermen didn't like the name's Catholic connection—anti-Catholic sentiment was far too ripe. And so it was that Anna Swan entered the historical record as the Infant Giantess. They said she was ninety-four pounds; they said she was four feet, seven inches tall. They assumed the Reverend Blackwood was Alexander Swan. They described Anna's mother as a woman of small size and interesting appearance.

That weekend, Haligonians filled Temperance Hall, a great meeting place near the center of town. While Ann Swan fussed with her daughter, the Reverend stood onstage and embellished the story of Anna's birth, adding such colorful details as a biblical storm, a broken carriage, and a crippled horse. Here was another one of Anna's encounters with revisionist history—but this time she, unlike the audience at Halifax, had the benefit of knowing the facts had been rearranged.

"Why isn't he telling the *truth*?" asked Anna.

"The truth," said her mother, "is rarely entertaining."

When she was at last brought to the stage, Anna clutched for the comfort of her mother's hand. She was almost as tall as her mother, and a murmur shot through the crowd. Distracted by the true wonder of her size, people barely heard the formerly arthritic Reverend turn the topic toward his own hands and the possible miraculous properties of Anna's touch. The price of admission, he announced, included an exhibit of Anna's possessions: the swaddling clothes, the shoes, the crib that had buckled under her tremendous weight. But for an extra fee, they could also receive her healing touch.

A dozen people came forward, including a tiny girl with brittle hair. Not yet twenty, she had a shoehorn face that was pinched tight, as if she held back some terrible pain. Anna wondered if she might collapse. But the girl with the brittle hair maintained her poise and paid her fee with the great dignity of one giving alms. She reached out and took Anna's hand.

"It's very nice to meet you," said the brittle girl.

"Hello," mumbled Anna.

There was an awkward pause as she continued to cling to Anna's hand, as if hoping to draw as much of the giant's strength as she could. "Is it working?" asked the girl. "Please: how do I know if it worked?"

She spoke with such earnestness that Anna felt a duty to respond. But while she was smart enough to know she needed to be comforting, she was ill equipped to think of a comforting thing to say. She looked to her mother, who sighed.

"You'll know soon enough," said Ann to the brittle girl.

It was as close to the truth as they could come. Ann didn't know if her daughter had miraculous powers; Anna didn't know either. *They* would know soon enough, too.

The visit was a great success, and they left Halifax with their pockets full of coin. The Reverend offered to invest their share of the money, and Ann Swan agreed, allowing herself to become steeped in the fantasy of wealth.

They returned to Tatamagouche to find themselves faced with a furious storm. Incensed that his will had been defied, Alexander had whipped the people into a frenzy. In a rage, he had told his neighbors the Reverend had stolen his wife and child away. He told them the man was a fraud; he told them that, far from being guided by God, the formerly arthritic Reverend had nearly killed Ann Swan on the night of Anna's birth.

If not exactly driven from the town, the Reverend found himself quietly pushed in the direction of anywhere else. He was gone by the end of the summer. He left behind all of his sermons; he also took every dollar he had promised to invest on behalf of the Swans.

"Good riddance," said Alexander. "Nothing but fruit of the poisoned tree."

"Poison or not, we needed it," Ann Swan moaned.

That night she conscripted her enormous daughter to help her tear down Alexander's sign. If pilgrims returned, they would be more than welcome. And if that *New Yorker* returns, said Ann Swan, *he* will be welcome, too.

The New Yorker *would* return, but not for many years. In the meantime the pilgrims, fearing Alexander's rage, stopped coming. As life returned to some new brand of normal, Anna's parents made an unspoken agreement to rewrite the story of her earliest days. It was just one more encounter with revisionist history; and since no one spoke of her past, Anna came of age remembering events that might have been part of a fevered dream.

TWO

A Shame Before God

Sant Julià de Lòria, 1900

AS FOR ANDORRA, she was born in the afternoon less than two months after her pregnant mother stumbled into the parish of Sant Julià de Lòria, the southernmost settlement of that principality that so neatly divides France and Spain. Newly nineteen, Andorra's mother arrived on foot with her younger sister, a bottle-shaped girl who many mistook for a mule; she arrived bearing all their luggage on her back. This was typical of a girl who had decided that loyalty would be her eternal trait. It had been this loyal girl who had helped her beautiful sister hide her scandalous condition from their family. Their various ruses had been truly clever, but no farce lasts forever; one morning their grandmother walked into the ornate bathroom just as Andorra's mother was stepping from the bath. Only recently, a man in America had learned to weld porcelain to iron, and because of this genius, the girl's olive body was a sharp contrast to the stark white of this imported claw-foot tub. With her grandmother at the door, nothing could save her. Elionor Noguerra did not even have a towel; there was nowhere for her protruding belly to hide.

Elionor made no attempt to hide the name of the father. Until recently, she and her loyal sister had been tutored by an intelligent youth who had been called home to attend to his father's death. Everyone had seen the attraction between the tutor and his eldest pupil. No one was surprised when, on the day he left, Elionor flooded her pillow with tears. But now, just weeks later, that protruding belly had proved the tears had not been the sorrow of unrequited love.

Her father was a captain in the Spanish Armada. Obsessed with the new—that claw-foot tub was only one of many wondrous imports from around the world—he was still a man of certain traditions. As she prepared for dinner on the day of her discovery, Elionor trembled at the thought of her father's wrath. Yet she was determined to endure it; the Captain had taught his daughters the value of sailing through storms. She went down to dinner with her chin held high. But her father barely met her gaze. Dinner was held in an opulent dining room that boasted several tall windows overlooking the garden. Elionor had barely stepped into the room when her father pointed through the glass to where the dogs tore at their mutton by the base of a mint-colored hedge.

"You have acted like a dog," he said. "Now you can eat with them."

You don't sail through a storm by turning back at the first crack of thunder, thought Elionor. As calmly as she could, she claimed her usual seat and asked her father to pass the salt.

Captain Noguerra did, but not in the way she would have liked. He flung salt in her eye and struck her across the face. "It will be a great miracle if I don't strangle you in your sleep," he said. "And it wouldn't be a crime. You are a shame before God."

Elionor looked across the table, where her grandmother was slurping her soup. The woman's expression announced she was forever on the Captain's side. She had exorcised all maternal instinct when it came to her granddaughters, for they both reminded her of their mother, who had abandoned the family shortly after giving birth to Elionor's loyal sister. The story was that she had fallen in love with a famed aviator who had whisked her away in a hot-air balloon.

"The sins of the father pass to the son for three generations," her grandmother said. "But the sins of the *mother* pass on as well."

With four months left to her pregnancy, Andorra's mother was locked inside the house, and everyone knew that if she survived the birth, she would be sent to a convent. Everyone also knew that if *the baby* survived the birth, it would certainly be drowned. The Captain suffered his little children. But he brooked no bastards.

Fortunately, the young tutor had not disappeared. He had continued to write to Elionor ever since he had returned to his home in the southernmost settlement of that principality that so neatly divides France and Spain. Each letter was poorly disguised as a lesson in literature; in fact, they were lessons on love. As an intellect, he had the poetry of Petrarch and Shakespeare on his side; he could also quote at length from the many novels and plays of Lope de Vega. Using their words, he wove his heart into dozens of paragraphs, each written in his scrawling script. He sent them to Madrid in the satchels of the smugglers who favored the principality's roads. Exactly how he had access to these rough men was not something Andorra's mother would learn for many months; Andorra herself would not learn it for years. At the time, it hardly mattered to Elionor, who found the letters as intoxicating as the wine, tobacco, and opium that had been in the smuggler's bags.

For safety, the letters were written in code and sent to Manuela Sofia Noguerra, that loyal sister, who fooled everyone into thinking the letters came from a female friend. This put the loyal girl at the center of the lovers' affair. It was Manuela who first dreamed of the marriage between Elionor and her tutor. At fifteen, Manuela Noguerra had the incurable optimism of youth and easily believed every pretty word the tutor had ever written.

Intoxicated as she was, Elionor was much more realistic. Men are very good at loving women, she said. But only until they have to marry them. "He may not accept me. What if I go all that way only to be exiled again?"

"He'll marry you." Manuela assured her. "He'll give us both a home."

"Men don't like to be surprised," said Elionor.

"He won't be," said Manuela. "I've already told him the two of you are on your way."

"The *two* of us!" Elionor Noguerra flew into a rage. "He might not *want* to be a father! He might *already* be a father!"

"I wanted to give him time to prepare," said Manuela.

"All you did was give him time to escape."

But Elionor reluctantly packed a bag, on the sole condition that Manuela pack one as well. Though four years apart, the two sisters might as well have been Siamese twins. It was Manuela that gave Elionor the courage to leave. *If I am exiled,* she thought, *at least I won't endure it alone.*

Their adventure was cursed from the moment it began. The roads were hardly safe for women, and they were forced to disguise themselves as men, just like the women in so many Shakespearian plays. But where Shakespeare might have given them comical circumstances, God authored much more serious events. Either their disguises were too convincing or not convincing enough; either they came up against thieves or ran the risk of blackmail and rape. Years later, Andorra would wish that she knew more of these adventures, but no one ever spoke of them; it became known in the family as the Most Interesting Story Never Told. What *was* known was that the women avoided public places, dealt with inclement weather, and were forced to kill their donkey after it became lame. They ate the carcass and continued on foot. They crossed into the Principality of Andorra on a blustery afternoon, completely unaware that during their travels the nineteenth century had ended and a new era had begun.

Their sluggish pace allowed them ample time to study the armies of sheep and the dominating outline of the Pyrenees before, at long last, they staggered into Sant Julià de Lòria. Spread through the trees, the parish was built entirely around sprawling farms of tobacco. There was a small square used for festivals, and this was flanked by the church to the north and the general store to the south. The girls stopped at one to thank God for their safety before crossing to the other to obtain directions.

Here the tutor's lessons came in handy. He had taught them Catalan, a subject in which both had excelled. Elionor Noguerra held her breath as Manuela spoke to the clerk. This was the moment. They would be told the tutor had mysteriously disappeared. They would not even be offered a place to spend the night.

The clerk checked his watch. "You might as well wait. He should be here any moment."

"You know him?" said Manuela.

"Everyone knows him," said the clerk. "He's the richest man in town."

"How do you know he's coming by?" asked Manuela.

"He comes every day. He waits for the mail like a Jew waits for the Messiah."

To Manuela, this proved that her faith in the tutor had not been misplaced. But Andorra's mother would not be lifted from her dismay. "If he's the richest man in town, he probably has an army of lovers," she said. "If he's the richest man in town, a different woman probably writes him every day."

"We'll know soon enough," said Manuela.

They took a seat on a stone that rested outside the store. Ten minutes later, a dusty and familiar face appeared on the road. The richest man in town did not *look* like the richest man in town. Unshaven and shabbily dressed, he still looked like a tutor. He even had books under his arm.

He froze when he saw them.

"Now watch," whispered Elionor. "He'll turn like the fox and run."

She held the air tight in her lungs, hoping it might protect her heart. There was no need. A moment later, Geoffrey del Alandra sprang toward her. Manuela beamed with pride. As for Elionor, she exhaled a long breath, perfumed with relief.

THE WEDDING HAPPENED with great speed, and though everyone in the parish attended, few knew it for what it really was. The town believed they were celebrating a marriage that had happened months before. This lie had been spread by Geoffrey's twin sister, the hideously stunted Noria Blanco. The twins' mother had died giving birth, and in her absence Noria had become the great matriarch of the house. On receiving Manuela's letter, Geoffrey had warned his sister of Elionor's approach—and her condition. Noria Blanco had no objections to the way the child had been conceived; like all great matriarchs, she had viewed the matter in purely practical terms.

"A baby is a legacy," she said. "And all great legacies have to claw their way into the world."

Noria Blanco immediately began to tell people that Geoffrey had married a girl in Madrid. Forced to abandon her after their father's death, he had been in agony due to the conviction that he would never see his wife again. This was easily believed, for the richest man in town had kept to himself ever since his return. He had buried his father with great pomp and dutifully taken over the business of running the farms of tobacco. Throwing himself into his work, he had shunned all festivals and had not stepped within spitting distance of an eligible girl. The townspeople had believed him to be mourning his father; now they saw he had been mourning his absent wife, too. The tale made for a heartbreaking scenario. Thanks to Noria Blanco, the richest man in town was now applauded for his loyalty and lauded for his romantic disposition.

The cost of the priest's silence was five gold coins, a pound of barley, and a case of imported wine. In exchange, he married Andorra's parents in secret and casually forgot to include the incident in the church's registrar. The next day, the celebration was held. It came as a great relief to the *other* young lovers of the parish. As was tradition at the time, betrothed couples could only announce their engagement during another marriage feast. Until Elionor's arrival, there had not been a wedding in Sant Julià de Lòria for several months, a circumstance that had caused more than a dozen romances to stop dead. It was with great joy that the bridal party marched to Geoffrey's elegant manor, a cathedral of stone built on the crest of a hill. They adorned Andorra's father with a wreath of *Adonis vernalis*, otherwise known as pheasant's-eyes, otherwise known as the official flower of the principality. The flowers were poisonous, and their traditional presence was said to be a bittersweet reminder of all those who could not be there to join in the celebration. With this wreath of poison flowers around his neck, Geoffrey del Alandra was hoisted onto a donkey's back and paraded through the streets. The march ended at the church, where, in lieu of a religious ceremony, the couple was blessed by the same priest who had quietly taken their bribe the day before. His poker face was exquisite: no one ever suspected that he knew the baby about to burst from Elionor's belly had been conceived in mortal sin.

The celebrations continued for several weeks. Now that other couples were free to marry, one marriage feast simply bled into the next. The chaos was still being enjoyed when the supreme moment came. Geoffrey was carousing with some of those rough smugglers, whose activities were never questioned and whose acquaintance he had still never explained. As for Elionor, she was at the stove attempting to fix an oversalted stew. Having added more water, she was tasting the concoction when the first great tremor seized her frame. She nearly choked; the tension caused her to snap the wooden ladle in two. As she fell, she glanced at the clock on the wall: It was just after nine o'clock in the morning, forty-seven days into the dawn of the twentieth century.

At once, Manuela Noguerra took control. Before leaving Madrid, she had questioned several midwives on the proper procedure in case the stress of the journey caused a premature birth. Now she could finally use the knowledge she had learned. She exiled the men from the room and locked her and her sister away. For the next nine hours, Elionor and Manuela wrestled with a baby who did not want to be born. Andorra was happy in the womb; she resisted birth with every last ounce of strength.

Beyond the bedroom, in the main room of his father's great stone house, Geoffrey paced by the hearth and took solace in the batches of wine supplied by his smuggler friends. Throughout those nine hours, Noria Blanco threatened to break into the birthing room, and each time Geoffrey held her at bay. "Manuela brought Elionor here," he said. "She'll get the baby here, too." His confidence masked a terrible fear. His mother had died giving birth; so had the many women in his library of books and plays. His body was firm, but his blood secretly trembled, and by the start of the ninth hour, he was convinced Elionor would never make it out of this day alive.

But Captain Noguerra had taught his daughter well—she was still a girl who could sail through a storm. She was screaming with life when, just after six o'clock, Andorra finally shot free. At just over eight pounds, the baby was large but not extraordinary; there was no reason for anyone to guess what was to come.

Elionor fell into the deepest sleep of her life. Geoffrey, now drained of his fear, opened the doors of his house to yet another raucous celebration. As was custom, it was a purely male affair. They arrived with gifts while the women hid in the kitchen and prepared the food. Manuela Noguerra was the happiest she had ever been; Noria Blanco was the happiest *she* had ever been, too. Both had been in mourning for the lives they had known—Noria's father was gone, and Manuela knew she would never see any of her family again. Each mourned the death of the comforts of the past. But the best cure for grief is hope: a baby brings with it unending optimism and great potential. Noria and Manuela would never get along so well again. Working from the kitchen, the stepsisters merrily doled out ewe's-milk cheese, spiced salami, fresh bread, and bottles from Geoffrey's secret supply of aguardiente.

By midnight the drunken men had taken to singing songs around the hearth while one of the smugglers strummed a broken guitar. Everything about the music was out of tune, so no one noticed when a terrible cry filled the house: it was drowned by the cacophony of the men. But the sound woke the infant Andorra. She had slept through the music but could not bear this terrible cry: she knew before anyone that the sound had come from her mother. She released a tragic wail as Elionor clawed her way from the room. Holding her stomach, shrieking as she leaned against the wall for support, she made her way into the other room, where the men continued to roar out their song. Distracted by their celebration, the men didn't notice her even as she flailed. At last, she did the only thing she could: she crashed into the table of food. Down she went, against the wooden table, cracking the legs and sending plates and goblets into the air. The men turned from the hearth to see Elionor collapsed on the floor, surrounded by salami and cheese in a gown stained brown with piss.

The music stopped. A pestilent stench filled the room. As Geoffrey helped his wife to stand, his great terror returned. There was excrement along her backside; a trail of dark blood leaked down the insides of her thighs.

Elionor remained weak and fevered for several days. Despite assurances that this was a common aftermath of birth, Geoffrey wandered from room to room in a state of horror that he no longer bothered to hide. At last a surgeon arrived from another parish and diagnosed the problem. A gaping hole had developed between the womb and the bowels. He guessed that Elionor's birth canal must have been too narrow and had been torn open by Andorra's arrival.

The surgeon called the hole a fistula and proclaimed it to be an ancient disease, one that had been sent to afflict women since the dawn of time.

In the hall outside the bedroom, the surgeon reproached them all. "If only I had been here," he said. "There might have been something I could have done."

Manuela Noguerra began to cry. "Then it was me. It's all my fault."

"Stop that," said Geoffrey. "What could you have done?"

"She could have summoned a professional," said the surgeon.

"It took you three days to get here," snapped Geoffrey del Alandra. "Were we all supposed to wait?" To the loyal Manuela he said, "This was no one's fault. No one is to blame."

"No one but your wife," said Noria Blanco.

"What does *that* mean?" said Geoffrey.

"God only punishes those who deserve it." His sister shrugged. Already she was looking at Elionor as the people of Troy must have looked at the first soldier emerging from the Trojan horse.

The surgeon announced the fistula would remain with Elionor the rest of her days. Sex was impossible: her genitals began to erode and now leaked without warning. The condition also meant that her breasts were merely aesthetic; her nipples turned inward, and baby Andorra could not find a way to drink. Her cries of hunger caused the house to tremble. Noria Blanco refused to turn herself into a wet nurse and directed all eyes to the loyal Manuela. Fed a special concoction of herbs, tea, and beer, Manuela was made to force Andorra into her chest, but the baby only wept; this was not her mother's milk. It was days before the constant suckling finally produced a miraculous flow. The ruined Elionor could only watch from afar. As for the richest man in town, he became a melancholy wreck.

Publicly, Noria Blanco let it be known that Elionor had developed consumption, but the truth was an open secret and Noria began to plot to send Elionor away. Near the edge of the valley, by the banks of the Valira River, there stood an abandoned hut whose origins were largely unknown. It was Noria's plan to use this house as Elionor's refuge. She could survive on a small remittance, away from the eyes of the world.

"Send me away," said Geoffrey. "The shame is mine."

"Have you thought what Elionor might do to her?" asked Noria. "I've seen it happen. It's like a madness in women. They start to think it's all the baby's fault. Then they do something without meaning to, because, deep inside, their souls want revenge."

Meanwhile, Noria went to work on Elionor herself.

"One day Andorra will be the age where she remembers you. Do you really want her to remember you like this? Do you really want her to grow up cleaning away your shit and your piss?"

Beaten down by shame, Elionor agreed to the one thing she had feared ever since leaving Madrid: exile. Again, there was no question of Manuela's staying behind; like all mules, she was hitched to something larger than herself. As soon as Andorra had been weaned, the sisters left the house behind. Each of them wept as they walked. The richest man in town also cried, but it was a masculine weeping, done only where it could not be seen. As for Andorra, she did not cry at all. Her terrible wails stopped the same day her mother left. Her only response was to grow: within a month of the exile, she was too large for her crib. Within a year, she was the size of a girl twice her age.

THREE

Opening Day

Detroit, 1937

O N THE FIRST DAY of the 1937 baseball season—her last in Detroit—Andorra packed her clothes with the skill of a veteran pitcher. From the dresser, she lobbed one ball of clothes after another into the trunk. Each one was a perfect pitch. This talent used to amuse the children, but right now they were distracted by the trunk itself. They had never taken a vacation; the notion of travel was a marvelous thing.

"Anna Swan was born in Nova Scotia," Andorra told them. "It was a place called Tatamagouche."

"Tatamagouche!" said Gabriel.

"Tatamagouche!" repeated Gabriella.

"How do you spell Tatamagouche?" asked Rowena.

"What does *that* matter?" asked Gabriel.

"I want to get it right," sniffed Rowena.

Of course you do, thought Andorra. The girl had been named for Rowena Moira Kelsey, her paternal grandmother, who had been called the Irish Queen of Burlesque. Rowena had her grandmother's red hair and coat of freckles, but that was where the similarities ended—she was far too serious to ever be a Burly-Q Queen. She wanted to be a writer; at the age of four, she had scrawled a brief report about Gabriel and Gabriella's birthday party; at eleven, she had written about the start of the Great Depression; and at fourteen, she had written about the death of her father. Now, two years, six months, and eleven days later, she was recording a giant's departure from Detroit. And she wanted to make sure she had all the details, right down to the proper spelling.

"T-a-t-a-m-a-g-o-u-c-h-e," spelled Andorra. "P. T. Barnum sent a man there to take Anna to New York."

"Who's P. T. Barnum?" asked Gabriel.

"A man who had his very own museum," said Andorra.

"Boring!" said Gabriel.

"Boring!" echoed Gabriella.

The twins were restless, and she knew why; they wanted to go down to Navin Field and sneak inside to watch the game. These days, Gabriel wanted to play shortstop for the Tigers; and since Gabriella wanted whatever her brother wanted, she wanted to play shortstop, too. She had trailed her brother into the world and had been following him ever since.

"It wasn't a *boring* museum," she said, lobbing a ball of stockings into the trunk. "It was a place for entertainment. They had lots of exhibits with giants and dwarves. She was paid twenty-three dollars a week in gold." Andorra was reciting from memory everything she knew, all of which came from the only book she had found on the subject: an encyclopedic volume entitled *Whoozits, Whatzits and Other Freaks of the Globe.* The only other mention of Anna Swan had been in Barnum's autobiography, which contained little information other than the delicious fact that Anna had been "an intelligent and by no means ill-looking girl."

"She married another giant," Andorra went on. "He was a soldier in the Civil War."

"*Another* giant!" said Gabriel.

"How many giants *were* there?" asked Gabriella.

"Not many," said Andorra. "A handful."

"A handful of giants!" said Gabriella, and she shook her head in awe.

"Do you think they were all like you?" asked Rowena.

"I don't know," said Andorra. "I suppose so."

"Was Anna Swan like you?" asked Gabriella.

"Of course she was, dummy," said Gabriel. "Why else would they have asked Mama to play her in the movies?"

"Don't call your sister dummy," said Andorra. There was no force in her voice; the scolding was purely automatic. She was wondering the same thing as Gabriella. *Was* Anna Swan like her? Or was that a ridiculous thought, as ridiculous as assuming that Gabriella might be like Shirley Temple simply because they were both girls?

"What about the man she married?" said Rowena. "Was he anything like Tata?"

Like the scolding, Andorra's reply was a reflex response. "No one was like your father."

"How could he have been like Tata?" snorted Gabriel. "Tata wasn't a giant."

"Mama said he was a soldier," said Rowena. "Tata was a soldier, too."

"Tata fought in the *Great* War," said Andorra. "Anna's husband fought in the *Civil* War. He was a captain in the Confederate Army."

"The Confederates!" said Gabriella. "Who were they again?"

"They were the ones who shot President Lincoln."

This last remark came from the doorway, where her father was leaning against the frame. He seemed to have appeared out of nowhere, although Andorra knew he had probably been lurking this whole time. The man who had once been the richest man in town was now a shaggy dog. His hair and beard were unkempt, and his slender eyes were completely gray. But there was strength in him; this dog could still froth at the mouth. Rutherford had promised nothing but a single role in the Anna Swan picture, but Geoffrey del Alandra was convinced this was the first step toward total exploitation. "You just wait!" he had argued the night before. "They want to see you sold to the world." Quietly, she wondered if he was right. She had done a screen test for Rutherford Simone, and there had been a nerve-racking week while it had been jettisoned across the country. She had chosen something from *Macbeth*, hoping that Shakespeare might lend her a little sophistication. But it probably wouldn't have mattered. Certainly, her portrayal of Lady Macbeth had not been without merit. But, as Rutherford had said, she was a giant being hired to play a giant; like so many other women in Hollywood, she had probably been hired on the strength of her measurements alone.

Andorra turned back to the children. "Anna Swan had two babies, but they both died. One of them is still on record as the largest baby ever born—twenty-three pounds."

"How did Anna Swan die?" asked Rowena, pen poised.

"She died of heart failure," Andorra replied. "She had a weak heart, like me."

"You don't have a weak heart," said her father.

"She always says she does," muttered Rowena.

"I don't *always* say it," said Andorra.

"Dad always said she had a *possibly weak* heart," said Gabriella.

"Where was I?" said Andorra, anxious to change the subject.

"You were dying of heart failure," smirked Gabriel.

"*Anna Swan* was dying of heart failure," corrected Rowena.

"They buried her in Ohio," said Andorra. "She and her husband were living in a town called Seville. They had built themselves an enormous house with high doorways and giant chairs."

"So it's like this place," said Gabriel.

"We should go live there," said Gabriella. "It would probably be *better* than this place."

"Anywhere is better than *this* place," said Gabriel.

Andorra wanted to chastise her son, but how could she? The house was an old coat, worn through right to the seams. The wallpaper peeled and the rats ran rampant through the walls. Winter brought an arctic chill while summer brought terrible heat. And there was that one particular ghost, that one shadowy memory who had left his mark on everything from the bookends to the crooked painting hanging in the hall.

Geoffrey, on the other hand, had no trouble scolding Gabriel. "There's nothing wrong with this place," he grumbled as he moved into the room. "It's a home, isn't it? What right have you to complain?"

"Who's complaining?" said Gabriel. "I just think it would be better to live in a giant house in Ohio."

"Well, it isn't going to happen," said Geoffrey. "All of us are staying here."

"Except Mama," said Gabriella.

"Mama's staying here, too," said Geoffrey. His eyes found Andorra's. There it was: that gaze of steel.

Andorra stayed firm. "Mama *is* leaving," she told the children. "But she'll be back as soon as she can."

She pitched a ball of stockings at the trunk, but by now Geoffrey had positioned himself so he was between her and the luggage. He had only to swing an arm to swat the stockings away. Out on Navin Field, it would have been a sacrifice bunt; in here, Geoffrey never even left the plate. He grabbed more clothes from the trunk and threw them across the room. Her skirt landed on the dresser, while a yellow slip, as large as a blanket, landed on the lampshade and changed the color of the room. Everything came down with a sudden case of jaundice.

Geoffrey pointed to the children. "At least take them with you. You heard them—they think anywhere is better than here. So bring them along."

"We've been over this. They're only paying for me. Rutherford said I'm going to stay in his sister's house. There isn't room for all of us."

"You ask me, it's nothing but a lousy shame," said Geoffrey. "What sort of mother leaves her children?"

"Mine did. And *her* mother left for a man in a balloon. Maybe it's in the blood."

"That was different."

"Mama was sick. Mama was sick, and we're poor, but it all amounts to the same thing."

Her father slumped down to the bed and adjusted the black mourning band around his arm. He wasn't wearing it for her husband. It was for her mother—word of Elionor's death had reached them sixteen years before.

"Why don't you run downstairs and wait for Mr. Simone?" Geoffrey said to the twins. Andorra glanced at the clock. Rutherford was coming in a taxi; he would be there any minute. "Tell him your mama needs help with her luggage."

"Since when does she need help?" said Gabriel.

"She's stronger than a taxi driver," said Gabriella.

"Do we have to wait?" asked Gabriel. "The game is going to start."

"Don't you want to say good-bye to me?" asked Andorra.

"Good-bye to you!" snickered Gabriel.

"Good-bye to you!" snickered Gabriella.

"Oh, just give me a hug." Andorra crouched and opened her arms. Her great body was built for twins; even at sixteen they fit perfectly inside her. "Stay out of trouble," she said.

"Where's the fun in that?" Her son winked.

Gabriella laughed as the pair scampered away. They're really their own universe, thought Andorra. You could separate them, but it would be like tearing a hole in the world.

She took the yellow slip off the lamp, returning the room to its proper shade. Rowena continued to skulk over her notebook, her red bangs falling low over her eyes.

"They lost their father," said Geoffrey. "Now they're losing you, too."

"It's *one* movie," said Andorra. "I'll be back in a few months."

"You'll have to stand in front of film crews and actors and say all those lines," warned Geoffrey. "You think you can do that? Have you forgotten how you get?"

Andorra had not forgotten; the last time she had stood in front of a crowd, she had been fifteen and had fainted dead away. But there was no point in thinking of that now. She could only hope that when the time came she would find that she had either outgrown her fear or that her particular brand of stage fright was reserved strictly for the stage.

"Someone has to do something," said Andorra. "We're all going to end up sleeping in the rain."

It was the right thing to say; it made her escape completely practical. But Andorra knew logic had nothing to do with why she said yes to Rutherford Simone.

Geoffrey wandered to the window, chewing the inside of his mouth. With Rowena absorbed in her notebook, Andorra was able to quietly reach beneath the pillow and remove a blue shirt. A man's shirt. A husband's shirt, though no one would know that but her. She had slept with it every night since she became a widow. Geoffrey saw no shame in wearing a mourning band for sixteen years, but it embarrassed Andorra that she still needed this shirt just to fall asleep. She slipped it under her blouse, even as she shut her eyes and forced her imagination west.

Hollywood. She knew nothing about it. At the occasional movie, condemned to the back row, Andorra had only been mildly impressed by the black-and-white wonders of the screen. Her husband had been the same way. A theater actor, he had decreed that the cinema lacked the enchantment of the stage. They seemed to have passed this disinterest on to the children: the twins rarely spoke of Hollywood stars or the latest cartoons. As for Rowena, the few times *she* had seen a picture, she always had the same complaint: "They're not very well written." All this meant that her family was unimpressed with the fact she was going to Hollywood. Andorra was equally unimpressed. She didn't care that she was going to *Hollywood*; she was *going*, and that's what mattered. They were collecting emptiness in that house. Empty purses, empty cupboards. She was out of things to pawn and trade and sell. She couldn't bear to be here. And even if she could, even if her weak heart (or *possibly weak* heart) could withstand the void, there was a deeper truth she had been aware of ever since she had killed her husband two years, six months, and eleven days ago: she did not deserve to be here.

"You should bring this," said Rowena. She reached into her mother's nightstand and pulled out the May 1929 issue of the *North American Review*. "Show them what *real* writing is like."

Andorra could barely glance at the magazine. She had hoped to be a writer once upon a time—she herself was the wellspring for Rowena's aspirations. But that May 1929 issue contained the only story she had ever published. *In the days just after the war, Katharine moved through the plague-ridden city just to give her future husband a shave* . . . Like her eldest daughter, Andorra had stolen everything from the world around her. That story in the May 1929 issue had the resonance of a photograph: the names had been changed, but every sentence was still a perfect snapshot of the past.

"You better keep it," she said. "It's the only copy we have." She swept those crimson bangs out of her daughter's eyes. "You're going to write about today, aren't you?"

"I kind of have to," said Rowena.

"So? How would it begin?"

Rowena showed Andorra the notebook. *My mother ran away on the first day of the baseball season; she was gone by the opening pitch.* Andorra envied that sentence. She envied the handwriting, too. Her own writing was terrible—the pens were always too small.

"I'm not running away," Andorra said. "Runaways don't come back."

"When *are* you coming back?"

"Well, let's see. It's opening day of the season. What if I'm back by the end of the World Series? That would have a nice poetry to it, wouldn't you say?"

"Sure," said Rowena. "But life isn't really all that poetic."

Rowena was right. Life *isn't* all that poetic. Andorra wouldn't be back by the end of the World Series. She would miss the entire season; she wouldn't even be there when it started to snow.

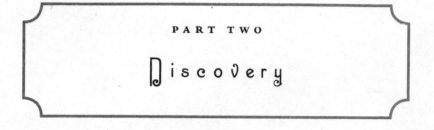

PART TWO

Discovery

FOUR

The Ambassador of Goodwill

Tatamagouche, 1861

THIS WAS SOMEONE ELSE'S WORLD; it had not been designed for the likes of her. Her mother continued to produce children, but since all of them were of average size, Anna Swan grew up under the impression that she was an aberration. Loneliness became a second skin. At the schoolhouse, she sat on the floor. When she walked into church, she thought she heard a distinctive break in the congregants' song. What could she do but retreat? In search of refuge, she turned to books, one of the few pleasures where her size couldn't get in the way. But even in the sanctuary of literature, the truth of her existence found a way to break through. In Greek myth, the Titans devour their children; in British stories, Jack defeats a giant who eats cows. *This is how people see me*, thought the not-so-little girl. *They think I'm going to swallow them whole.*

She prayed for something to arrest her growth, but she had only to visit the tailor to see that her prayers were being ignored. For this reason, she came to loathe Johnson Clarke, the diminutive thing who worked tirelessly to renew her wardrobe throughout the years. Famed for both his skill and the terrible assortment of blackheads splashed across his face, he broke into an ugly grin each time she appeared in his shop: she was his one connection to notoriety. Anna came to hate that smile. She wanted to connect him with normalcy; she dreamed of making the ugly tailor frown.

One rough April morning—it was 1861 and she was almost

fifteen—Anna trailed her mother into Johnson Clarke's shop. Having slept badly, she was full of petulance and was prepared to make the next round of measurements as difficult as possible for the ugly tailor. But instead of blackheads and a bald head, she found only smooth skin and a mop of shaggy hair. A young man was struggling with a bolt of fabric. He emitted a wonderful string of curses; when he saw Anna, he emitted even more.

"Damn and double damn!"

"Language!" snapped Anna's mother.

"Sorry, ma'am," said the young man. (He was clearly *not* sorry.)

"Where's Mr. Clarke? Annie needs a new dress."

"I always thought Pa was making it up," said the young man, who continued to gape.

"Don't gape!" snapped Anna's mother.

"Sorry," said the boy. He said it to *Anna*—and he clearly *was* sorry.

It was hard to see the resemblance between the boy and his father. Barely eighteen, Gavin Clarke was long and smooth, resembling something that might be used to push a gondola down a Venetian canal. He only knew a little about tailoring. He had been living with his mother in Toronto, but she had fallen to cholera, and he had been brought to Tatamagouche to be his father's apprentice. "Pa's gone to measure a funeral suit," said Gavin. "He might be back by tonight."

"At least take her measurements," said Ann. "That way your father can get started when he returns."

"I think we have her measurements written down."

"They're probably out of date," sighed Anna's mother.

"My measurements are *always* out of date," sighed Anna.

Reluctantly, Gavin led her to a curtained stall at the back of the store. He released the sash and brought the curtain down around them, effectively hiding them from her mother (or rather, hiding *him*; Anna's head was clearly visible over the top). It was musty and dank:

he bore the rich smell of shaving soap and sweat. When he approached her with the measuring rope, she saw that his hands were shaking. His eyes moved away from her enormous bust, but seconds later he was staring at her again. He seemed to have no control over his own gaze. A small thrill went through her. She was accustomed to making people uncomfortable—but *this* was a discomfort of an entirely different sort.

"Perhaps you'd feel better if you took some of the measurements yourself," he said.

"Do you think I can do it properly?"

"It's the easiest thing in the world."

"If it's so easy, why are tailors always doing it themselves?"

"An excuse to touch girls. I'd reckon that's why they invented tailoring."

Anna laughed. She took the rope and wrapped it around her body. Her hands were precariously close to her own breasts, and she thought she saw him blush.

"Well?" he asked. "Are your measurements out of date?"

"Definitely." Anna returned the rope. She had kept her thumb on the new number so that he would have no choice but to brush the top of her hand.

Gavin made notes in his father's ledger, an impressive record that chronicled Anna's history one millimeter at a time. "Incredible," he murmured.

"Maybe to you. I just wish it would stop."

"It will."

"We'll know soon enough." Anna shrugged. "I might keep growing until I burst."

Gavin almost laughed. But he must have seen that she was serious. He examined the ledger with a studious air. "If you want my professional opinion, you're already slowing down."

She decided not to mention that he was only an *apprentice*; he was hardly experienced enough to *have* a professional opinion. He knelt and slipped the slipper off her foot—Cinderella and her prince but in reverse. There was a tear in her stocking, allowing the soft place at the crest of her foot to poke through. In taking the measurements, it seemed to her he touched this spot more than was needed. At one moment he even rested his hand over the tear so his skin was touching hers. Was this on purpose? She felt a surge of lust, not quite understanding it. His skin was hot, a warming pan fresh from the stove.

Right then, Ann Swan pulled back the curtain. Anna recoiled and drew back her foot. (The moment looked innocent enough, but she was absurdly struck with shame.)

"We're leaving," said Ann Swan.

"We're not done," said Anna.

"There's no time," said her mother. "He's here."

"Who?" said Anna.

"The *New Yorker*. He's back. Hurry up—before your father drives him away."

At once, Anna pushed her foot back into her shoe. She grabbed her bonnet and fled the shop, pausing just long enough to send a slight curtsey Gavin's way. She pictured him standing in the tailor shop, measuring rope in hand, clinging to the sensation of her soft foot for as long as he could. *She* was certainly clinging to the memory of his slender hands; her foot, she imagined, still pulsed from his touch. Distracted by the return of the New Yorker, Anna did not spend much time wondering what any of this might mean. But her heart knew. It had begun to quiver in her chest, as if in preparation of all that was to come.

FOR THE LAST ELEVEN YEARS, H. P. Ingalls had returned like clockwork; for the last eleven years, the spring thaw produced

the New Yorker along with his dappled horse. Like Gavin Clarke,
H. P. Ingalls had his own professional opinion about Anna's future—
but as far as he was concerned, she was not done growing at all.

Alexander Swan had continued building signs in the vain hope
it would keep the New Yorker away. Ann Swan, meanwhile, had continued to have her enormous daughter tear them down. This had
become part of the clockwork, too. Spring came. Alexander built a
sign. Ann and Anna tore it down. On this particular spring in 1861,
they were halfway through the routine. The sign was still standing;
its message was the longest it had ever been:

ALL PILGRIMS, NEW YORKERS, AMERICANS,
MANAGERS, AGENTS,
ENVOYS, SCOUTS, REPRESENTATIVES,
AND BUSINESSMEN
WILL BE SHOT.

Coming home from the tailor shop, Ann Swan was terrified this
might be the day the sign drove H. P. Ingalls away. She needn't have
worried. Nobody obeys anything in New York, and New Yorkers
carry this habit wherever they go. Both H. P. Ingalls and the dappled horse walked on by—the horse was a New Yorker, too.

"Still haven't learned to read," grumbled Alexander.

"I'm just an ambassador of goodwill," said the New Yorker.

"I'll add it to the sign. How do you spell ambassador?"

Just then, Ann Swan and Anna returned in their carriage, out of
breath as if they had been pulling it themselves. "Mr. Ingalls!" Ann
exclaimed, and she let the man help her to the ground. This was
another part of the clockwork. Whenever the New Yorker came,
Alexander was rude while his wife was gracious. Since losing her
money to the Reverend Blackwood, she was hesitant to trust the
smiles of men. But she trusted H. P. Ingalls.

The New Yorker had been returning for eleven years, but it had only been in the last three that he had learned of Anna's weakness. Achilles had his heel and Goliath had the divot between his eyes; as for Anna, she did not have the strength to withstand the kindness of strangers. She weakened as H. P. Ingalls thrilled her siblings with toys and clothes; she blushed when he handed her mother a pair of golden candlesticks. She became speechless when she herself was presented with a brand-new book. In that isolated patch of Nova Scotia, there were few books. Except for her stories of ogres and giants, Anna had only the Bible and *Ivanhoe*, and each had been read dozens of times.

"It's called *Jane Eyre*," said H. P. Ingalls. "My sister can't get enough." He presented it to her wrapped in old copies of *The Toronto Globe*. Anna tore off the wrapping and turned the book over in her hands. It was a first edition, and its spine was hardly worn.

While Anna turned the book over in her hands, her mother brought the New Yorker into the house to fix some tea. Alexander, anticipating the usual heated conversation, sent the rest of the children out into the yard. He did not exactly go for his rifle, but he positioned himself beneath the place on the wall where it hung. If the New Yorker saw this, he blithely ignored it. Ann Swan was his ally; he focused all of his attention on her.

"So how's Annie getting along?" he asked.

"Still growing," said Ann.

"I was hoping you'd say that."

"Actually, I haven't grown all that much," remarked Anna. "Gavin Clarke seems to think I'm done."

"Who's Gavin Clarke?"

"The tailor's son."

H. P. Ingalls laughed. "Well, I guess he should know."

"We're still not interested," said Alexander wearily.

"You just aren't being practical," said the New Yorker. "Every time

I come here, you have more children." On that day in 1861, Anna had four sisters and a pair of brothers; unaware of his real purpose, they each considered the New Yorker a favorite uncle who came and disappeared at whim. "What exactly are your measurements, if you don't mind me asking?"

"Of all the nerve!" said Alexander.

"Sit *down*," said Ann Swan.

"It's all right," said Anna. She told him the numbers. H. P. Ingalls whistled. She had sprouted almost three inches since the previous spring.

They drank tea while Anna sat on the floor and stared reverently at her copy of *Jane Eyre*. Not daring to crack that virgin spine, she turned instead to those pages from *The Toronto Globe*. To wrap his gift, the New Yorker had used the editorial page, which was giving some very strong opinions on the matter of a few shots that had been fired at a place called Fort Sumter.

"Your country's at war!" exclaimed Anna.

"War's a strong word," said the New Yorker. "It's just a skirmish that'll be done by the first snow."

"I wouldn't be comfortable sending Annie to a country at war," said Ann Swan.

"Good thing it's not a war."

"We're not sending her anywhere," said Alexander. "Annie's going to teachers' college in Truro."

"Is that a fact?"

The New Yorker turned to Anna, who gave an unhappy nod. At home, she was a strain on the family's resources. It was time she started to prove her worth. Other women could hope to marry, but Alexander wanted Anna to find good, solid work. *He probably doesn't think I'll ever be a wife*, Anna thought with disdain. *In his world, women have few options—and giant women have even less.*

"This isn't some sideshow," H. P. Ingalls said. "Barnum has

nothing but the utmost respect for propriety. His museum is a celebration of the extraordinary. That's your Annie. Do you think I'd be here if she were anything less? We already have three giants, and they're wonderful things, but they're all men. I really do think she might be the only lady giant in the modern world."

Anna glanced up. She wasn't sure what had startled her more—that Barnum had *three* giants or that he had three giants who were *men*. Her heart, already quivering from her encounter with Gavin Clarke, now shook like a trembling fist.

"*Three* giants?" she said. "Is that all there is? Or are there more?"

"Oh there are plenty more," said the New Yorker. "I've seen a handful with my own eyes over the years. Right now there's just the three, but that's enough. Get them all together and they become a thunder."

A thunder of giants! Her mind reeled at the thought.

"Have you really never seen a lady giant?" asked Ann Swan.

"Never in all my years," said the New Yorker.

"She's not a lady giant," said Alexander. "She's a lady like anyone else."

"You don't really believe that, do you?"

"I want *her* to believe it." Alexander put a firm hand on H. P. Ingalls's arm. "Time's up."

The New Yorker tipped his hat. "Until next year, then."

"When are you going to give up?"

The New Yorker fixed a hard gaze on Alexander Swan. "When you let her make up her own mind," he said. Then he turned to Anna, who was still trembling at the thought of P. T. Barnum's thunder of giants. "What do you want, Annie? Do you want me to leave forever?"

Here was something new to the clockwork: no one had ever asked her this before. Anna knew what Alexander wanted her to say; she knew what Ann Swan wanted her to say, too. But what did *she* want to say? New York. War. That thunder of giants. Best to play if safe while she sorted it all out.

"I suppose there's no harm in you coming back," she said.

H. P. Ingalls clapped Alexander on the back. "Looks like you're building yourself another sign," he said.

THE NEW YORKER'S GRIN lingered in Anna's mind well into summer. She read and reread *Jane Eyre*, always using the paper from *The Toronto Globe* to mark her place. She read the book to her sisters; she read the book to her dog. She liked the way Jane Eyre kept reinventing her life. One minute she was with her evil aunt; the next she was a governess at Thornfield Hall. Anna also liked how, at the end of the book, when Jane and her great love return to Thornfield Hall, it was *Jane* who had to show him the way. "Being so much lower of stature than he, I served both for his prop and guide."

Being so much lower in stature! thought Anna. *Imagine if that could ever be so!*

In the autumn, she left for Truro. Like Jane Eyre's time at the Lowood School, Anna's time at the teachers' college felt like an "irksome struggle"; it was a gloomy place consumed by deep snow and impassable roads. Worse, it was called the Normal School, an irony lost on no one. The faculty members had been warned of Anna's size, but they were not equipped to handle it. "Little children *might* respect you," the teachers told her. "But no one over the age of ten will ever take you seriously." Sure enough, when she took her walks on the college grounds, the youth of Truro followed and gawked as if she had just escaped from the zoo.

She did not write home of her troubles; instead, she risked a letter to Gavin Clarke. She had been thinking of it for days, and at last, during a wintery evening when the wind and snow had buried her in the dormitory, she put ink to page. She described the school and her teachers; she masked her loneliness with invented incidents and friends that didn't exist. She agonized over how to sign such a letter, and in that agony she finally became aware of the hope that was burning in her chest. She began to fear sending the letter; she became suddenly terrified he wouldn't respond.

But, to the relief of her throbbing heart, he responded swiftly. His own letter was filled with the gossip from his father's shop. In America, H. P. Ingalls's summer skirmish had evolved into a war, and in Nova Scotia this had led to fears of annexation. Mother England had sent troops to defend the borders. Yet nobody could agree on where their sympathies lay. "Some people say they're fighting to free the slaves," wrote Gavin. "If so, then we're for the North. But some say they're fighting about money and power. Everyone thinks the North will invade. All the men have to join the militia. It's become a <u>mandatory thing</u>." From the intensity of his underline, she knew that *impressment* impressed him. He was a boy, wasn't he? He liked the idea of war. Anna liked the idea, too. She liked the idea of Gavin's long body draped in militia gray; she liked the idea of *Gavin* period. She imagined him with a rifle growing hot in his hands; she imagined him injured and needing to rely on her—as both a prop and a guide.

Their correspondence continued, but it was hardly enough to keep her afloat; she continued to drown in her own isolation. *Jane Eyre* became an obsession; she read it until she didn't have to read it because she knew so much of it by heart. "What do I want?" she asked herself one night, and in response she quoted Jane Eyre, who answers the very same question in chapter 10: "A new place, in a new house, amongst new faces, under new circumstances. I want this because it is of no use wanting anything better." Suddenly, Anna knew that she could finally answer the question H. P. Ingalls had put to her last spring. She wanted to be in New York; but she didn't want to be there alone. She supposed she should be thinking of men her own size— men like those giants in the American Museum. But if she married

a giant, then she would always be a lady giant. If she married someone like Gavin Clarke, then she could be what her father had wanted:
just a lady, like anyone else.

This was what she wanted. To marry Gavin and go to New York.
To be both celebrated *and* have a normal life.

When the snow thawed, she dropped out of college and returned
home. The New Yorker returned like clockwork, didn't he? But this
time the clockwork would change; *this time,* she thought, *I'll make
that clock bust a spring.*

"Teaching just isn't for me," she told her parents.

"Then what *is* for you?" asked Alexander.

Anna held her tongue. She knew what her father would say if she
told him what she was thinking: *New York is for me. A new place and
new circumstance.*

She held her tongue with Gavin, too; she was too scared to confess her dreams. He startled her. Now nineteen, there was a fire in
him and he merrily kicked at the world. He stalked through the
town, eager to find a way to prove himself. He had lost interest in
the militia; he adored having a rank but did not believe they would
ever be called upon to fight.

"Why would America want to fight two wars?" he asked one day.
"It doesn't make any sense."

"It *doesn't* make any sense," agreed Anna.

"You're both too young to understand," said Alexander. They were
all in the tailor shop, waiting for Gavin's father to provide Alexander with his latest pair of pants. "Every time you turn around, the
Yanks have their claws in something else. They want this whole con-
tinent to themselves. They think it's their destiny."

"The only way we'll ever see action is if we take the regiment and
go down to Maine," said Gavin. "We could offer to join up."

"That's treason talk," said Anna. "We're supposed to be neutral."

Gavin revealed a folded piece of newsprint that he had torn from the *Royal Gazette*. "Look! They'll give us money and clothes. If we get an honorable discharge, they'll give us land. You even get a bonus if you bring your own gun. I'm telling you: every one of us could be rich."

"The only people who get rich in a war are those who don't fight," remarked Johnson Clarke.

"Politicians and munitions men, they're the ones who get fat." Alexander nodded. "The rest of us grow poor trying not to get shot."

"I'm telling you," said Gavin, "we all need to go down and give those rebels what for."

"Those rebels are our bread and butter," called his father. "What do you think this war is doing to the price of cotton? And you want to go fight them? Have you no shame?"

Gavin leaned in and whispered in Anna's ear. "I'm going to do it," he said, his breath hot on her neck. "I'm going down to Maine, maybe even New York. I'm running at the end of the week."

Anna hardly knew what to say. She loved that she knew something about Gavin that no one else did. But did it have to be *this?*

Johnson Clarke was still distracted with her father's fitting, so Anna leaned down and whispered back to Gavin, blowing her own warm breath into his ear. "You can't go off to war," she said.

"You just wait. One day I'm going to be all big and fine. In my boots I might even be as big as you."

"You're going to get hurt."

"What I'm going to do is save the life of some Southern belle."

"You wouldn't want a girl from the South."

"I would if she was rich. Can you imagine me as a war hero with a rich wife? I can't wait to look in the mirror and see *that* staring back at me, I'll tell you that."

He had puffed up his chest, and she hated him. So arrogant! So cruel! "Go right now, if you're so excited," she snapped.

"Keep your voice down."

"You don't even need to pack. Why would you? There's nothing for you here. So why don't you just pick up and leave?"

She meant to make a dramatic exit. She meant to turn away in a single great motion so the frills of her skirt whipped through the air. She meant to exit with the sort of magnificent gesture that would obsess Gavin Clarke for the rest of his life. But as she turned she stepped on his foot, and the bones cracked like fallen leaves.

"Damn and double damn!" Gavin sprang into the air. His cries drew the attention from the others in the shop. Anna tried to help, but Gavin pushed her away. He gingerly put his foot on the ground but drew it back almost at once. "I think it's broken! You better hope it's not broken! If it's broken, I'll never speak to you again!"

"Don't be a fool," said Anna.

"You did that on purpose!" he hollered.

"Oh, enough. It was an *accident*."

"The *hell* it was! You're trapped, so you think everyone else should be, too!"

Her cheeks flared. "I'm not trapped. I'm going to New York just as soon as I can!"

"Why don't you then?" snapped Gavin, and he began to limp away.

"You don't mean that," said Alexander Swan. Anna had forgotten he was there. "You don't want to go to New York, do you, Annie?"

"The *hell* I don't!" said Anna. She called after Gavin. "I *will* go to New York. I'll go and I'll marry a merchant or a New York banker or maybe even P. T. Barnum himself!"

She stormed from the shop and went to the edge of town, hoping that by some amazing coincidence this would be the day when H. P. Ingalls returned. But his timing wasn't *that* good; it would be another three weeks before the New Yorker appeared. By then, Gavin Clarke would be gone, having limped stubbornly out of town on his injured foot. She would not allow herself to weep, even though he would leave without saying good-bye. After he left, she gripped her heart and forced it to sit still. In New York she would have her new place and new circumstance. She might even have something more. There was always Barnum's thunder of giants. Surely one of them would give her a normal life. She may have been the only lady giant in the modern world, but in New York, she knew, she would never be alone.

FIVE

The Not-So-Little Girl

Sant Julià de Lòria, 1905–1910

IT WAS IMPOSSIBLE to protect Elionor from the news of Andorra's size. According to Manuela Noguerra, who returned to the house periodically for food and supplies, Elionor wept when she first heard of her daughter's incredible growth. Her grandmother had warned that the sins of the mother are passed along; and here was Andorra, suffering as she grew.

Needing to tell Andorra something about her mama, the loyal Manuela informed the not-so-little girl that Elionor had gone to America. (To the romantic Manuela, America was a lost horizon as exotic as the moon). As for Andorra's father, Manuela told her niece he had taken up a life of solitude in the west wing. Forbidden to go near the rooms, Andorra was five before she found the courage to search for her father. Unsure why the wing was prohibited, she braced herself for spirits, ghouls, and all manner of deadly things; instead, she found only covered furniture and broken antiques. The west wing was empty. The windows were shut; the walls covered in dust. No one lived here. Having summoned all her bravery to come here, the not-so-little girl experienced the first great horror of her life: her father was gone.

She told no one about the secret of the west wing and returned in silence to the unhappy life she shared with Noria Blanco, a woman who was impossibly ugly both inside and out. It hadn't always been like this. She had once been engaged to a musician whose blindness kept him from noticing her terrifying looks. But on the day of the wedding, he was kicked in the head by a mule. Ever since, Noria Blanco had been entirely alone. Solitude had twisted her heart. She was now like the forests of the principality: dense and dangerous.

Noria had little sympathy for Andorra's strange condition, and almost at once she began to isolate the girl. It was years before Andorra would read the story of Rapunzel; when she did, she wondered if Noria had read it for inspiration. Noria Blanco did not exactly imprison Andorra in a tower, but she worked as hard as any witch to keep her away from the outside world. Andorra didn't go to school, and she never played with the other children of the parish. In a town as small as Sant Julià de Lòria, though, nothing could keep the truth of Andorra a secret for very long. From the window of her room, the not-so-little girl could easily see the *little* little girls as they stood near the gates of the house. They were forever pointing. Forever whispering words Andorra would never hear.

It wasn't until she was six—and already three and a half feet—that Noria Blanco summoned the same physician who had discovered the hole in Elionor's womb. This time, he made no diagnosis. How could he? There was nothing to diagnose. Size is not a disease.

"But she's growing *too much*," said Noria Blanco.

"How much is *too much*?" asked Andorra.

"Look in the mirror," snapped Noria.

The physician turned to Noria and lowered his voice. "She's perfectly healthy, but that doesn't mean there's no cause for concern. Scientifically speaking, the larger the animal, the shorter the life. It's the heart. It just starts to wear out."

Andorra blanched. She had heard every word—the physician had not lowered his voice enough. After he was gone, she tried to force herself into her aunt's arms. She wanted to hide from the terror the doctor had left in his wake.

"Is my heart going to stop?" she asked.

"It's very rude to eavesdrop," said Noria Blanco, and she pushed the child away. "You poor thing. I won't be around forever. Who will care for you when I'm gone?"

"What about Manuela?" asked Andorra.

"She has her loyalties. I'm not sure they involve you."

"Won't Mama come back for me?"

"I doubt it very much."

"And Tata?" asked Andorra carefully.

Here Noria paused because the truth was that Geoffrey del Alandra was not as far away as Andorra thought. Dutiful as ever, he had continued to run the business his father had left behind. But it had nothing to do with tobacco. The tobacco farms ran themselves. The *real* family business was smuggling; the *real* family fortune had been made using the principality's dense forests to transport contraband between France and Spain. This was why Geoffrey had always been such good friends with the smugglers, whose criminal behavior was quietly ignored by everyone in the parish. The smugglers paid good money for their passage and furnished the isolated parish with many goods they would not otherwise have. Geoffrey, like his father before him, could have orchestrated the business dealings from home. But he was eager for escape.

So although it was true he disappeared for months at a time, he always returned, and during these times, he indeed stayed in the west wing of his father's house. Andorra only *thought* the wing had been deserted that night months before when she had crept inside; in fact, Geoffrey had been hiding behind the couch. He had been wide awake, for he was plagued by such terrible dreams that he had trained himself in the art of insomnia by keeping sharp stones in his pockets so that every movement caused him pain. He spent most of his nights standing on the banks of the Valira River, staring across at the shack where Elionor and her faithful Manuela now lived. Andorra wouldn't know this for many years; not until she was a young woman would she learn how her father had prayed to catch a glimpse of his wife. "But I didn't want to see her as she was," Geoffrey would tell his daughter. "I wanted her to appear to me as she had been; I wanted her only if she was cured."

In those early years of the twentieth century, though, this information was still years away. For now, Andorra was just a not-so-little girl, and Noria Blanco knew that Geoffrey was nothing but an echo of a man, lost even to himself.

"Your tata prefers his isolation," Noria told her niece. "You can't really count on him at all."

The young Andorra could only conclude that her parents' absence had everything to do with her great size. Size may not be a disease, but it was definitely a curse. She began to stare in the mirror and tell herself to shrink. "*Stop!*" she told her reflection, as if it were a dog being trained to sit. But her reflection ignored her, as reflections often do. Like her missing parents, like her body, like everything in this world, her reflection had a terrible will of its own.

It was her eighth Christmas when the loyal Manuela appeared bearing a gift: a letter, all the way from America. It was from Elionor, who claimed to be writing from a house on some golden American street. She said she had become an actress, a darling of the stage. Andorra clutched at the envelope. She didn't comment on the fact the letter had no stamp or postmark. She knew little about the laws of the postal system; this was the first letter she had ever received.

Andorra disappeared to her room to read (and reread) the letter, while, downstairs, Noria scowled at the loyal Manuela.

"An *actress?*" said Noria.

"That was my idea," said Manuela.

"Is any of this necessary?"

"Elionor begged me."

"*Elionor* asked you to do this?"

"She likes the lie. She says it's better than the truth."

"Nothing is better than the truth. Better we tell Andorra everything."

"She has enough problems," said Manuela. By then, Andorra was four foot three.

Noria Blanco chewed her lip. "Very well. But in exchange, you're going to do something for me."

The next day—Christmas Day—Andorra came downstairs to find Manuela Noguerra was joining them for the Christmas feast. "It's time that we discuss the next stage of your education," said Noria Blanco.

Andorra's weak little heart grew tense. So far, all the stages of her education had involved private lessons with Noria Blanco. The *next* stage could only mean one thing. "Am I going to school with other children?" asked Andorra.

"That would be a terrible idea," said Noria. "Other children won't like you. No. Manuela has agreed to take part in your education."

Andorra's heart relaxed. She liked this idea; she was terrified by the thought of those *little* little girls prancing through the schoolhouse with their whispered words. "How long will we do this?" asked Andorra.

"Until you're the same size as everyone else," said Noria.

"Will that ever happen?"

"You'll know soon enough," said Manuela.

Noria Blanco announced she would be teaching poise, etiquette, and a woman's duty to the family tree; Manuela Noguerra would be in charge of language, geography, and literacy. "Your first assignment," said Manuela, "is to write your mother back."

"Is my mama very important?" asked Andorra.

"Oh, yes," said Manuela. "She's one of the most important people in town."

Although she hated being taught by Noria Blanco, Andorra came to adore her time with her strange but loyal aunt. Manuela was an ideal teacher who repeated much of what Geoffrey had taught *her* back in Madrid. Having not lost her romantic ideals, she was the perfect counterbalance to Noria Blanco's pragmatic ways. Had Noria Blanco taught geography, for instance, Andorra would have seen only a map of the principality, beyond which were all the dragons that cartographers said flew across dangerous lands. But to Manuela, the world had no dragons. On the day of their first lesson, she unrolled a map of the world and pinned down the corners with pieces of shale. Andorra stood over the world and learned for the first time that, no matter how large she became, she would still be one of the smallest nations on earth. *There I am,* she thought. *A prick between France and Spain, one hundred and eighty miles long.*

"Where's Mama?" she asked.

"You tell me," challenged Manuela.

The not-so-little girl knew her mama was the most important person in town; she didn't know exactly where that town was. After some consideration, she traced a line that cut through Spain, crossed the Atlantic Ocean, and landed in America—*South* America. Manuela took her niece's hand—already, it dwarfed her own—and moved it up through Mexico and into the United States.

"Are there many theaters in the *United States?*" asked Andorra, saying each word with care.

"Hundreds," said her aunt. "Your mama performs in them all."

"One day I'm going to see Mama act in America."

"Who knows? Maybe one day your mama will return on her own."

"I'll have to stop growing first," said Andorra.

"What does that mean?"

"I know it's why they left. If I stop growing, maybe they'll return."

"Your father isn't gone. He's in the west wing."

"Nobody is in the west wing," said Andorra, releasing one of her secrets into the world. "I've been there. I've seen it myself."

A shiver went through the loyal Manuela. "Your parents didn't leave because of your size. Size is not a terrible thing. My grandmother believed that giants were good luck."

A giant! It was the first time anyone had ever used the word to describe Andorra—at least in her presence. "Am I a *giant?*" she asked.

"Not yet," said Manuela, kissing her niece's forehead. "But if you are, then you're lucky. My grandmother touched a giant when she was a girl, and it changed her life."

She told her the story as it had been told to her. Manuela and Elionor's grandmother had been an orphan, abandoned by her parents because of a terrible affliction: she suffered from epileptic fits.

"What are epileptic fits?" asked Andorra.

"Something that's *really* a curse," said Manuela. "It's like a great storm that takes over your whole body for a short time and makes you shake without stopping. Her parents left her at an orphan's asylum and disappeared. When she grew up, my grandmother went to a place called Halifax, where she tried to be a lady's maid. But she lost her job after a seizure struck just as she was ladling soup into her mistress's bowl. Desperate, she went to see someone called the Infant Giantess, who was rumored to be a saint."

"What's an Infant Giantess?" asked Andorra.

"She was like you," said Manuela. "She was a not-so-little girl."

"And your grandmother touched her?" said Andorra.

"That's right. And as far as I know, she never had a seizure again."

As the story went, the frail girl—she was known for her brittle hair and shoehorn face—was completely transformed. Her confidence improved, she was transformed from a dour maid into a cheerful bit of sun. This change did not go unnoticed by a Spanish sailor who was docked in Halifax while his ship was making repairs.

He wooed her, and she, having never been wooed, was easily won; she sailed home with him to Madrid, where they retired to a small town not far from that prick between the border of France and Spain.

"That story is a lie wrapped in an exaggeration," said Noria Blanco.

They turned and saw the stunted woman standing in the door, arms crossed in front of her flat little chest. They hadn't known she was there.

"My grandmother swore it was true," said Manuela.

"Your grandmother was a fool," said Noria. She was tottering a little, and her breath bore the rich smell of aguardiente. "Read your Bible. Giants are terrible people. That's why the Lord destroyed them in the flood."

"Don't say such things!" Manuela tried to cover Andorra's ears.

"I don't have to say it. God already has." Noria Blanco gave her niece a piteous look. "None of this is your fault. It's the sins of the mother. You'll just have to find a way to live with it."

She staggered away and her footfalls filled the house.

"I don't know what to do," Andorra complained. "Or rather, I don't know what *not* to do. I just want to be what she wants me to be."

"To hell with her," said Manuela. "You're going to be something better."

NORIA BLANCO GREW HARSHER. More and more often, she was caught with aguardiente on the breath. The household was a runaway cart, careening toward a mountainous wall; the crash came the day Andorra's breasts began to sprout. She was almost eleven, but this sudden sprint to womanhood so startled Noria Blanco that she resolved to finally take charge of Andorra's fate.

"I'm taking her to the capital," she told Manuela. "Nobody knows us there. She's still heir to Geoffrey's money. Someone will want her."

"I don't want to go to the capital," said Andorra.

"Don't be difficult!" snapped Noria. "Remember the story of Job. The test is how we respond to the challenges the Lord provides. We all must find a way to endure."

Andorra's poor little heart shook. She had been in virtual isolation her entire life. The thought of the capital—of *anywhere*—was euphoric. But not if it meant marriage. Not if it meant dealing with *men*. She had no understanding of men. That terrible doctor was one of the only men she had ever seen.

"This is absurd," said Manuela. "She's only ten."

"Not anymore," said Noria Blanco. "From now on, if anyone asks, she's seventeen and a half."

Tormented, Manuela Noguerra thundered back to the Valira River and demanded Elionor reclaim her rights as a mother. But by then, Elionor had been living with her terrible condition for almost a decade. She had learned to survive but not how to triumph. There are other curses besides size and fistulas; shame is a curse, too, and it had seeped into Elionor's bones. "A husband is not always a bad thing," said Andorra's mother. "At least she'll be provided for."

"*You're* being 'provided for'!" Manuela Noguerra swept her arm around the dilapidated shack, pointing to the rotted wood, the flies, the cracked plates. "Is *this* all you want for her?"

"It might be the best she can ever hope for."

"Maybe Geoffrey will help. He's still her father."

Andorra's mother smiled sadly. "You always had too much faith in him."

"And you never had enough."

"Why put your faith in something made of stone?"

"I wish you really *were* in America," spat Manuela. "You'd be a lot more good there than you ever were here."

It was the closest she ever came to betrayal; it was the harshest thing that loyal girl had ever said.

Two mornings later, Manuela Noguerra shook Andorra awake.

It was a week before Christmas and she had decided to give her niece a gift. "Get dressed," she said. "We're going to see your father." Stunned by the news, the not-so-little girl practically threw herself into her favorite dress. She put on soft flat slippers and wore her hair down in order to lessen her height. She was still fighting with her hair when Manuela returned to lead her to the west wing.

"You look beautiful, *mi amor*," said Manuela.

"I just hope I look like I've stopped growing," said the not-so-little girl.

Geoffrey del Alandra had only just returned from his latest trip with the smugglers. They found him, dirty and hairy, lying on one of the covered couches. He was an echo of Noria Blanco; as her twin, he bore the resemblance that made it seem to Andorra she had been staring at him all her life. The room had the odor of iniquity—of tobacco, of opium, of unhappy thoughts.

"So it's you," said Geoffrey. He was toying with a broken guitar, idly plucking its one remaining string. "Well, come on over. You might as well give me a kiss."

Manuela led Andorra to the couch. Andorra grimaced at the smell as she kissed his cheek. He grimaced too as her shadow fell over him. How absurd it had been to ever hope she could appear as something small! Encased by the low ceiling, her condition was all too clear. She understood then what she was—or rather, what she was on her way to become.

Manuela had probably practiced a speech full of pretty phrases, but upon seeing Geoffrey in beard and rags, she was suddenly filled with rage. After Andorra kissed her father's cheek, the loyal Manuela slapped the very same spot. This so stunned them that no one moved until Manuela, so relieved by the act, performed it a second time. Now Andorra's father tried to roll away. But he wasn't fast enough, and Manuela beat him with her fists, driving him to curl into a ball at the foot of the couch. At last, Andorra stepped in and grabbed her loyal aunt by the wrists. They were both surprised by her strength. The not-so-little girl was able to drive her aunt toward the other side of the room.

Geoffrey struggled to sit up. His face was red and bruised, and the attack had drawn tears instead of blood.

"I knew it!" crowed Manuela in triumph. "You aren't made of stone at all."

They began to tell him everything that had been happening in the house, but it wasn't necessary. He was aware of everything. His crime was not ignorance; it was indifference. Andorra suddenly saw the weakness in her father. It wasn't a weakness of body—the months of travel had kept him strong. But, like her, he had a soft heart. His spirit was cracked.

"Elionor calls me a romantic," said Manuela. "But so what? You accepted your responsibility once. There's no reason you won't do it again."

"I don't know what you would have me do."

"Noria's right about one thing—Andorra should be taken away."

"I don't *want* to go away," said Andorra.

"You deserve to be something other than someone's embarrassing secret," said Manuela. "You *both* do."

She told Andorra to wait outside. Andorra, feeling out of her depth, happily fled from the room. She nearly fled down the stairs, too, but at the last moment she positioned herself outside the door. She wanted to be nearby in case Manuela attacked Geoffrey again.

"There's nothing for you here," Andorra heard her aunt say. "Nobody wants you to stay."

"What about Elionor?" asked Geoffrey.

"Why would she want you here? What good have you ever been to her?"

Andorra heard a muffled sound. She wondered if her father was crying again.

"You will steal money from your sister," said Manuela. "You will leave using those secret roads you know so well, and you will get as far from here as you can. Go anywhere you like. Go to America, if you want."

"America's not the place you think it is," growled Geoffrey. "Whatever you've heard, it's probably nothing but a lot of myths."

"I know they like freedom there," said Manuela. "Maybe they'll give her the freedom to be whatever she wants to be." Her voice softened. "You can be something else, too. You want to escape this place, don't you? Then *escape*. In America, you can have a history made up entirely of lies."

They summoned Andorra back into the room, and when they told her their plan, she pretended to be hearing it for the first time. She did not weep, but there were tears on her cheeks. She didn't want to leave. She *definitely* didn't want to leave with her father. He was hardly the hero she needed. How could he ever lead her through the world?

"I want you to come," she told Manuela.

"I have to stay here."

"How long will we go? How long will I be away?"

"Forever," said her aunt.

"Does Noria know about this?"

"Noria definitely does *not* know about this. And we have to keep it that way."

"Do I get to say good-bye?"

"Say good-bye," said Manuela. "Just don't let her *know* you're saying good-bye."

Andorra fought to find something good to look forward to. "If we go to the United States, can we see Mama act?"

The faithful Manuela, who had started the lie, could not bring herself to end it. She looked at Geoffrey and then back at her niece. "You'll know soon enough," she said.

. . .

THE NIGHT BEFORE CHRISTMAS EVE, the not-so-little girl
did as she had been told: she said good-bye but did not let Noria know
she was saying good-bye. "Good night, Auntie," she said to the stunted
woman. Noria Blanco barely replied. She was so drunk on wine that
she could do little more than blink. Later, bundled in a cloak, possessions packed tightly into a single valise, Andorra walked right past
Noria's room. The door wasn't even closed, and her last glimpse of
her terrible aunt was the sight of the woman sprawled on her stomach, drooling into a pillow and emitting the type of snore reserved
for mythical beasts.

She met her father at the back of the house, and together they
slipped into the trees. Like the Rapunzel she was, Andorra fled
the tower and never looked back. She imagined the air smelled
different, even though they were only steps from the house. But
the thrill of freedom was quickly tempered by her father. Instead of
leading her to the smuggler's roads, Geoffrey took her to banks
of the Valira River—and as they walked, he told her who they were
going to see. She had received her father for Christmas; now she
was receiving her mother too. Andorra would have many weeks
(and months and years) to consider this ambush. One has to be
careful what is told to children; one has to be careful what is *untold*
to them, too.

"I'm sorry," said Geoffrey. "I just thought the longer we waited,
the worse it would be."

The young Andorra took the truth in silence: it was a bitter pill,
and she actually felt herself struggle to swallow it whole.

"Who wrote me those letters?" she asked.

"Your mother. But she wrote them from here."

"She's been here the whole time."

"We both have."

"Here but *not* here."

"Here but not here," said her father.

"And now we're going to say good-bye?" said Andorra.

"If we see her," said Geoffrey.

"And it's a real good-bye? She knows when we say good-bye that we're really saying good-bye?"

"She should. Manuela told her we're leaving."

"But doesn't she want to come with us?"

"She may want to," said Geoffrey "But I don't think she will."

When they emerged from the trees, they were not far from the pathetic shack that Elionor had made her asylum. They appeared at the worst possible time. By now the parish physician had developed a special apparatus that Elionor could wear beneath her dress, one that caught the urine and feces as they leaked away. The doctor was especially proud of this device, which he championed as the height of ingenuity. It involved a small cup that rested between her legs and funneled into a small bag strapped around her thigh. This bag always needed to be cleaned. This was what Elionor was doing when her husband and daughter stepped from the trees. They came into view just as she was spilling her own shit into the earth.

Andorra believed she remembered her mother at once, but it would be a wonder if this was true. She had been an infant when Elionor left and in the time since, the woman had aged almost twenty years. She was brittle and frail. Some of her hair had actually fallen out.

"Mama," said Andorra softly. "Mama, hello."

Her mother stopped at the sound, the empty bag in her hand. She might have been a wild deer, frozen in place, a heartbeat away from escape. Then Elionor's body shifted—perhaps she was turning toward Andorra, perhaps she was turning away. But the ground was wet with her filth, and she slipped. She fell hard. Elionor looked at her hands, now covered with shit and piss, and released a small cry of horror that resembled the squeak of a lost bird. Then she did as she always had: she ran away. In a moment she was gone, cowering behind the broken door of the shack.

Andorra misunderstood the moment entirely. At ten years old, she was almost five and a half feet tall. In her mother's face, Andorra imagined she saw nothing but terror and rage. Terror at her daughter's size. And rage because she had been caught with her shame spilling into the world.

"Elionor!" her father called. "Elionor!"

With pained silence, Andorra turned away. It was just as Manuela had said: nobody wanted them there. Because she believed this, it was that much easier to leave.

SIX

A Clean Slate

City of Los Angeles, 1937

THEY ESCAPED DETROIT by train only to be delayed in Chicago—Rutherford the Traveler was eternally misreading timetables. The train for California didn't leave until Saturday, forcing them to spend three awkward days in the Windy City, wandering down Michigan Avenue as if they were friends when they hardly knew each other at all. At last they boarded the *City of Los Angeles*, a great locomotive which held a compact world of domed dining cars, observation rooms, lounges, and sleeping berths that folded into the walls. Andorra did not have to suffer the indignity of riding coach, but the moment she saw the tiny sleeping car, she knew it would be a test of endurance. She had thirty-nine hours and forty-five minutes ahead of her; she would spend every minute packed as tightly as a wrapped gift.

Rutherford's brother-in-law had refused to pay for a flight. "I've waited for her for years," said Chester Smith. "You think I want to risk putting her in one of those death traps?" Andorra thought the producer's name made him sound like a little boy, but there was no youth in the man: he was an ancient sixty-six. He had made his fortune in silent film and was the star player in a dozen legends, from being the man who had discovered Errol Flynn to adopting the dog that had mothered Rin Tin Tin.

"Most of the stories aren't true," said Rutherford. "He's really his own myth. He's a bit of a tyrant but he'll probably be a pussycat to you. For all he's done, he'll think you're the peak of his career."

He laughed as he spoke. He was laughing at *everything* now; Rutherford the Traveler had become Rutherford the Victorious. After years of exile, he was finally returning home. He waxed poetic about the joys of the Pacific Ocean and the glorious food they would eat at places like the Brown Derby and the Armstrong-Schroeder Café. Andorra could only guess at the *other* joys Rutherford was looking forward to. He was, after all, on his way to a reunion with his wife. He struck her as being as loyal as her faithful Manuela and she imagined that until now he had been living a chaste and sexless life.

The longest part of the ride took them through the Midwest, which was such a blight on the eyes that the porters suggested they pull down the shades. Omaha and Nebraska were wastelands where the faces of the people on the station platforms were wizened like rotted fruit. In places called Happy Creek and Bright Meadows, children ran alongside the train pleading for food. Somewhere in Utah, the train came to a violent stop because a man was lying facedown on the tracks—this was unique, Andorra learned, not because of the man, but because the conductor had actually stopped the train in time. At last, Andorra obeyed the porters and pulled down her shade; if she had wanted to see desperation, she would have stayed in Detroit.

She tried to distract herself with books and magazines, but there was a brutal impatience to her thoughts. In a notebook stolen from Rowena, she turned to writing to her lost mother. It was a habit she had started after Elionor's death, an embarrassing business made worse each time she dropped the letter in the mail. Rowena was forever recording her surroundings, and so was Andorra—but while Rowena dreamed of being the next F. Scott Fitzgerald, Andorra wanted only to be a girl who could speak to the past. The letters

almost certainly ended up in some dead-letter office—she never provided a return address—but she wasn't ready to stop any more than
she was ready to stop carrying her husband's blue shirt, which even
now sat inside her blouse, carefully nestled against her skin.

She wrote furiously in Catalan, and the train jostled her pen.

*This trip reminds me of when Tata and I went to America. We
rode third-class on a ship called Amsterdam. I wasn't nearly as
big as I am now, but poor Tata grew thin from giving me all his
food. He developed a terrible cough and became terrified the border people would think he was diseased, but when we got to the
border, nobody was looking at him. You ever want to sneak into
a country, bring a lady giant! No one noticed Tata was sick, and
they let him in. It was the first time I was grateful for my size. Now
I am again. The thing that shamed Noria and made you flee in
terror when you saw me—that thing is now saving my life.*

She glanced over at Rutherford the Savior. She had thought he
was asleep, but in fact he had been watching her as she worked. She
recognized the look on his face: he was lost in wonder.

"Sorry," he said, glancing away.

"Best to get it out of your system now."

"Is that even possible?"

"Oh, sure. After two or three years, you won't even notice."

He grinned. "Do *you* ever get used to it?"

"Depends who does the staring."

They were in the dining car, and the coffee cups rattled as the
train wound its way through Nevada. At least she *thought* it was
Nevada; she had not dared to lift the shade. The clock was closing
in on midnight, but neither of them could sleep. Rutherford lit a cigarette and sucked on it with the grandeur of a movie detective. God,
he was small. And so *compressed*! He was sharper and cleaner than

he had been in Detroit. They must have wired him money. There was something of her husband in Rutherford. Same eye color. A similarity in the face. She was surprised to find him handsome. Not devastatingly handsome, as her husband had been. More like casually handsome, as if even he was unaware.

He said, "Can I ask you the question that everyone asks?"

"Seven-eleven. Three-hundred and twenty-two pounds."

"And how often do you wish you were smaller?"

"I don't know. How often do *you* wish you were taller?"

He laughed. "Touché."

"Can I ask *you* the question everyone asks?"

"Five-two. About one hundred and twenty pounds."

Andorra smirked. What they must have looked like, sitting side by side! They were a tower and a shack, a mountain lording over a stone. "Listen," she said. "While we're revealing things, I think you should know: I tried performing once, a long time ago. It didn't go well."

"You survived your screen test."

"That was just you and me. The truth is, I get terrible stage fight. My husband was the same way. He could deal with it, but I never could."

"He was an actor?"

"Five-six. One hundred and fifty pounds. Devastating good looks."

"He must have been successful."

"Not really. The truth is, he was never very good." She added sugar to her coffee and gave it a rhythmic stir. Dat. Dat-dat-dat-dat-dat. Dat . . .

"Buy me some peanuts and Cracker Jack," sang Rutherford.

"What?"

"You were playing "Take Me Out to the Ball Game.""

She glanced down at the spoon in wonder. "My husband liked baseball. The way he talked of it, he could have played for the Tigers."

"Can I ask how he died?"

Oh, that? I killed him.

"Some men beat him up. We think they were trying to rob him. They roughed him up, and he hit his head."

"We should change the subject."

"Yes, we should." She fought to find a new topic. "Was Anna Swan ever in Halifax?"

"When she was young. They took her there on some sort of tour."

"My great-grandmother claimed she touched a lady giant in Halifax."

"What do you know! It was probably her. Not a lot of lady giants in the—"

There was a sudden jolt, and the scream of the breaks swallowed his voice. Andorra flew forward. The legs of the dining car table buckled, and Rutherford's ashtray rolled to the floor. The train ground to a stop. She and Rutherford exchanged looks. Another suicide on the tracks?

A portly porter ran into the dining car. "Just a small fire in the engine room," he said. "They're putting it out now. There's no reason for alarm."

Rutherford wrung his hands. "We better not be late getting in. You're already slated to meet some important folk tomorrow at four o'clock."

But Andorra would not keep that appointment: when the sun rose the following morning, the *City of Los Angeles* was still in the middle of Nevada, two miles from the town of Caliente. Rutherford, whose anxiety had not allowed him to get a drop of sleep, was belligerent when he finally tracked down the portly porter as he waddled through the train, unhappily mopping the sweat from his brow.

"How long until we get under way?" demanded Rutherford.

"No way to tell, sir," said the porter. "A few folk are walking into town to send telegrams. You may want to do the same."

Rutherford removed his glasses and pinched the bridge of his nose. "Is it really so bad if we're late?" asked Andorra. "Can't we just meet the men at the studio another time?"

"Some of the studio heads are headed to Europe," said Rutherford. "We would need their approval for the budget. If we miss them, the whole film could be delayed." He sprang to his feet, returning the glasses to his face. "I'm going to find the telegram office. Why don't you come? You can send a wire home."

Andorra wasn't really interested in writing home. She was still smarting from the cold attitudes that had surrounded her departure: the twins' hurried embrace, her father's biting words. But she was equally tired of the cramped quarters and a ceiling that brushed the top of her head. She followed Rutherford into the desert air, passing the portly porter, who goggled at her even as he reminded them to return as soon as they could.

The Nevada air burned the inside of her throat. Rutherford was a terrible sweater; for such a small man, he produced a rainfall that trickled down his cheeks. She was a terrible sweater, too, and the addition of her husband's blue shirt didn't help. Secreted beneath her blouse, it was another layer that locked in the heat. Discreetly, she reached through her buttons to shift the shirt around. She didn't dare take it out, not wanting to suffer through the explanation of why she had a man's shirt under her own.

Caliente proved to be the sort of small town where all the necessities could be found on a single main strip. Andorra immediately began to draw the eye, after which it wasn't hard to find the telegram office— people practically leapt at the opportunity to help the sweaty giant and her equally sweaty companion find their way. The telegram office was inside Gower's Drug Mart, a tiny piece of heaven, thanks to its being "air-cooled to perfection," just as the sign in the window claimed.

They each stood dripping at the postal counter, lording over a blank telegram slip. Rutherford wrote with a fury—he seemed to not care about the expense—but Andorra paused over hers, the pen sliding around in her large sweaty hand. For a woman who never stopped writing to her dead mother, she found herself at a loss for words. She toyed with what to say but felt her power over language slipping away. So she turned to Shakespeare—*he is our voice*, she thought, *whenever we don't know what to say.*

TRAIN DELAYED.
"I AM EVEN THE NATURAL FOOL OF FORTUNE!"

She sent the message even though it left her unhappy. But why should she be surprised that she couldn't write a telegram? She hadn't known what to say to her family in two years, six months and—what was it now? Fifteen days? Sixteen? The train ride was playing havoc with her mourner's clock. But she still felt the same gnawing fear that had gripped her ever since her husband's death, that unwavering certainty that she might, at any moment, reveal her crime. So she had reverted to silence. Now it was a habit. When it came to the family, she could scold, discipline, and command. But simply *talk*? That talent had left months ago.

"We'd better leave tomorrow," Rutherford remarked. "That's all I'm going to say. I'll push the train if I have to. Odysseus took ten years to reach Penelope—I'm not nearly as patient."

"I haven't seen my home in years," said Andorra.

"Then it was never your home," said Rutherford the Philosopher. "If it was your home, you'd have gone back."

They headed back for the door, but she was loath to step back into Nevada's inglorious heat. Rutherford seemed to hesitate, too, pausing by the entrance to wipe the sweat from beneath his glasses. At the drugstore counter, a swarthy soda jerk was fixing phosphates and ice cream sundaes. "Do we have time?" she asked, motioning to the counter. Rutherford looked like he was about to object, but then he too was taken by the snow-white balls of vanilla as they dropped neatly into a glass. The soda jerk—and everyone else—marvelled at Andorra as she took her place at the counter. She had to sit sideways on the stool, and when her ice cream float came, she had to concentrate to make sure the glass didn't slip from her hands. As for Rutherford, he ordered *two* floats, one of which he tried to swallow in a single gulp.

"Do you like being a talent scout?" she asked.

"It's a little piece of hell. All you do is make promises you know they won't keep."

"Like the one you made me?"

He shook his head. "You're different. You're not going out there to be an actress. I promised you one film, and you can bet your last dollar it will be made. If it wasn't for Anna, Chester Smith wouldn't even be here. She's the reason his parents met. *That's* what the movie's about, you know."

"I thought it was about Anna Swan."

"It's about how Anna Swan brought Chester's parents together. Everyone loves a love story." Rutherford checked his watch and then took another long gulp of his phosphate. "Chester Smith isn't his real name. That's just his *nom de film*. His real name is Gavin Clarke Junior. Gavin Clarke *Senior* knew Anna in Tatamagouche. But I'll tell you the other reason they want to make this picture, if you promise to keep it between us. My wife's a foundling, but nobody knows it. After having Gavin Junior, their mother became a little touched. Not insane, just feeble. She died in an asylum."

"What does that have to do with Anna Swan?"

"The official story, or rather the official *unofficial* story, is that my wife was found in an outhouse."

"And what's the *unofficial* unofficial story?"

"That her real mother is Anna Swan."

Andorra nearly choked on her soda. It bubbled up into her nose, and she quickly grabbed a napkin to cover her face. "Is that even possible?"

Apparently it was. At the time his wife was discovered, Rutherford explained, her parents had been living in Seville, Ohio—the same town where Anna retired toward the end of her life. The couples had been friends, making it easy for the Foundling to spin a compelling fantasy: perhaps not surprisingly, she had seen the whole thing like a movie in her head. Fade in on the Giantess who wants children. Cut to the Giant Husband who keeps giving her children that die. Dissolve to Another Man who finally gives the Giantess what no one else can. Quick cut to him "finding" a baby in an outhouse.

"Is there any evidence that Anna Swan was pregnant a third time?"

"No, but so what? There's not much evidence of anything except a tiny handful of the truth. My wife thinks she was given to the Clarkes after Anna's husband guessed the truth. Anna's first two children died because they were enormous. The moment Anna gave birth to a normal child, her husband probably knew he had been betrayed. At least, that's how my wife sees it."

"What does Chester think of all this?"

"Like me, he has decided that silence is the better part of"—and again a sound drowned out Rutherford's voice. He was destined to always be interrupted by that Hollywood-bound train. This time, it was the whistle. Faint and distant but all too clear.

"Son of a bitch!" said Rutherford Simone.

They were gone in a moment, leaving only money and half-finished sodas in their wake. What a sight they were as they raced through the desert wind! Rutherford the small, Andorra the immense! They weren't the only ones tearing through the town. Other passengers ran, too, and the stampede seemed to delight the locals, who stopped in the street to gape and point. But in the race to the train, Rutherford and Andorra were easily left behind. He had short legs and was out of shape; as for Andorra, she was too cumbersome to ever be fast. Each movement was more like a thunderous hop.

At last, full of pants and grunts, they broke the crest of a hill and saw the train in the distance. Other passengers were already leaping on board. Then, just ahead of her, Rutherford toppled over his ankle and crashed to the ground. He rolled twice and came to a stop. Another blast from the train whistle, another warning of what was to come.

She stopped over Rutherford the Heap. "Are you all right?"

"I'm fine, I'm fine. Go. Run."

So she did, and Rutherford, hobbling a little, was soon once again at her side. As they closed in on the train, she caught sight of the portly porter standing near the back of the car. He was watching them with a great big grin on his face, wide as the desert itself.

His voice reached her. "You didn't need to run. Don't you think we'd notice if *you* weren't on board?"

His laughter taunted them even as Rutherford and Andorra, nearly exhausted, reached the edge of the train, holding the stitches in their sides and sucking Nevada's cooked air into their lungs. Rutherford's pants were torn, and his face was full of sand and grime. As for Andorra, her brazier had snapped open, and her hair had come loose. She ran her hand through the tangle of her blouse to tuck it back into her skirt, and that was when the hot breath died in her throat. Her hands scrambled even as she glanced back at the desert behind her. Nothing. It was true. The blue shirt was gone.

"All aboard!" said a voice from the front of the train. And that whistle went again.

"Wait," said Andorra. "Can you wait?"

The portly porter frowned. "We gotta get a move on, miss, now that everyone's here. What's the trouble?"

She had to bite down on the reply. She couldn't admit it; she wouldn't. "Never mind," she muttered, and she helped Rutherford stagger into the train.

In the privacy of her berth, she crawled to the floor to nurse her aches and pains. In order to fit, she had to lie in an awkward way, bending her throbbing legs into a crooked shape. She barely noticed the discomfort. Her mind was rifling through the contents of her trunk in the hopes of finding something else that had once been her husband's: a scrap of handwriting, a stray sock. There was nothing, of course. His belongings had all been handed down or given away. The blue shirt had been the only thing left.

With a jerk, the train began to move, and Andorra shut her eyes to press out the light. *Well*, she thought, *I wanted to leave Detroit behind*. I have. She would cross into California with nothing of the past; she would arrive in Hollywood with swollen knees and a clean slate.

PART THREE

Love

SEVEN

The Top of the World

New York City, 1863

P. T. BARNUM'S AMERICAN MUSEUM towered over Broadway and Ann Street with the glory of a great cathedral. It was five floors of waxworks and trick dogs; it was a hundred rooms of living statues and industrious fleas. There were lectures and full-scale theatrical plays. There was a menagerie of exotic pets. There was an oyster bar and the hair of Pocahontas and the Cyclops's retina floating in a jar. There were snow-white albinos, ink-dark aborigines, conjoined twins, a living skeleton, an army of miniature men. And, of course there was the thunder of giants: a trio of behemoths, each between seven and nine feet tall, who astonished visitors daily with their feats of strength. Yet on the first floor, inside the Great Lecture Hall, something far greater could be seen. Beyond the hall's arched doorway, for the price of twenty-five cents, a visitor could see a girl, sixteen and a half years old and said to be eight feet tall. It was January 1863; she was thought to be the only lady giant in the world.

By that frosted winter, this lady giant had been in New York for seven months. Since her opening night, her performance had never changed. The Great Lecture Hall was actually an elegant theater with a balcony, mezzanine, and tiered boxes for the upper class. Full-stage theatricals were known to occur there, but for this performance, no pageantry of costumes was needed—the lady giant was pageant enough. The performance always began with a clever juggler, who nimbly kept silver balls afloat while cracking jokes based on the news of the day. During that frozen January, the news was entirely about the Civil War. Far from New York, battles were happening in Texas, Missouri, and Arkansas. In the lecture hall, that deft juggler insulted the Confederates while maintaining a patriotic fervor to keep the fighting spirit high. Then, whenever he sensed he had outstayed his welcome, he would change his tone. Stepping onto center stage, he spoke in a grave voice that might have been shot from a gun.

"And now, ladies and gentlemen, I give you what you have all been waiting for—but please, no applause! Nothing but awed silence will do for this magnificent wonder! The book of Genesis tells us our world was once filled with giants, and today the Good Lord has given us an example of that magnificent breed in the form of a woman, nearly one hundred inches high. Remember, no applause! Hold your breath and marvel at the sight that is the Nova Scotia Giantess, Miss Anna Swan."

And there she was. Stepping out from behind a curtained portico at stage left, she was usually emerald-green from the neck down—her color of choice. She wore jeweled necklaces, and her dark hair, molded into a peak, sat high atop her head. Someone had worked hard to erase both her clumsiness and her Nova Scotia brogue. Her speech was as graceful as her movements: she had become the ideal. Stunned murmurs always shot through the crowd. Despite having paid to see a giantess, many did not believe that this was what they would see. Barnum was famous for his humbugs. Skeptics doubted that the Cyclops's retina had really once been inside a Cyclops, but they could not doubt Anna Swan. This made her unique among the exhibits for the simplest of reasons. She was exactly as advertised; she was the real thing.

The other giants could stand onstage and perform feats of strength, but Anna, as a woman, was expected to be more genteel. No one wanted to see *her* lift a cinder block over her head. Instead, she impressed the audience with her favorite hymn, singing in a pretty voice as her enormous goiter wobbled with the great precision of a violin. Then she gave a brief lecture on the history of Nova Scotia before being joined by a tiny dwarf in military dress (Barnum knew that a small boat always makes the ocean seem larger—and vice versa). Together, this unique pair enacted a scene from *Macbeth*. It was pure comedy to see the dwarf play the brutal Macbeth, but it was equally alarming to see his villainous wife portrayed with such seriousness that the absurd scene quickly ascended to solemnity. They always lightened the mood with a comic sketch about the dwarf's hopes to fight in the war, after which Anna would sing "Amazing Grace," making sure to dedicate the song to all the men fighting in the War of Rebellion.

It was at this point in the performance that, on a blustery day in the second week of 1863, something happened that had not happened before. Glancing into the crowd, Anna caught sight of a familiar face, a dead ringer for a boy she had not seen since he had limped out of Tatamagouche nearly eight months before. A wet chuffing sound escaped her lips. The doppelgänger sat near the stage in the blue uniform of a Union soldier, but it was clear that his fighting days were done. The left sleeve of his jacket was folded at the elbow, with the cuff pinned to the shoulder; if it was Gavin Clarke, then he would never thread a needle again.

Someone coughed. Only ten seconds of silence had gone by, but that's a lifetime on the stage.

She recovered her voice. It was custom, for her finale, that she answer the one question everyone wanted to ask. She called out for an "average girl" who would volunteer to step onto stage so their measurements could be compared. On this January afternoon, an ugly young schoolteacher was pushed into the limelight. As the grotesque thing made her way to the footlights, Anna turned back to the crowd to find a second volunteer who would have the honor of taking the measurements themselves.

She stared at the one-armed boy who looked like Gavin Clarke.

"Ladies and gentlemen," she said. "At this time I'd like to call upon another volunteer to take the measuring rope in hand. Usually, I'm not so particular, but I'm feeling a little homesick today, and so I would like to add a little caveat. Would all those people who have come to us from Canada please stand?"

Across the auditorium, a few dozen people rose from their seats. For a second, the one-armed soldier didn't move. Then he rose, too.

"How many of you are from my own colony of Nova Scotia?" she asked, voice shaking.

Most of the people sat back down. Now there was just the one-armed soldier and a single obese man whose skin poked through his shirt. She wished she had never started this game. But there was nothing to do but see it through to the end.

"And of the two of you, which of you has spent a morning walking across the frozen Northumberland Strait to Prince Edward Island?"

The obese man fell away, and the one-armed soldier became the city on a hill: the eyes of the world were upon him. Anna's heart sank. It was no mistake. By then, she was accustomed to seeing injured men in the crowd. She had seen bandages and hardened scars of blood; she had even seen men who had lost limbs. But none of these men had ever been anyone she knew, and in this moment the entire war, once so distant, came crashing through the roof with a cannonball's speed.

If pity could manifest itself, then Gavin would have clambered to the stage in a fog. He was barely twenty and had already given an arm to save a country that wasn't even his.

Anna took his only remaining hand, squeezing it with affection even as the tears came to the corners of her great brown eyes.

"Tell them who you are," she said softly.

"Speak up!" yelled someone.

"Tell us who you are!" Anna said loudly.

"Sergeant Gavin Clarke, ma'am. Fortieth Infantry."

A whoop from the crowd—a patriot or someone else from the Fortieth? There was light applause, and Gavin waved his cap. Anna collected her strength. How many times had she thought of Gavin since coming to New York? Yet never once had she pictured him with anything worse than a broken nail. She had thought him untouchable, an Achilles without a heel.

"I can see you've given a lot for this war," she said. She regretted it at once. A dumb thing to say. Absurd and idiotic.

"I gave all I could give," Gavin said. "I just wish I hadn't left my arm in Virginia."

He winked even as a nervous laugh went through a part of the crowd. Anna covered her mouth to swallow another cry. A new thought had come to her. What if he *couldn't* take her measurements? Had she singled him out just to humiliate him?

"Do you think you can help us take some measurements, Sergeant?" she asked nervously.

"I'm sure I can manage," he said.

So she handed him the measuring rope. The dwarf reappeared with a stool, and Anna took her place in front of it. Gavin climbed on top, moving with care, wincing slightly as he aggravated the pain in the arm that appeared to stop just above the elbow. He held the edge of the rope to the top of her hair, and let the rest drop. He called out the result ("Ninety-five inches!") before stepping down to measure the hideous schoolteacher. Then he wrapped the rope around Anna's waist and called out the result again ("Fifty-two inches!"). In a flash of inspiration, he used his singular arm to his advantage. His thumb was still marking the length of Anna's waist, and instead of measuring the schoolteacher, he circled the schoolteacher, wrapping the rope around her. This created a rather dramatic effect: the rope went two and a half times around the woman's body, thereby demonstrating the true enormity of the Nova Scotia Giantess without a single word.

The audience hooted and broke into applause. Gavin smiled broadly, and Anna thought she saw the actor's triumph, the great thrill of success.

Anna curtsied to the crowd and then to her volunteers. The schoolteacher was already darting off the stage, but the one-armed sergeant lingered to return the rope. This allowed Anna the chance to lean down and leave a whisper in his ear: "Stay in the Hall. I'll send someone to get you after the show."

After her bows, she paused long enough to give instructions to the juggler before slipping through the curtained portico. Beyond it was a spiraling staircase that ended at the Top of the World, her name for her fifth-floor rooms that afforded a glorious view of the city below. But Anna didn't get as far as the top of the stairs. Emotion overtook her long before, and she fell into the shadows as tears filled her throat. She was holding a lantern, but the light went out, and in the dark she saw Gavin's arm, lying in the field, left behind like a lost coat.

She heard movement. There came the light of a torch, and then a one-armed shadow passed. He brushed right past her, walking carefully to keep his balance, for there was no way for him to hold onto the wall. She called his name and rose out of the dark. Because he was on the higher step, they were suddenly eye to eye. She could not help it: she fell back into tears even as she threw her arms around him.

"Your poor, poor thing."

But her words were lost in his howl: she had squeezed his bad arm. She released him at once, flushing red with shame as she recalled the other scream she had caused just after cracking his foot nearly eight months before. Why was she always causing him pain?

"Damn and double damn!" he cried. But the fury did not stay in his face: in hospital, Gavin Clarke had learned to swallow his complaints. "It's not too bad," he whispered. "I'm hoping it'll grow back."

He told her how a pair of Confederate bullets had lodged in his arm. Gangrene had set in, and two months ago the doctors had lopped off the arm. Even now the wound was still swaddled and sore.

She brought him to the Top of the World. Several suites on this floor had been designed to house Barnum's thunder of giants, and the tremendous furniture met all of Anna's peculiar specifications. In her sitting room, she left him to drown in one of the enormous chairs while she slipped into the bedroom to clean her face. She was determined not to cry again. The last thing he needed was pity. She splashed water on her cheeks and wiped her eyes clean.

"I'm glad you remembered me," he called from the other room.

"Does that really surprise you?"

"I don't know. So much has happened, it feels like a lifetime ago."

"*Two* lifetimes," she replied. A year ago she was at the Normal School feeling decidedly *un*-normal. Now she was a star attraction and Gavin was a man without an arm. Was it even possible? She returned to the other room, wondering if even now he might prove to be an illusion. This was Barnum's world, after all. Nothing was ever what it seemed.

Slowly, almost as if she herself was unsure of the narrative, she told him all that had happened since he had limped out of Tatamagouche. With her parents in tow—a mother elated, a father sour as rot—she had journeyed to New York through a magnificent combination of wagons, boats, trains, and, for one brief hour, a reinforced canoe. They had been fearful of everyone they met. It was wartime, after all, and on the steamship it had been impossible to tell the travelers from the spies. Only Anna herself could not be mistaken for anything other than what she was; only she had been the young woman who towered over the sea. In New York, a carriage drawn by two magnificent Clydesdales had carried them through the dirty streets toward the corner of Broadway and Ann. "From New Annan to Ann!" Anna had said to Ann Swan, and even her growling father had to admit there was something auspicious in this strange concordance of Annans and Annas and Anns.

Her father handled the negotiations of her contract with P. T. Barnum, who turned out to be a dapper man with a plump face, curly hair, and a nose as soft as a spot of shit. Alexander Swan demanded draconian terms. His daughter was to be provided with room, board, and wardrobe. She was to be given a female attendant, at Barnum's expense. Her education was not to be neglected. And she was to be paid in gold. (The war meant Alexander didn't trust America's paper money.)

"I think he thought he would sabotage me," Anna told Gavin. "I think he expected Barnum to turn him down and send me home."

But Barnum agreed to every condition. Anna still remembered the way her father's jaw had gone slack even as her mother had swallowed a laugh. When her parents finally left, Alexander predicted that Anna would follow within the month. Anna replied by holding her father close and crushing him tight against her giant breast. "I *want* this," she told him, quoting her Jane Eyre. "I want this because it is of no use wanting anything better."

Thus began her life in New York as one more crack in Barnum's thunder of giants. As promised, Barnum had supplied her with a tutor, a dour thing who had erased Anna's brogue and worked to instill nothing but good sense and decent morals. Yet the bulk of her time was spent serving as chaperone, for almost at once Barnum's trio of male giants had viewed her as the water sent to slake their thirst. They fell over her and fought to win her affections. Colonel Routh Goshen—every inch of the name was a Barnum creation—plied her with flowers. Jean Bihin, the enormous Belgian, gave her both chocolate and language lessons. And there was Angus

MacAskill, the behemoth from Cape Breton. Coming from Canada, with a Nova Scotian brogue of his own, he seemed to believe no seduction was needed. To MacAskill, the winning of Anna's heart was a fait accompli.

All of this attention had been wondrous, until Anna realized that she had fallen victim to the same curse that had struck Helen of Troy: men were fighting for her solely because of her looks. If she were any shorter, they would have looked the other way.

"Surely you can see yourself loving *one* of them," said Gavin.

Anna shrugged. None of them were interested in her ideas; not one of them had even read *Jane Eyre*. Still, she understood the practicality of such an arrangement. A marriage to Jean Bihin or Angus MacAskill had a certain symmetry to it. She would be a bookend finding its mate.

A sound at the door caused them both to turn. It was Miss Eaton, the tutor and chaperone who had helped turn Anna from a farm girl into one of Barnum's star attractions. She was nineteen but built like a fourteen-year-old boy. A puritanical girl of strong Hoosier stock, she believed in propriety above all things. Because of this, Anna knew she would think it scandalous that her charge had spent fifteen minutes alone with an unmarried man. But Miss Eaton's disapproving glare melted when she saw Gavin's kepi on his lap; it vanished altogether when she noticed the pinned sleeve of Gavin's coat.

"You brave soul," said the girl. "You have our sincerest gratitude for everything you've done."

"The doctor did most of the work," said Gavin. "I just drank whiskey and looked away."

Miss Eaton frowned in confusion. She had not a humorous bone in her body.

"Forgive me," said Gavin. "Gallows humor. A consequence of the war."

"This is Sergeant Clarke," Anna said. "He's an old friend."

Miss Eaton was still staring in sorrow at Gavin's pinned sleeve. "You'll come back, I hope," she said "We should convince Mr. Barnum to let you give a lecture on your experience."

"Actually, I did want to speak to Mr. Barnum about something. It's the other reason I came today. I was hoping Annie could work me an introduction."

"Of course," said Anna. "Is it about money? I'm sure he could find you work."

"Nothing like that. I'm still in the army. I'm fairly mobile, so they have me working as an attendant at the hospital. That's what brought me here. Believe it or not, I'm actually one of the lucky ones. There are men who are bedridden and full of pain. I was hoping Mr. Barnum might allow some of his attractions to come down and raise their spirits."

"A magnificent idea!" said Miss Eaton. "You have a charitable heart, Sergeant Clarke."

"It's a marvelous thought," said Anna. "And I know P. T. will approve. He's happy to do anything to support the war, you know."

"You'll come, won't you?" said Gavin. "I know they'd all get a thrill out of seeing the only lady giant in the world."

Anna blushed. "I'll come if you'll take the measurements."

"Agreed." And he stuck out his only hand, which Anna swallowed in her grasp.

That night, long after he had gone, Anna studied the sleeping world from behind frozen glass. She stared out at the tops of the buildings wrapped in a great polar bear quilt that Colonel Goshen had procured especially for her. For months she had been steeling herself for the inevitability of marriage to a man whose only similarity to her was their enormous size. But those male giants didn't know her. They certainly didn't need her. Once again she recalled the passage in *Jane Eyre* when Jane brings the blind Edward Rochester back to Thornfield Hall. "Being so much lower of stature than he, I served both for his prop and guide." *If a woman is to marry,* thought Anna, *she should be more than just a prized fish.* No, Gavin wasn't blind; no, she wasn't of lower stature. But it amounted to the same thing. She could be his prop and guide. He just needed to ask.

BARNUM, AS EXPECTED, was thrilled with the idea of bringing solace to the convalescents; his only regret was that he hadn't thought of the idea first. He happily began the arrangements to send his battalion of human curiosities into the field, but paused at the thought of sending Anna herself. As a Canadian, she was a British subject, and her country was neutral.

"She's raising the spirits of injured men," argued Miss Eaton. "It's not as if she's taking sides."

Barnum scratched his fat little chin. "She's raising the spirits of *Union* men. She is, by implication, waving a flag."

He had come to see Anna at the Top of the World and had interrupted a brutal game of whist. Anna was happy to throw down the cards—she was losing terribly. "I don't care if I am waving a flag," she said. "I want to do it. I support the war."

"No intelligent person supports war."

"I support the *cause* of the war."

"And tell me," said Barnum. "What is the *cause* of this war?"

"Slavery."

"Ha! Slavery is probably the last thing this war is about. This is about *democracy.* The South says democracy is about letting people choose how they want to live—even if they want to live with slavery. But we say democracy isn't an excuse for people to be cruel. Cruelty is not a thing that any government should sanction."

"You're not in your lecture hall," said Miss Eaton. "Don't give us a lecture."

Barnum broke into a grin. "My point is that Annie is a celebrity now. We have to be careful about how she is perceived."

"No one can blame me for going to visit a hospital. And it doesn't matter what you say, because I'm going whether you like it or not."

"You're on contract. I control where you perform."

"Then I won't perform. I'll just visit. I'm sure they could use volunteers."

Barnum's scowl only lasted a moment. Then the fierce expression broke, and he gave a good, hearty laugh. "Lord knows I love a stubborn woman! All right, Annie. You go down and do what you can. I'm sorry for objecting. This war does funny things to your brain: half the time, you never know how you should be."

Not long after, on a glorious and frigid Monday, Anna left the intersection of Broadway and Ann for the frigid shores of the Bronx. Barnum had tried to send along some of his other attractions—he had even suggested sending the entire thunder of giants—but Anna had subtly convinced him that she would be more than enough. She didn't want to journey out there with Angus McAskill or Col. Goshon; she wanted to see Gavin entirely on her own. Of course, Anna was never entirely alone. With Miss Eaton at her side, she traveled swiftly in the same great carriage that had met her when she and her parents had first arrived in New York. She was even taken by the same driver and the same team of Clydesdales, both of whom shuddered and snorted as they raced through the frost.

Gavin was stationed at the hospital at Fort Schuyler, an old building that stood in the earth like a crumbling fist. Upon their arrival, they were met by a doe-eyed private on a crutch, who gawked at Anna's approach before breaking into a wide grin. "I had to trade rations to make sure I was the first to see ya!" he proclaimed before leading them inside. Anna wrapped her cloak tight: the ancient stone did little to keep out the chill. Down they went through the labyrinth of halls toward dank gloom and the putrid smell of infection. From somewhere in the distance, she could hear the faint howl of men who writhed in corners unknown. A horrible place, thought Anna. A far cry from the Top of the World with her polar bear quilt, hot water bottles, and stockings knit by her mother's hand.

Gavin was in one of the larger wards, changing a set of fouled sheets. His movements were impressive; he had adapted quickly, moving as if he had claimed only one arm his entire life. "Nothing compared to a winter on the North Shore, eh?" he laughed.

"This can't be good for the men," snapped Miss Eaton.

"It's actually better when it's cold," said Gavin, breath billowing out of him. "We freeze to the point when we can't feel a thing."

Most of the patients had gathered in another ward to await Anna's arrival. Gavin warned them that the crowd was larger than he had thought—the hospital had its share of civilians on staff, and some had brought their families. "They're all excited about this," he said. "Most of them can't afford to go to the museum."

"I'm happy to do it," said Anna, but what truly thrilled her was the way Gavin spoke to her. With respect and sincerity. And was that gratitude? "Let me help with that," she said, plucking a clean sheet from a nearby trolley. Her numb hands found a way to shake out the sheet. Whatever liquid had seeped into the mattress had frozen, for when she spread out the stiff linen, the bed crackled in the cold. Gavin took the other end, and together they finished the bed, tucking in the corners just the way both of their parents had taught them to do when they were young.

At last Gavin led her to the other ward while Miss Eaton trailed behind. She waited in the hall while he stepped into the room to silence the audience. The howling wind was in her ears, and she did not hear much of what was said. Some variation of what he had heard at the museum a few weeks before. He ad-libbed some of it, but she recognized her cue. He told them to hold their breath; he told them to marvel at the sight that was Miss Anna Swan. Then she swept into the room and nearly stumbled on a puddle of piss that had frozen to the stone floor.

The audience was different than any she had seen. The beds had been arranged in a semicircle, and in each one boys and men lay steeped in wounds and amputations, their frozen blood hanging off of their bandages, their dark infections sitting like scales on the skin. More men stood around them, dwarfing the uninjured with their crutches and slings. Anna only saw the tragedy. She hardly noticed the children or wives who had come to see her; she barely saw the way everyone's breath hung suspended in the air.

Swallow the horror, she thought. *Remember your lines.* "Who would like to hear a song?" she asked, and the strength of her voice impressed even herself.

It was a great success. When it was through, the men and women gathered around her. Not quite able to recall those days in Halifax when she had touched people's hands, Anna imagined this to be the first time she had ever met her audience. She was completely overwhelmed. One by one Gavin introduced her to the soldiers who had nearly lost their lives in Shiloh, Yorktown, Antietam. She tried to be gracious, only to feel like a fraud. Who was she to thank them for fighting for a country that wasn't even hers? Still, she shook hand after hand and sweetly answered every question about her life. She could see what it meant to them. Her life was history to her but a fantasy to everyone else. They had only known war, while she had known the top of the world.

Later, Gavin offered Anna and Miss Eaton supper in a private ward. Famished, she ate heartily at a small table stationed next to a roaring hearth. The meal was meager, but she hardly cared. She was filled with a great glow of satisfaction. For the first time since she had started performing, she finally felt she had done something of worth. She was biting into an icy apple when she noticed Gavin watching her, half of his face lit by the glow of the hearth. Then he looked sharply away and, with a slight stutter, asked if the women would mind if he smoked. Anna liked this—Jean Bihin and Colonel Goshen certainly never asked before lighting their pipes—so she gave her permission without waiting for Miss Eaton to acquiesce. It didn't matter. Wrapped in a shawl and exhausted by the day, Miss Eaton had fallen asleep.

Anna watched as Gavin rolled a cigarette with a single hand, keeping the paper and tobacco pressed against his lap.

"You do everything so well," she remarked.

"I feel like a clumsy oaf." At last the cigarette was rolled, and he gave her a sheepish grin. "I can roll the cigarette, but I have trouble lighting it."

He came round the table and sat next to her. She had trouble with the matches—her fingers were too large, and the sticks dropped to the floor.

"We're quite the pair, aren't we?" smirked Gavin.

Resolutely, Anna tried again. The match struck, and her large fingers managed to hold onto to the flimsy stick. She leaned forward and Gavin sucked in the flame, and their eyes met across the cigarette even as the smoke rose up between them.

"See?" she said. "You've got one arm, and I'm far too big, but we could still figure out how to conquer the world."

"Is that what you want to do? Conquer the world?"

"Maybe. I probably can't do this forever."

"You probably could. Barnum would see to that."

"I'm sure I'll do something else."

"Like run off with one of your giants."

"I don't have to run off with one of them. I'm my own person. I could run off with anyone I choose."

"Yeah, I imagine you could." Gavin smoked for a moment and

glanced at the sleeping Miss Eaton. Then he leaned forward and lowered his voice. "I'd like to confess something to you, if I may. I wanted to write to you."

She didn't dare move. His eyes had locked into hers. "You did?"

"I kept thinking about the last time we saw each other. That stupid fight in my father's shop. What was it even about? Then one day our infantry met up with another unit, and someone told me that some regiment in Lexington had a captain who was eight feet tall. They were calling him the Kentucky Giant."

Anna ran a finger along her empty plate. Another male giant. Why not? There were at least three in the Union. Why shouldn't the Confederates have their own?

"Some of the others didn't believe it. But I did, and it got me thinking of you. I wanted to tell you. And once I started thinking about it, I wanted to tell you everything else. The names of the men. The lousy marching. How scared I was. They were so anxious for me that they threw me into battle right away and I could barely hold my gun. I could have written anyone, I suppose. But for some reason, you were the only person I wanted to tell."

Anna spoke softly, willing Miss Eaton to stay fast asleep. "So why didn't you?"

"You said you were going off to New York. I knew you were enjoying all your success. I guess I figured you didn't want to hear from me. That museum, it's sort of like its own little paradise, isn't it?"

"That museum is a bit like a dream," she confessed.

"You sorry I brought you out here into the real world?"

"Not at all. I was thinking I should come back."

"You want to perform again?"

"I don't care what I do. I'll make beds so long as it helps."

"Will Barnum let you?"

"I don't care if he won't. He wants me to be a good and decent person. What sort of good and decent person doesn't help people in need?"

Gavin looked at her in wonder. "You've become something really brash and bold, Annie. Or were you always like that and I'm just noticing now?" He glanced down at his cigarette. "It's gone out. Light it again?"

Once more, she struggled with the matches; once more, her thick fingers struggled with the tiny sticks. The match came to life and she raised it toward him, only to find him leaning in close. He was stretched in an awkward way so that their faces were of equal height. Only the length of a cigarette between them. "We're really quite the pair," he said again, and then there was nothing between them at all. His kiss landed on the corner of her mouth. He was shadow and stubble and coarse skin. She tasted his tobacco. She smelled something medicinal emanating from his wounded arm. There was the crackle of fire and the gurgle of Miss Eaton's snores. Sight and taste, smell and sound. The only thing missing was touch. The kiss had happened too fast; she had barely felt it at all.

Gavin drew back. They studied each other in the faded light. She knew a promise had been made, and she would spend the rest of the night trying to decide exactly what it had been.

EIGHT

The Empty Mountain

Detroit, 1912–1915

RAWN BY THE FACTORY whistles of Ford and GM, a tide of immigrants swept into Detroit in the spring of 1912. Two Andorran exiles followed in their wake. They were exhausted from their journey, which had taken nearly sixteen months, first because Geoffrey del Alandra had misread the map and then because their trans-Atlantic steamer encountered three terrific storms, each of which blew them further off course. Now, at last, they were stepping into the Eight-Fingered City, so called because the great machinery of the automotive world tended to devour hands. This did not surprise Geoffrey, who had been introduced to the automobile during their bewildered trek through Europe. "Iron tigers!" he proclaimed. He found them so loud that they could only inspire mistrust. As for Andorra, she saw them as cages with wheels. She had not stopped growing and for nearly a year and a half she had been suffering on steamships and trains. She was tired of suffering; in the automobile she saw a punishment as humiliating as a pillory.

Fortunately, her father's plan wasn't for them to ever *ride* in an iron tiger; he merely hoped to live off those who did. In quick succession, he found work at Ford and established a home for his daughter in a pair of rooms on Elsa Street. Most émigrés chose their living quarters based on where their clans had collected: the Russians went to Highland Park, the Syrians to the Lower East Side. But there was no Andorran neighborhood in Detroit. Geoffrey's appearance on Elsa Street was due entirely to an advertisement that had been printed in French. Coming from the prick between France and Spain meant he and Andorra easily understood an *à louer* for what it was.

The house on Elsa Street was owned by Mrs. Holt, a young widow whose husband had died of old age. This aged husband was one Andorra would remember in her prayers because, in addition to giving his wife French, Mr. Holt had left one other thing that made him invaluable: a house with high ceilings. Although Andorra had to stoop to get through the door, she *never* had to stoop once she was inside. As it was later explained, Marianne Holt's husband had been a terrible claustrophobic, and each room had been designed to mimic the open space of a country field. Every hallway was wide, every room had a large window. The bathroom was as expansive as it was tall. This could only thrill Andorra, who had struggled with toilets her entire life. They were as much a humiliation as the steamship or the cramped compartments of the train. On the trip to America, she had been almost happy when the bad food had left her constipated; now, in the bathroom on Elsa Street, she saw she could finally sit without banging her knees on the wall. Paradise in a water closet.

"I trust the house is to your liking," said the Widow. She was speaking in French; for months it would be the only common tongue between them. "Breakfast and dinner are at seven, and I insist on punctuality. You're welcome to use the kitchen during the day, but try to stay out of the cook's way—assuming you can!" Then her eyes widened, and she clasped a hand over her mouth. "Oh God, I'm sorry! That was terribly rude."

"Not half as rude as *some* of the things we've heard," said Geoffrey.

"No, it was awful. Tell me you forgive me."

Andorra was stunned. No adult had ever asked her this before. "I forgive you," she said solemnly.

"Good!" said the Widow. "The two of us should be good friends. I prefer being friends with my borders. It makes the whole thing a lot more pleasant." She gave a girlish laugh; it clearly pegged her age at twenty-three and a half. "Most of my family have disappeared," she admitted. "The family I was born with have all died. And the family I married into threw me away."

"Why?" asked Andorra.

"Why else? They thought I was a gold digger."

Andorra didn't understand. The Widow had interpolated the English word into her French phrase, *Ils croyaient que j'etais une* gold digger. "What's a gold digger?" Andorra asked.

"Someone who marries for money instead of love. We need to teach you a little English."

"We need to teach her a *lot* of English," said Geoffrey. "Finding a good tutor is our top priority."

"But I can do it!" exclaimed the Widow.

"Are you a teacher?"

"Better! An actress!"

Andorra frowned. She wondered if the French word for actress—*comedienne*—meant the same thing in America as it did back home.

"You misunderstand," said Geoffrey. "I want someone who can teach us to speak."

"Yes, yes. I can do that."

"But I want to learn to speak it *well*."

"Actors *have* to speak well," said the Widow. "Speaking is our bread and butter. Please say yes. It would give me something to do. It'll be just like the language-lesson scene of *The Life of Henry the Fifth*, only not as dull!" She gave Andorra a broad, compassionate grin. "Would you like it if I taught you to speak American?"

"I want to learn English," said Andorra.

"Oh, nobody speaks *that* here," laughed the Widow.

"You can add the cost of the lessons to the rent," Geoffrey said.

The Widow waved him away. "Keep your money. You can pay me back in other ways."

Andorra assumed this meant her father would be expected to run errands or help with household repairs; it would be many years before she discovered that from that first day, Mrs. Marianne Holt already had something else in mind.

THEY WOULD STAY ON ELSA STREET throughout the years of the Great War. They were the Widow's only borders, and the house became their castle, the Widow their adopted queen. Geoffrey wrote to Manuela upon their arrival, but it was a full year before they received a reply. Sant Julià de Lòria was not on any postal routes; letters were often held at a French post office for months until enough mail had collected to warrant a journey into the parish. This meant the Andorra in Detroit would always be behind the times when it came to news about the Andorra in Europe. (When the Great War came, she knew only that it had spared the principality, which declared war on Germany only to find itself ignored. The post office would go there only when needed; the Germans decided there would never be a need to go.)

Geoffrey proved himself a tireless cog in Henry Ford's great machine. He was expected to work six days a week, nearly fourteen hours a day, an exhausting regimen that never once provoked a complaint. Having lived among the smugglers, he was satisfied to finally be supporting his daughter in an honest way. Anxious to make up for all his years of failure as a father, Geoffrey went overboard in his effort to keep Andorra pleased. All his extra money went to keeping her enormous body warm, fed, and clothed. Thinking he was being kind, he even gave her full dominion over the bed. But the frame was not nearly large enough, and so they dragged the mattress onto the floor. This is how the pair slept for many years: with Andorra on the floor and Geoffrey curled on the couch.

Andorra was twelve when she arrived in Detroit, and at first she could hardly wait to explore the city. She begged the Widow to take her shopping on Woodward Avenue and out to explore the wilderness of Belle Isle Park. She was eager to study the world; what she was not prepared for was the way the world studied *her*. In the principality, she had stared at the other children through the window and wondered what it was they whispered as they stood outside her house. Now she knew. She had heard it on the boat when they crossed the Atlantic, and she heard it in the streets of Detroit. She was too large to play with children her own age: they assumed she was an immature adult. As for the *real* adults, they just stared at her with wild curiosity. Her features were young, and it was only on second glance that it became clear she was larger than she should be. That was when the whispering began. Like that physician who had told her about her weak heart, they always lowered their voices—but they never managed to lower them enough.

"Better find a David," said one. "There's a Goliath in town."

Then there were the streetcars and ferries—even the sidewalks themselves conspired against her. Everything was too narrow, and she returned from the city with a coat of bruises that stretched from tip to toe.

"How did you like it?" asked her father.

"Everyone *stares* at me," said Andorra.

"People are ridiculous," said the Widow. "You're not even six feet."

"She's twelve, and she's already the size of a *man*." Geoffrey sighed.

"I'm larger than a man," complained Andorra. "I'm already larger than you!"

Geoffrey blinked and then laughed in astonishment. It was true. Stepping up to her, he saw his not-so-little girl was a little higher than the top of his head.

"I think I've seen enough of Detroit," said Andorra. "I think to-morrow I'll stay home."

But if Andorra wouldn't come to Detroit, Detroit seemed to decide it would come to her. Gossip traveled fast in the Motor City, and the very next day the first in a long parade of callers appeared on the Widow's porch. The first visitor was in advertising but, before long, they had been assailed by producers, circus agents, and newspapermen, each plying Andorra with complicated contracts and promises they didn't intend to keep. Small bands of peeping promoters began appearing in the bushes around the Widow's house. It became such a nuisance that in 1914 she finally placed a sign in the window:

THE HOLT BOARDING HOUSE
NO VACANCY
ALL MANAGERS AND PRODUCERS WILL BE SHOT.
AGENTS WILL BE EATEN ON SIGHT.

"Eaten by *who?*" asked Andorra.

"Eaten by *whom*," corrected the Widow.

"Eaten by *whom?*" said Andorra.

"You, of course," said the Widow. "And if you won't do it, I will. Serves the gold diggers right."

Hating the attention, Andorra burrowed deep into the house on Elsa Street and rarely emerged. It made for a good cocoon. The only other person who came by was the Widow's cook, a Russian immigrant who seemed unmoved by Andorra's size. ("I am used to big person," the cook said. "I am daughter of Cossacks!") And with the Widow taking charge of her education, Andorra saw she could secure her destiny as a girl who would never go to school. When she did go outside, she never went beyond the six blocks that surrounded Elsa Street, a small neighborhood that included two churches, a synagogue, railway tracks, a park, three barber shops, a Russian travel agency, a Hungarian photography studio, and a hat shop run by Swedes. What she knew of the outside world came from the newspaper or from whatever was spoken of in the house. She was so carefully tuned to these conversations that she quickly noticed how, for six months out of the year, something shifted in the attention span of those around her. Discussions hinged on what was happening at a mythical place called *the Corner*. Her father came home talking about men named Ty Cobb and Sam Crawford. She thought they were coworkers, but in fact they were celebrities; as part of his cultural assimilation, Geoffrey had adopted the city's heroes as his own. Cobb and Crawford played something called baseball; the Corner was the arena where the spectacle took place. Andorra quickly learned everything she needed to in order to understand the sport that obsessed Elsa Street—and Detroit, and Michigan, and all of America. That this sport would eventually bring her grief—that it would have everything to do with how she would kill her future husband—was hardly something the not-so-little girl could have known. Yet even then she understood that baseball was a mischievous thing.

THOUGH THE WIDOW CLAIMED to be an actress, Andorra rarely saw her prove her worth. The Widow occasionally went on auditions but spent most of her time seeing plays and attending the parties thrown by the cast and crew. Her husband had left her financially secure, and thanks to this legacy she could dabble in the arts without the pressure of needing to succeed. "Mr. Holt didn't trust the theater," she explained. "I don't really blame him. When we met, I was in a musical comedy called *That's My Pig!* Can you hear the exclamation mark in the title? That's the sort of thing Mr. Holt wanted to save me from."

Her talent may have been in question but her passion wasn't. The Widow adored the theater and believed it was the best way to teach Andorra about the world. She used Chekhov's *The Cherry Orchard* to teach Russian history while Ibsen's *A Doll's House* introduced Andorra to the subject of women's rights. When it came to the task of speaking *American*, the Widow turned to the plays of Eugene O'Neill. But she also turned to Shakespeare, who was the Widow's own personal God. (Exactly how she hoped to use a *British* playwright to teach Andorra *American* was something that made sense only in the mind of the Widow herself).

For her first English lesson, Andorra was introduced to Act III, Scene IV of *The Life of Henry the Fifth*—this was the language-lesson scene that, according to the Widow, was "the dullest thing Shakespeare ever wrote." Written mostly in French, the scene concerns a French princess who worries about her impending marriage to an English king. To prepare herself, she asks her maid for a few English words. By the end of the scene, she has learned to say "d'hand, de fingre, de nailès, d'arma, d'elbow, de nick, de sin, and de foot." And so, with her copy of Shakespeare in hand, Andorra and the Widow would reenact the scene with Andorra playing the role of the princess. "D'hand, de fingre, de nailès, d'arma, d'elbow, de nick," Andorra repeated again and again.

"Someone once told me that in Shakespeare's time those words were all dirty," the Widow said in French.

"Because no one ever washed?" asked Andorra.

The Widow laughed. "Not dirty as in *dirt*. Dirty as in *obscene*. Each word was a sexual pun."

"What's a sexual pun?" asked Andorra.

"Oh, you'll find out soon enough," said the Widow.

Already she had more faith in Andorra's love life than Andorra herself. Andorra doubted she would *ever* learn about sexual puns, or love, for herself. By now, it was 1915 and she was six and a half feet. Still sprouting, she felt that every moment brought her that much closer to touching the sky. What man would want to love *that*?

The Widow, meanwhile, was having no trouble learning about love and sexual puns. She had money and she had beauty: she was a siren to every bachelor in Detroit. While Andorra was contending with her own parade of agents and producers, the Widow dealt with her numerous suitors, each cut from a different cloth, yet each with their hearts firmly on their sleeves.

"Listening to men in love is a dull and terrible fate," she lamented to Andorra one day. "But I really can't turn any of them away. Henry the Fifth had to go through war to get his princess. We all have to do the same. I just wish I didn't always have to face them alone." Suddenly her eyes lit up; she was struck by inspiration. "*You* should sit with me when they visit!"

"Wouldn't I make them uneasy?" asked Andorra.

"That's the whole point! If I like them, I'll send you away. But if I *don't* like them, then we can have a little fun."

Andorra had to admit she liked the idea. Marriage didn't interest her, but men had finally started to have a mysterious appeal. Because she doubted she'd ever have to understand a sexual pun, men could only provoke an academic curiosity, the sort a zoologist might have for a wild boar. Which was, more or less, how the Widow saw the men who came to her. The very next time one of these boars appeared, Andorra took a seat next to the Widow. She was much too large for the chairs, so they took an ottoman and placed it against the wall. Then they moved the sofa next to it, allowing the two bachelorettes to sit together side by side. When the latest boar finally arrived—a spindly rake with bad breath—Andorra was introduced as the Widow's chaperone. Andorra waited to see if she would be sent away, but it was clear the Widow had already passed judgment.

"Andorra and I were about to start our language lesson," the

Widow said. "Which lesson should it be, Andorra? Should we do the one with all the dirty words?"

"I'm not sure that's appropriate," stammered Andorra.

"You may be right," said the Widow. Then she turned to the wild boar. "What do *you* think? Where do *you* stand on the subject of dirty words?"

The Boar coughed and loosened his tie.

"I'll tell you what," said the Widow. "You just sit over there, and if any thoughts come to you, you let us know." Then she turned to Andorra and showed her elegant hand. "D'hand!" she said.

"D'hand!" said Andorra.

"In Shakespeare's time, *hand* was a phallic symbol," said the Widow to the Boar. "You do know what a phallic symbol is, right?"

"Right," said the Boar.

The Widow wiggled her fingers. "D'fingre!"

"D'fingre!" said Andorra.

"That's a phallic symbol, too," said the Widow.

"Well, sure," said the Boar.

He never said much else. Even after the Widow explained the *rest* of Shakespeare's sexual puns, he only continued to cough and loosen his tie. As soon as he could, he stumbled out of the room and ran from Elsa Street. His tie dangled behind him; he was never seen again.

"Are they *all* like that?" asked Andorra.

"Oh, no," howled the Widow. "Most of them are worse!"

The Widow was still wiping tears from her eyes when Geoffrey came home from the factory. He had the afternoon paper with him, but he dropped it to the floor when he learned the Widow had used Andorra to abuse her wild boar.

"She's not a toy for your amusement," he growled.

"They're all just a bunch of gold diggers," said the Widow. "Why shouldn't we have some fun at their expense?"

"Because you're using Andorra's size to do it," said Geoffrey. "It's exploitation, and it makes you as bad as those men who keep coming to the door."

Andorra frowned. She didn't *feel* as if she had been exploited. It had seemed to her as it had to the Widow: nothing but a bit of harmless fun.

"You're overreacting," the Widow said to Geoffrey. "That boar wasn't uncomfortable because of her *size*. He was uncomfortable because we talked about *sex*."

"That's even *worse!*" roared Geoffrey.

"Don't be such a puritan," said the Widow.

"Uh-oh," said Andorra. She finally noticed the newspaper Geoffrey had dropped. Geoffrey had probably not noticed the headline—his reading was poor, and he only bought the paper for her—but Andorra wondered how she had not immediately seen the large dark letters that seemed to scream into the world:

LUSITANIA SUNK BY GERMAN SUBMARINE
128 AMERICANS DROWNED!

As the Widow and Geoffrey continued to argue about what had happened with the wild boar, Andorra scanned the first few paragraphs. Isolated on Elsa Street, the Great War in Europe had been a distant thing. Her only reason to fear had been its impact on the Andorra she had left behind. Now the battles struck closer to home. The sinking of the RMS *Lusitania* was being hailed as a great disaster and a possible act of aggression that could drag America into the war. The notion terrified Andorra, who looked over at her father, so tall and strong as he argued with the Widow. Would they ask him to fight? Would they send him overseas? Surely he was too old to be in the army. Yet she realized with shame that she didn't actually *know* her father's age. Since coming to America, he had developed a

boxer's face, which meant he always looked like he was healing from
a bruise. Yet he hadn't started to wrinkle. Did this mean he was
young enough to join the army?

There was a knock at the door and the Widow went to answer it,
leaving Geoffrey and his daughter alone. She showed him the paper
and explained what it said. "Are they going to make you part of their
army?" she asked.

Still hot from his argument with the Widow, Geoffrey's tense
expression suddenly broke. "*Mi amor,*" he said and kissed her giant
hand. "War isn't coming. That's just newspaper people trying to sell
papers. They're exploiting this sunken ship just like they want to
exploit you."

"But what if you're wrong and they go to war and force you to
fight?"

"Only a fool would make me a part of their army," he assured her.
"If they ever try, we'll just leave. We're escape artists. We will always
know when it's time to run away."

It was then that they heard the Widow's voice from the front
door. "Someone get me some paint! And tell me how to spell ambassador!"

Andorra didn't know it, but May 7, 1915, had just become even
more important than it already was; her future husband had just arrived.

HE WAS THE SON of the Irish Queen of Burlesque; he was also
the son of the man who had discovered her. Zachariah Kelsey had
made his fortune scouting talent and now ran the Detroit division
of one of the largest talent agencies in the country. It was his great-
est hope that his only son would follow in his footsteps, and it was
with this in mind that he had dragged the boy to see the Giant of
Elsa Street. Nicholas Kelsey, six months away from his nineteenth

birthday, stood pouting in the front hall while Zachariah attempted to convince the Widow of his good intentions.

By the time Andorra and Geoffrey arrived, the Widow had Zachariah trapped between her and the door. "If you'll just hear me out," Zachariah was saying.

"Another producer?" said Geoffrey.

"This one swears he's an ambassador of goodwill," said the Widow.

Geoffrey lunged forward, and Zachariah slipped to the side, deftly moving away from the door and farther into the house. Andorra stayed where she was. She had barely noticed the so-called ambassador of goodwill. There was Nicholas Kelsey, slender and strong and short. There was Nicholas Kelsey, whose good looks devastated her like a small bomb. His blue eyes sparked even though they were half-concealed by the brim of his Detroit Tigers ball cap—out of embarrassment for his father, he had pulled the hat low over his head. Andorra was so taken by him that she barely noticed the argument his father was having with her own.

"She has no interest in performing," Geoffrey was saying.

"I think I could persuade her," said the Ambassador of Goodwill. "It's not as if I'm expecting her to be *given* away. I'm more than happy to discuss a reasonable price."

By *price*, the Ambassador had meant *percentage*, for he always took a cut of his client's wages. But to Andorra's father—and to Andorra herself—it sounded as if he was looking for a way to purchase a prized steer. No wonder, then, that Geoffrey threw a punch at the Ambassador's head. The punch was sloppy, and the man easily weaved away. But Geoffrey attacked again. His oiled hands stained Zachariah Kelsey's lapels, and the Ambassador, known for his vanity, knocked the greasy hands away. All at once the men became Grecian wrestlers: they grappled at one another right there in the front hall, releasing bullish snorts as they tried to throw each other to the floor.

The Widow screeched, but Andorra continued to hover in silence. Nicholas watched the men with dismay, looking like a boy who hoped to disappear—while Andorra looked like a girl who hoped he'd take her along.

"How . . . tall . . . is . . . she?" gasped Zachariah Kelsey. (Geoffrey had wrapped an arm around his neck.) "The greater she is . . . the more . . . I'm prepared to offer."

"We're not interested in your offers," said Geoffrey. He squeezed, and Zachariah's eyes began to bulge. Then he let out a cry as something latched onto to his leg: the Widow had entered the fray.

The Ambassador of Goodwill looked to his son. "Help me!" he wailed.

"I didn't want to come here in the first place," said Nicholas.

Zachariah flailed, and in his thrashings he kicked the Widow in the head, forcing her to let go. She cried out as she fell back. Distracted by her cry, Geoffrey loosened his grip, and the Ambassador squirmed free. He slipped down and then scrambled back to his feet. The Widow leaned against the wall, holding her leg. Geoffrey and Zachariah stood panting. And Nicholas and Andorra? They remained where they were, completely statuesque. A boy staring at his feet, a girl staring at a boy.

"You just aren't being practical," said the Ambassador. "Do you know what kind of life I could give her? And the money! I know how hard it must be to make a living."

"She's not interested," growled Geoffrey. The men were inches apart.

"Maybe I should talk to her myself," said the Ambassador.

"I'm not interested," said Andorra, and she finally stepped forward.

Zachariah gaped: he had not known she was there. Nicholas gaped, too. She had been staring at him, but he had yet to notice her. Father and son froze in surprise. The light was coming from another direction; her shadow could not fall over them, but they each *imagined* it had. Her great size seemed to dominate the world.

"Five hundred dollars a month," said the Ambassador.

It was a good price. In those days, Geoffrey barely made twenty-five dollars a week. But he wasn't tempted. "Snakes usually offer much larger apples," he said.

The Ambassador of Goodwill tried to clean his lapels. "Five twenty-five, plus room and board when I take her on the road."

"I'm not interested," said Andorra again.

"Five fifty a month. I've seen one or two giants in my day, but they've all been men. I really do think you might be the only lady giant in the world."

"She's not a lady giant," snapped Geoffrey. "She's a lady like anyone else."

"You don't really believe that, do you?"

"I want *her* to believe it," said Geoffrey. He purposely laid a greasy paw on the Ambassador's arm, further ruining the coat. "I'd very much like you to leave."

The Ambassador stooped to retrieve his hat, which had fallen during the fight. Nicholas turned to Andorra. He was even shorter than she had thought—he barely made it to her breasts.

"Don't hold this against me," he said softly. "I take after my mother." Then he gave her a sly wink even as he pressed the ball cap lower over his head.

Geoffrey followed the Ambassador onto the porch, slamming the door behind him.

"We should have tried to eat him," said the Widow.

Andorra ignored her and peered through the crack in the door. The men were still on the porch. She couldn't quite see them, but she could hear them easily enough; it seemed that Zachariah Kelsey was determined to be the sort of ambassador who outstayed his welcome.

"You don't fool me," he was saying. "You want to manage her and keep the coin for yourself. It's the only thing that makes sense. Otherwise, you're just a damn fool."

"What are they saying?" asked the Widow.

"Shhh!" said Andorra.

"Have a safe trip home," said Geoffrey. "Try not to get shot."

"You really think she can live like a lady?" said the Ambassador. "You think some boy like my Nicholas is just going to marry her? Look, if you were rich, you could marry her off no matter how big she was. A man will marry a mountain if it has enough gold in it. But right now she's just a big, empty mountain. And I'll tell you who will want her: men less honorable than me. Men who will want to use their new wife as a way to make themselves rich."

"She doesn't have to marry," Nicholas remarked.

"Then she's a spinster. Then she's nothing but some lonely woman. Let her be a giant and the whole world could be hers."

Footsteps and then the voices died away.

"Never mind him," sighed the Widow. "He's just another boar."

Andorra—the big, empty mountain—didn't reply. She simply peeked through the curtains and watched Nicholas walk away. She barely heard her father return, even though he slammed the door shut and bolted it tight.

"The nerve of the man!" he hissed. He looked to the Widow. "Did he hurt you? If he hurt you, we can take him to court."

Andorra saw the Widow smile—she was touched by Geoffrey's concern. "Never mind the court battles," she said. "I'm a little bruised, but I'll live."

Andorra stared at the now-empty road. "Am I really a big, empty mountain?" she asked in Catalan.

Geoffrey turned white as he realized his daughter had heard the conversation on the porch. "You listen to me," he said. "You aren't a mountain. You forget everything that man said."

"But will anyone ever want to marry me?"

"A man will marry anyone he's in love with. You just have to show him that you're more than the sum of your measurements."

That night she plucked at her dinner; the next morning, she picked at her breakfast. Geoffrey frowned, worried that his daughter was getting sick. Andorra didn't know the trouble either. She had learned a lot about the world since coming to Detroit; but on that morning after the *Lusitania* sank, she still didn't know that a loss of appetite is the first sign that a girl is thinking about love.

NINE

"It's Like Staring at the Moon"

Hollywood, 1937

HOLLYWOOD. MOVIE LAND. The Hills. Born twelve years before the *Lusitania* sank—before Andorra started thinking about love—it took its name from a ranch in the Cahuenga Valley whose owner had seen the word *Hollywood* on the gate of a Chicago estate. By 1897, the region had a post office, a hotel, and a population with the dubious practice of leaving promissory notes in lieu of cash in the register of the general store. Andorra was still in her principality when the first Hollywood movie was made, but she was somewhere between Europe and Detroit when the man who made it was murdered in his sleep. "His name was Francis Boggs," said Rutherford the Historian. "No one remembers his films but everyone knows he was killed by his Japanese gardener. That's Hollywood. You come here to make movies and they remember you for something else."

The *City of Los Angeles* crested a hill, and then the station loomed before them. Somehow, that great locomotive had made up for lost time. They were only ten hours late. Andorra had missed her appointment with the executives at the Studio but not by much; the clock on the station wall told her it was a sensible six o'clock. Next to it, she noticed a single word painted in black letters on a white sign: WELCOME. The simplicity surprised her. She had been expecting spotlights and marquees. Even an exclamation mark would have made sense—*WELCOME!* At least there was a crowd waiting on the platform. She had expected there to be crowds here, one potential audience after another dotting the horizon as far as the eye could see. As the train slowed, she studied the lean faces and hair sculpted with cream. Worn suits and ties. The odd woman, dressed in somber clothes.

"Journalists!" said Rutherford.

"How can you tell?"

"Trust me—they have a distinction all their own." He quickly cleaned his glasses with the end of his tie. "Say nothing—I'll do the talking."

"Just remember: seven-eleven, three-hundred and twenty-two pounds."

They had barely stepped off the train when the flashbulbs went off, each one a small exploding star. But these flashbulbs were only popping in her vicinity; the cameras were not really pointed at her. They weren't pointed at Rutherford either. Rather, the photographers—and the journalists, the porters, the passengers, everyone, really—had turned their attention to a mountain of a man who was swaggering toward the train. He held his hat in his hand, revealing hair with so much pomade that it might have been painted to his scalp. Oh, he was handsome. Not *devastatingly* handsome, like Nicholas, but they were in the same league. She didn't recognize him. She knew little of the movies, so why would she know Grover "Grove" Wilson, star of gangster films, westerns, and a single adventure flick with Rin Tin Tin?

The reporters turned their attention to the actor, clamoring as they scrambled toward him.

"We should get our luggage," said Rutherford.

But suddenly Grove Wilson was upon them. In his time, he had kissed the hands of stars like Jean Arthur, Mary Pickford, and Myrna Loy. Now he took Andorra's giant paw and added it to the list.

"Darling!" he said, far louder than was needed. "It's so *good* that you're here."

"It is?"

Rutherford caught on faster than she did. With sudden vigor, he sprang into action. "I'm glad you found us, old man," he said, clapping the actor on the back.

"Your wife got your telegram." Grove laughed. "We told the press I was coming to meet a true Hollywood giant. Always good to make a dramatic entrance, no?" He turned to Andorra. "Come, let's get you out of this madhouse."

Andorra was still confused. "Am I coming with you?"

"Of course you are," said Rutherford. "But why don't we give the cameras at least one photo? These people have to eat, after all."

Grove Wilson guided her toward the reporters. Almost at the same time, the photographers took a step back—it was the only way they could get *all* of her in the shot. Grove put his arm around her waist and delivered that clean smile that had been painted on movie posters from coast to coast. At the last moment, Andorra realized she was supposed to smile, too.

They escaped into the parking lot, where a beautiful iron tiger waited to carry her away. Elegant and grand, its engine was tucked under a long black snout that gave way to a cab with red leather seats. Grove produced bright blue sunglasses and a kerchief she could use to save her hair from the wind. "This beauty might as well be a plane," he warned. "She doesn't drive—she *flies*. You've never seen anything like it."

"Actually, I have," said Rutherford. "This is *my* car." He ran a hand across the side of the car, irritation clashing with his good mood. "I told her not to let anyone drive it," he muttered.

There was no room for their luggage—there was barely room for *Andorra*—so they filled the trunk of a waiting taxi and told the driver to follow them into the hills. Rutherford drove—he practically tore the keys from Grove Wilson's hand. "This is a 1931 Duesenberg," he said. "It's the same car driven by Al Capone. It's a Lycoming engine. Eight cylinders, four valves per cylinder, double overhead camshafts." Andorra didn't know what any of this meant, but she hardly cared. All that mattered to her was that the roof came down; all that mattered was that she almost didn't mind climbing through the iron tiger's jaws.

The Duesenberg carried them away. She was instantly struck by the sprawling freeway, the rolling hills, the elegant sun. And was that an actual *palm tree*? There was a vague familiarity to this new world—it was the Spanish influence, the echo of things carried across the border by the Mexicans who had inherited so many things from Spain. No, this was not Sant Julià de Lòria, but Andorra thought she understood this place just the same. The droughts and dust storms consuming America did not seem to have come to Hollywood. She had the sensation of arriving on an island, unaffected by the rest of the world. Grove Wilson was right. The car *was* a plane. And she was very clearly soaring away.

Chester Smith lived with Rutherford's wife in an ornate house buried deep within the hills. Rutherford swore it was a palace. Look at that house, he said, and you'll know where all the money in America went. She couldn't see the house when they reached the front gates, but she could read the name of the estate, which was etched into a stone plaque:

WELCOME TO NEW ANNAN
ALL PILGRIMS WILL BE SHOT

Rutherford honked as he edged the car up one last hill. Then she saw it. The house—the palace—was a great animal basking in the sun. Manicured hedges of oleander lined a front lawn adorned with an immense stone fountain that shot water into the sky. In this New Annan, God was in the details. The railings were elaborate. Balconies rested on Greek pillars. Curlicues were etched into the stairs. The glory of the place dazzled her at once. This was what she should have seen when that train had pulled into the station; this was what she had always imagined Hollywood to be.

Rutherford's wife, summoned by that blaring horn, stepped through a pair of marbled front doors just as the April wind swept through the estate. What had Andorra been expecting? Certainly not a blonde who was this large; certainly not a woman who was this blousy. Jessica Simone was as short as her husband but infinitely larger in girth. She's lovely, thought Andorra. Big and bold, like a tropical storm.

"Why didn't you call?" she said. "You should have told us you were on your way." She wasn't speaking to Rutherford; her nasal voice was directed toward Grove Wilson, who was still helping Andorra out of the car.

"Those reporters were hungry," said Grove. "I wanted to get out of there before they ate us alive."

Rutherford the Romantic leapt up the stairs two at a time, racing to his big blond wife like, well, like a lover in a film. He opened his arms. The blousy Jessica, after a moment of consideration, stepped into the embrace and left a peck on her husband's cheek. Then she broke from Rutherford's grip and descended the steps. Andorra, still trying to extricate herself from the car, nearly did a pratfall as Jessica neared.

"My God!" She had seen Andorra's screen test, of course. But for all the power of film, there are times when it fails to capture the true wonder of real life. "Damn and double damn," said the blousy blonde. Then she shook her head. "Well, come on. Chester has got to see this."

She led them around the side of the house and stepped onto the back deck, where the California sun struck them like the spotlight that it was. A stone path wound its way past a garden toward a large fluorescent pool. Chester Smith was cutting his way through the water: he was gray as an old schooner and rhythmic in his strokes. They reached the edge of the pool at the same time he did. Grabbing the side of the pool, the producer hoisted himself onto land. His skin was worn like an old coat. Ribs protruded over the tufts of gray hair that sprouted on his chest. He seemed determined not to show how winded he was from the exertion of the swim.

Andorra drew herself up to her full height, making sure that she towered over him. She remembered what Rutherford had said about Chester Smith's importance; she wanted to prove she was every bit the salvation Rutherford Simone had made her out to be. But it was a hopeless cause. She could not save Chester Smith. In that moment, no one could.

"My God," said the producer. "It's like staring at the moon!"

He leaned forward to take her hand, and his face contorted at her touch. Those gray eyes rolled to the back of his head. A great convulsion rippled through him, and his body twisted like origami before rolling into the pool. Jessica screamed even as Rutherford the Fully Clothed dove in after him. Andorra only stared in horror. She had encountered unique comparisons before—her husband had excelled at them. But who had ever compared her to the *moon*? It hinted at an originality of vision that would never be explored. Here was an abrupt fade-out, and it smacked of terrible prophecy because it had been caused by something she understood better than most: the doomed producer had a weak little heart.

TEN

A Girl like Her

New York City, 1863

WHO WOULD HAVE GUESSED that a room of convalescing soldiers could ever be enamored with a girl like Jane Eyre? Certainly not Anna, who had taken to reading to the men at the hospital at Fort Schuyler in those first months of 1863. And certainly not Jane herself, who regretted that she did not have "rosy cheeks, a straight nose and small cherry mouth." But such things hardly mattered to the battered men. They adored *Jane Eyre* so much that Anna had read it twice by the time the East River thawed. The reading began as a kindness to a single blind lieutenant, but her voice had carried and taken Jane with it. Soon dozens of men had gathered to hear Anna read from her well-worn first edition. She was only dimly aware of the crowd; she was only dimly aware of the book, too. Able to recite many passages by heart, she often looked up and locked eyes with the only battered soldier who mattered. Gavin Clarke never missed a chapter. Always he could be seen leaning in the doorway, his single arm draped over his chest so his head could rest on his hand.

Fort Schuyler had become her domain; even Barnum gave up trying to put his other attractions at her side. Her schedule did not permit her to go there more than once a week. Throughout that winter and into the spring, Anna and Miss Eaton would spend their Mondays working as laundresses, nurses, and cooks. They changed bandages, doled out medicine, and prepared rough meals with the measly rations found in the hospital's canteen. The cuisine was so unhappy that Anna began bringing supplies bought with her own gold. With Miss Eaton's guidance, she gave the men their best meal of the week. She would finish the day with a reading from *Jane Eyre* before retiring to take her own supper with Gavin. As the weather warmed, the two began taking walks across the slushy hospital grounds. With Miss Eaton always at a discreet distance, there could be no repeat of that kiss that had so warmed Anna's mouth back in January. But she didn't need it. There would be enough time for kisses and everything that followed. She was as certain of this as she was of the thawing earth.

"You've done a real miracle here," Gavin told her one March evening as they strolled beneath the poplars. The trees, still skeletal from the cold, lined the stone walls that surrounded the hospital grounds. Gavin walked on her left side so his missing arm was hidden from view. But she was so tall that she could easily see over his head to that pinned sleeve that flapped so gently in the breeze. "The men really adore you," he went on. "They think it's a blessing that you keep coming here every week."

"I look forward to it. To be honest, it's become the happiest part of my week."

"Don't you like performing?"

She shrugged. "I'm starting to feel like a showpiece. When I'm here, I'm actually of use. I'm accepted, so I forget I'm not like everyone else. At the museum, I can't ever forget. How can I, when I'm always surrounded by dwarves and skeleton men?"

"And the other giants," said Gavin.

"And the other giants." Anna sighed. "I'm definitely happy to get away from *them*."

They were approaching a great white boulder that Gavin liked to sit on as he smoked, and he was already drawing his tobacco pouch from inside his coat. "How does Barnum feel about you coming here every week? Is he still giving you grief?"

"Not anymore. Some newspaper wrote a story about how I'm being all charitable, and it gave him all sorts of publicity. But he's still adamant that I remain neutral in any discussion of the war."

"And you don't like that."

"You can't live in a country at war and be neutral. You can't come to this hospital and not get some rock-hard ideas about what's going on. Which reminds me: I had a favor to ask of you."

"Name it."

As they stopped at the boulder, Anna stole a glance back at Miss Eaton, who was still far enough away that she did not think she would be overheard. From beneath her cloak she pulled a small bag of gold, a mere fraction of what she had saved since coming to New York.

"I don't like what this war is doing to folk," she said. "There's lots of people I could be helping. I have all this money. I won't just sit on it like the ogre on top of her horde."

Gavin, who had laid out his tobacco, suddenly forgot it as he measured the bag of gold. He weighed it in his hand and gave a low whistle. "Where do you want it to go?"

"Half to the Home for Indigent Woman. And the other half for the Colored Orphan's Asylum. Please say yes. Barnum will only accuse me of taking sides, and Miss Eaton would never approve. She thinks indigent women are all lunatics and the orphans should be sent back to Africa." Anna looked back at Miss Eaton. The chaperone had stopped a short ways off, apparently distracted by some birds flittering through the trees. Even so, Anna leaned down further. "Please, put it in your pocket. And keep it between us. Will you do that?"

"You continue to astound me," was all he said, and then the money vanished into his coat.

Anna turned away, embarrassed by her own pleasure. Now they had two secrets: the money and that most singular kiss. They had a furtive nature now, one that suggested a sly little world that was entirely their own. Whistling, he rolled his cigarette, and she, having perfected the art of striking a tiny match with mammoth hands, easily brought it to life. He smiled at her, and she felt herself spiral downward, almost as if she was shrinking into the damp spring earth. Like Jane Eyre, Anna did not have rosy cheeks or a cherry mouth. But here, beneath the poplars and lost in Gavin's smoke, it hardly seemed to matter at all.

WHEN SPRING TURNED TO SUMMER, the juggler who opened Anna's act donned a forage cap and took up the gun. He was not a patriot; back in March, Congress had passed the first national conscription act in American history. "It's now or later," shrugged the juggler before disappearing into the war.

"He's right," said Gavin Clarke when he heard the news the following week. "And at least if he goes now, he'll get more money."

"It's the end of democracy." Miss Eaton sniffed. It was a muggy Monday, the first in July, and the three of them were scrubbing the floors of the hospital's foul surgery. "Imagine: whole regiments comprised of men who don't want to be there."

"The war needs men," said Gavin. "Find another way to fill the regiments, and I'm sure the government will take it."

"More war and more soldiers," said Anna. *More patients, more blood,* she thought to herself. *More bullets in the eyes and arms left to wither on the field.*

Gavin seemed to read her mood. "No need to be morbid, Annie."

"This war is just going to go on and on. How can it not make you upset? You can't tell me you aren't the least bit upset. Look at what it cost you."

"Overworked doctors cost me my arm. They rushed their work, and an infection set in, and they lopped off my arm because it was the easiest thing to do. I've been in pain ever since but none of it has anything to do with the war or why it's being fought."

Anna wrung a bloody sponge into a bucket. "I thought you joined up for land and money."

"You can't live in a country at war and be neutral." He grinned. "You also can't *fight* in a war without picking up some ideals. I really believe this is a just war. America's a good country, which deserves to be saved. Even if they have to conscript men to do it."

Not everyone was as supportive of conscription as Gavin Clarke. Throughout those previous weeks the entire city had become infected with heated debate. Even the American Museum wasn't immune. Most of Barnum's human curiosities could easily avoid conscription, but those male giants were more than eligible. (Gavin argued that all three of them should volunteer. "If the South has that Kentucky giant on their side, why shouldn't we have some giants of our own?") Afraid of losing his prized attractions, Barnum rallied against conscription, though Anna knew his objections had more to do with himself than his business. The real reason her juggler had decided *now* was better than *later* was because Barnum had paid him three hundred dollars to go to war in his place.

That evening, after another humble supper and a reading of chapter 25 of *Jane Eyre*, Anna found her morbid thoughts return as she and Miss Eaton rode back to Manhattan. Staring out the window, past her own reflection at the gloomy night, she saw more than Gavin's lost arm lying on the fields of Virginia. She saw legs, too. And guns and bodies and flags and mud and shit and boys and horses and . . . she had to squeeze her eyes just to stop imagination's flood. It astonished her that Gavin could have seen it all for real and still support the war. Such fierce loyalty! He was barely twenty and already had all the great conviction of a man.

"I'm afraid I can't agree with your sergeant," said Miss Eaton suddenly. The remark came out of nowhere; apparently, *she* had been thinking about Gavin, too. "What's this war about, really? Some imaginary idea of what the country is supposed to be. The Rebels want to secede so badly, I say let them do it already."

"Then slavery will just keep going and going."

"Let it. We have enough missing brothers and sons without adding more to the lot." Quiet suddenly, Miss Eaton burst into tears. Anna, not knowing what else to do, awkwardly extended her arms in the cramped carriage and brought her chaperone close. The sobs were wild, but only for a moment. Miss Eaton was not one to suffer a loss of control for very long.

"Forgive me," she said, blowing her nose on a handkerchief. "I received news of my brother this week."

Anna was embarrassed. She didn't even know Miss Eaton *had* a brother.

"He was with the Indiana Seventy-fifth," Miss Eaton went on. "Now he's gone. *Gone.* Some artillery fire just washed him away."

"Oh, Rebecca. I'm so sorry."

Perhaps it was the use of her Christian name, but Miss Eaton suddenly stiffened and slipped out of Anna's arms. Anna glanced back at her window, allowing Miss Eaton a moment of privacy as she ran her handkerchief over her face. But the silence felt awkward, and she searched for something to say.

"This war will be over soon," said Anna. "Conscription will bring in fresh men and the South will surrender and that will be that."

"That will *never* be that. You said it yourself: this war will go on and on. If I were you, I'd get out of New York. Maybe leave America altogether."

"Where would I go?"

"Let Angus MacAskill marry you. Go back to Canada. And, for God's sake, take me with you. I want to get as far from this terrible place as I can."

Such was her sympathy in the moment that Anna impulsively made a promise she would keep the rest of her life.

"I'll take you wherever I go," she said. She could have left it at that, but Anna felt obligated to add a caveat. "But wherever we go, it won't be with Angus MacAskill."

"No?" Anna thought she heard the hint of a chuckle in Miss Eaton's voice. "No," she said again. "I imagine, if you have your way, we'll be traveling with someone *else* entirely."

The way she emphasized that *else!* Anna blushed in the dark. So Miss Eaton knew. She held her breath, urging the chaperone to continue. Miss Eaton had been watching Anna and Gavin for weeks. If she disapproved of Gavin, now was the time when she would speak. But the chaperone said nothing, and in that silence there was hope.

Anna spent the entire night lost in her fantasies. Hope may cure grief, as her father always said, but it did terrible things to a girl's ability to sleep. When the July sun rose the following day, she had managed little more than a light doze. Yet she went through her morning rituals with a sleepy joy, the sort that follows a night of revelry when magnificent things have occurred. Before leaving Miss Eaton the night before, she had told the chaperone to take a few days off to mourn. So this morning she was left to herself to dress for her performances on her own. She had just finished fixing her hair into the usual tower when she was startled by a knock at the door. Anna frowned. It was a hard knock. The knock of a man.

It was Colonel Routh Goshen. As always, he was in his faux military garb, a hodgepodge of dress stolen from European armies that Barnum had devised for the giant's use. Part of this costume was his magnificent pith helmet with a large floral crest that ran across the skull. Barnum insisted he wear it to increase his size; smaller than Anna, he was not quite seven and a half feet.

He shrunk even more as he removed the helmet and shrunk even more as he folded into a polite bow.

"I was wondering if we might have a word," he said.

"Of course, Colonel. Though I'm due onstage in a half hour."

"It won't take a minute." His European accent was polite and clipped. He enunciated his English with such care that his T's came out sharp like a sword. He ducked his head as he came inside—the rooms at the Top of the World were large, but the doorways were still small.

She had nothing to offer him except tepid water from a pitcher she had filled the night before. That was fine for him: he appeared to have a dry throat. The grippe? Or was it something else? He seemed nervous as he shuffled awkwardly in the middle of the room, shifting from one giant leg to the next. All at once, Anna thought she knew why he had come. Men, she had learned, don't get nervous around women unless they're about to discuss money or love.

Please let it be money.

"I'll come right to the point, Annie," said the Colonel. "Barnum wishes to send me on a tour of America. It would be a great delight if you were to come with me as my wife."

Anna turned away, occupying herself with the mirror and her hair. Well here it was at last, she thought. The unhappy proposal. She had been expecting it, but still she was surprised. If she had been forced to wager, she would have bet on Angus MacAskill to be the first to offer his hand. In the reflection, she caught sight of Colonel Goshen's twitching moustache. *Can you not even get down on bended knee, Colonel? Is there no romance in you at all?*

"I'm flattered, of course," she replied carefully.

"A year or so in America," said the Colonel. "Then more in Europe. I would very much like to return to my home. I'm from there, you know."

"Jerusalem, isn't it?"

"That's merely one of Barnum's inventions. But I'll happily tell you the truth—once we're married."

He tried a coy smile, and she tried one in return. "So it's to be bribery, is it?"

She had hoped to keep the mood light, but Colonel Goshen immediately turned serious once again.

"I think you will find I make an excellent companion," he said.

"Shouldn't a man and wife be more than just companions? Don't you think there needs to be something else between them? A passion of some sort."

"Well, of course that would be pleasant. But I think there are practical considerations. You need to take a husband, and I need to take a wife. Passion will come when it needs to."

"Do I really *need* to take a husband?"

"It is your duty," said Colonel Goshen. "I will make you happy, Annie. Certainly more than that oaf MacAskill. I know he's my rival in this, and I tell you, I can easily beat him down."

"Angus isn't your rival in anything," Anna said. She turned from the mirror, chewing the inside of her mouth. "I'm afraid it just wouldn't work, Colonel. I'm not interested in touring America. In fact, I've been thinking of leaving this business altogether. I don't think it's quite for me."

"But you're so marvelous at it. What else could you do?"

"Something more substantial. Maybe keep helping the veterans if I can. There are plenty of men who have been wrecked by this war."

"You'll leave yourself a spinster if you devote yourself to that."

"I don't see how you come to that conclusion. How does leaving show business lead to me being a spinster?"

"Where else but in show business are you going to meet your own kind?"

"My own kind?"

Colonel Goshen wrung his hands. "God made many races. Too many, I'd say. This war they're fighting, it's because one race is trying to live with the other, and it just can't happen. We all need to stay with our own. The coloreds need to stay with the coloreds, and normal folk need to stay with normal folk."

"And us *nonnormal* folk, we need to stay with each other, too?"

"Yes. Exactly." Now he finally dropped to a single knee. How was he to know it was far too late to do any good? He pressed her palm to his mouth but his moustache was nettles, and she grimaced at the touch. "Marry me, Annie. Why did God put us on this world if not to find each other?"

Anna took her hand away. "I don't know why God put me here. I'm sure I'll find out one of these days. And if I find a husband, I won't care whether or not he's *normal*."

Silence. Then Colonel Goshen coughed as he stood. "You've got fire in you, and that's a good thing. But in this matter, it will only take you down. Regular folk don't see us as wives and husbands. To them, we are trinkets. Pieces of amusement. You might as well accept it: if you do find a husband, he will be one of us." He returned his helmet to his head and went to the door. "Think it over," he said. "The offer will continue to stand until I leave."

"I assure you: I will not think of the offer again."

It was a vow she intended to keep. But she would, to her own irritation, remember the proposal well. She was, of course, destined to do exactly as her giant suitor had predicted. She had turned down a false colonel; a genuine captain was waiting for her in the days to come. On that summer day in 1863, however, Anna would not have guessed Colonel Goshen's prophecy had the vaguest hope of coming true. In turning him down, she had given voice to a grand idea. She would leave Barnum; she would do something true and honest and real. In that moment, she resolved that she would tell Gavin Clarke—it seemed important that he know before anyone else.

For the rest of the week, she kept her secret close. Counting the minutes until Monday came again, she endured her daily routine with a distant look, her mind set on strengthening her resolve.

She knew she would tell Gavin about her plans to leave the American Museum—but would she also finally question him about the promise he had made when he had given her that kiss? Enough bravery was needed to abandon the security of Barnum's employ. To also pull back the curtain and reveal her heart's desire? It struck her as an impossibly daring act.

Distracted by these thoughts, Anna barely noticed the odd difference in the American Museum as that hot July week gave way to a stifling weekend. For the first time in memory, the lecture hall was only three quarters full. Attendance dwindled throughout Saturday, and by Sunday, the hottest day in memory, the halls of the American Museum had fallen still. A performance was canceled, something that had never happened before. Still obsessed with her thoughts, Anna saw nothing foreboding in these events. "The heat has kept everyone away," she blithely told Miss Eaton before slipping back into her rooms. Gazing dreamily out the window, she barely saw the faint glow of flames. The night rang with the sound of a fireman's bell; but Anna's nerves were the only reason why she passed a troubled sleep.

In the morning, she rose earlier than usual and, as she had already plotted to do, left without telling Miss Eaton. She wanted no witnesses. She had slept so poorly the night before that she actually dozed off in the carriage, so she never noticed that the trip took longer than usual—the hired man who drove the carriage had been forced to take a different route.

"Somethin' odd's happenin'," he told her when they arrived. "Tried to turn onto two different streets and saw nothin' but a great herd of people marchin' like cattle and kickin' up a fuss."

Anna frowned. She had not heard a thing—she must have been sleeping deeper than she thought. "What were they yelling about?"

"Probably the draft," said the man. "Lottery was this weekend. Way I heard it, everyone got filled with rage the moment they pulled out the first name."

Anna reached for her purse. She had forgotten about the conscription crisis, as she had everything else. It angered her a little. What had she told Colonel Goshen? That she wanted to do something substantial? How could she do that if she let her own thoughts distract her from the things that mattered?

I really must pay more attention. Read the paper every day. I'm no longer going to just amuse the world. I'm really going to be a part of it.

She was slipping gold into the driver's hand when Gavin Clarke appeared behind her, wobbling and flushed red. He was so off-kilter that he nearly fell as he reached the carriage. He gave Anna no greeting—his attention was purely on the hired man.

"Are the horses still fresh?"

"Depends how far you need to go, I'd guess."

"Manhattan. How soon can you get me there?"

"Within the hour, if I don't spare the whip. But if I'm goin' to drive them hard, I'd better get them some feed."

Gavin pointed in the direction of the stables. "Be quick about it. I'll wait here."

A moment later, the driver was gone, and they were alone by the stone gates. Gavin still hadn't acknowledged her. He was pacing, right arm crossed over his chest, fingers drumming restlessly on his shoulder.

"Well, hello to you, too," she said.

"What? Oh. Sorry." He seemed to finally remember who she was. As if until now she had been just some stranger standing with him in the sun. "How bad is it down there?"

"Down where?"

"Manhattan. One of the doctors showed up late last night and said the whole city's gone mad."

"Do you mean the protest?"

"Doctor said it was more than that. Said it was becoming a battlefield."

"If it's that bad, maybe we should stay up here."

"I can't. I have to get to the asylum." He was still pacing: moving fast, talking fast, thinking fast. He was in a great panic, and she couldn't understand why.

The asylum? What asylum? Then, she recalled the favor she had asked the week before. He meant the Colored Orphan's Asylum.

"If it's about my money, never mind. That can wait until this protest, or whatever it is, has stopped."

"It's not about that," said Gavin, and at last he came to a halt. He fell against the stone wall of the hospital gates, ragged face thick with sweat. "You might as well know," he said. "I think I'm in love."

Anna merely frowned. As if he had switched to a foreign tongue and was saying something she couldn't possibly be expected to comprehend.

"It's all your fault, really," Gavin went on. "She works there. Her name's Susannah Brooks. She's an assistant to the owner."

Her legs felt weak. There was nothing to sit on. She glanced at the empty sky. Where are the clouds? When bad news comes, aren't there supposed to be clouds? "And this is my fault?" she said, her voice even.

"You're the one who sent me to that asylum," he said. "I never would have met her if not for you."

"But I only sent you there last week. How can you be in love with someone you've only known for a week?"

"I've seen her almost every day. It was instantaneous, Annie. A passion of some sort just hit us hard."

A passion of some sort. Well, that's what you needed. Hadn't she told Colonel Goshen that very thing?

Gavin had stopped moving. Talking about Miss Susannah Brooks seemed to calm him down. Apparently, she was tiny and short with long fingers and spindly legs. She was an orphan herself who had been adopted by a good home; until meeting the one-armed sergeant, she had had no aspirations other than ensuring other orphans were as lucky as she was.

"Now she wants something more," said Gavin.

"Let me guess," said Anna. "She wants you."

Gavin looked off toward the stables. "Thank God," he said. The hired man had clearly rushed the horses' feeding—they were already coming back toward the gate.

"What about me?" said Anna.

"If there's real chaos, she might be in trouble," he said. "I need to know she isn't hurt."

Anna grabbed his arm—his wounded arm—and spun him hard even as he cried out from the pain. "What about *me*?" she asked again, and something wet stung the corner of her eyes.

Gavin could only stammer. "What about you?"

"You *kissed* me," said Anna.

He was going to deny it. She could tell. Claim it was the kiss of a brother, a companion, a friend. Then his face fell, and he glanced away. "I'm sorry for that. I shouldn't have done it."

"Why do you say that?"

He searched for the words. "You're a wonder, you really are. And that night when I kissed you, I thought . . . well, I thought maybe I was brave enough to be with you. Because being with you would be an adventure. But I don't have it in me. It would take real conviction for a man like me to be with a girl like you."

A man like me. A girl like you. Anna backed away from him. She couldn't break his gaze. The wind came in. What was he talking about? Bravery? Adventure? What did any of that have to do with her?

Then the sound of the horses. The carriage was back. Wordlessly, Gavin climbed in, but when he went to slam the door shut, Anna reached out and caught the door in her massive grip.

"I need to get back there," she said.

"You should stay here."

"If there's chaos, like you say, then I should be there. Who knows? Maybe a girl like me can do something to help."

She climbed in and slammed the door. The carriage shook. Another silence hung between them, this one as large as Anna herself.

AFTER THE FIRST MAN WAS DRAFTED, a storm of discontent began to gather in New York. It rolled across the city until, late Sunday night, the clouds burst. Angry citizens came to the same conclusion: if the government wanted an army, then New York would give it one. On Monday morning, regiments of fury paraded through the streets. Enraged by the draft—and by disease, by low wages, by whatever else angered them—the people split into various throngs, each a lava flow that drowned whatever it met. Like the poet Walt Whitman, they sounded their barbaric yawp over the roofs of the world. Abolitionists were throttled. Republicans were beaten. The mob hated the war and the colored people who lay at its heart. They turned their wrath on the colored tenements, the colored factories, the colored shops. And the colored asylum? It was only a matter of time.

Anna and Gavin didn't get much farther than Central Park. On Fifth Avenue, just past Fifty-Eighth Street, they encountered a clutter of paving stones and old furniture blocking their way. The mob was on the other side of the blockade, howling with a hurricane's rage. The hired man immediately pulled on the reins, and the carriage made a violent jerk as the Clydesdales came to a sudden stop.

"We'll try cutting across the park and going around the other way," said Anna.

"It's only a few blocks," said Gavin. "I'll do the rest on foot."

He was gone before she could object, lumbering out of the carriage and stumbling away with his heartbreaking lopsided gait. *Let him go*, she thought. She had been stewing ever since leaving Fort Schuyler, and now she felt foul inside, as if her blood had turned to rot. Gone was her resolution to brave the chaos and do something of worth. She wanted only to crawl into her rooms at the Top of the World. How could she have ever thought of leaving? Didn't she know the American Museum was where she was safe? She poked her head out the window, telling herself she would instruct the driver to leave just as soon as Gavin disappeared. And disappear he did—right into the frenzy of rioters, who seemed to swallow him whole. Each of them wielded debris as weapons and yelled their cries of hate. Why were they clawing at him? Of course. He was in uniform. The army was no doubt somewhere trying to regain control. The mob probably thought Gavin was one more soldier trying to get in their way. Through the noise she heard Gavin's own voice and that was all it took: her body moved long before her heart had decided what to do.

With her great stride, traveling into the storm was the work of a moment. She arrived just as the mob was lifting Gavin into the air. At the sight of her, the turmoil came to a crashing halt. They may not have been sane enough to recognize that a single one-armed man in uniform was not a threat; but they could still recognize an eight-foot-tall Goliath for what she was.

"Put him down," she said. "*Now*."

And they did, to her great surprise. Putting her arm around him, using her own body as a shield, Anna turned back to the carriage. But the hired man had decided enough was enough. He and the horses were gone.

Cursing, Anna continued to shield Gavin as she moved them down the closest alley she could find. Stunned from the attack, Gavin allowed himself to be dragged along without a word. They spilled down the alley and emerged into another street. This was one was empty of people but full of rubble and waste. More blockades. Shreds of clothing. Remains of shattered windows. And blood and bile and a single mangled body, a tiny wisp who, from the distance, had all the bearings of a little girl. As they came near, she saw it was actually a woman, frail and emaciated. A weak woman. Perhaps she had been a beggar in life. But in death she was a stone. Her face had been crushed, an eye popped free so there was just a gaping void.

Vomit, moving with a will entirely its own, snaked its way up Anna's throat. She turned and threw up into the street. But Gavin Clarke had seen men shit themselves in battle and barely gave her a glance. His serenity was eerie. He had endured war and gritted his teeth while they sawed off his arm. The sight of a single dead girl did little more than provoke a solemn shake of his head.

"How can people do this?" said Anna. "How can this be happening?"

Gavin was already tossing away his cap. "You need to get to safety."

"What about you?"

"I'll be fine. The asylum's not far." Now he was fighting to remove his army coat. Clearly he wasn't about to risk another assault.

"I'm coming with you."

"Go to your museum. I don't need taking care of."

She bristled. Hadn't she just saved him from the mob? How could he dismiss her as if she were a pest? "You want to make sure your Susannah's safe," she snapped. "Well, I want to know that *you're* safe. I deserve that, at least, wouldn't you say?" The words were like her vomit: hot and otherworldly, born in the moment and not from conscious thought. In the moment, she actually believed that if she stayed with him long enough, he would find whatever courage he needed for a *man like him* to be with a *girl like her*.

It took them hours to crawl through the shattered streets. The mobs were everywhere, forcing them to duck into some alley or abandoned building to wait for the chaos to pass. Forced into side streets, they became disorientated and spent an hour going the wrong way.

New York was a jungle, overgrown with refuse, crawling with wild and terrible things. Storefronts had been destroyed. Shops burned. Colored men hung from lampposts. She was soon numb with horror and fatigue.

At last, thank God, the Colored Orphan's Asylum rose out of the earth like an oasis. Situated on the corner, it was a colossus of brick surrounded by a stone wall and accessible only by iron gates. The one on Forty-Fourth Avenue had been locked tight: an ugly chain lay coiled around the bars, a great metal serpent without a tail or a head. Exhausted as he was, Gavin found his strength to holler and rattle the gates. A gunshot was his reply. Beyond the gate, the old gatekeeper emerged from the shadows, holding a revolver as dark and ugly as the iron in Gavin's hand.

"Go on now! Get away from here." His hand dropped when he saw Anna. The old gatekeeper had probably heard of Barnum's thunder of giants. Clearly he hadn't yet paid his money to see any for himself.

Gavin clutched at the bars. "You know me! You know who I am. I've been here before. Look at me."

It was an effort for the old man to tear his eyes from Anna. He studied Gavin for a moment and then nodded. "You need to get off the streets, boy. Somethin' wicked is goin' on."

He stopped as both became aware of the locusts' buzz. Another faction of the mob had turned up Fifth Avenue; they were marching toward them, loud and full of fire. Anna grimaced and fell against the gates. Her head ached. Her lower back throbbed.

"Please," she said. "Please, let us inside."

Her word was enough; she was so startling that the old man probably would have listened to anything she said. He unlocked the gate, loosening the chain just enough so Anna and Gavin could slip through. Then the iron snake was coiled once again.

"Do you think they're coming here?" said Anna.

"'Course they are," said the old gatekeeper. "Coloreds aren't safe at all right now."

"Are there men up there?" asked Anna. "We'll need help."

She turned toward the asylum and saw that Gavin had already vanished: he was already staggering up a short winding path that led to the asylum's stone steps. Sluggish, ravenous, parched as a desert road, Anna moved after him. She stumbled a little before finding her footing, and when she glanced up, she was at the foot of the stone steps. And there, at the top, was Gavin with a tiny beauty tight in his arms. With no regard for propriety, he was kissing her hard on the mouth. It was a stronger kiss than any he had given Anna; a stronger promise, too, one he definitely meant to keep.

Susannah was a Snow White, sheer as lace, with a shock of black hair. Something awful corkscrewed its way around Anna's heart. And squeezed hard so she thought it might burst. Standing as she was at the bottom of the steps, the couple was a constellation floating high.

Susannah broke from Gavin and looked down. She couldn't have been more than fifteen. "You must be Anna," she said.

"Who else *would* I be?" asked Anna.

Down by the entrance, the gates screamed. Anna glanced back. The mob had stopped outside the stone walls and were beating against the bars.

"Get every man you can," said Anna.

"There aren't any men," said Susannah.

"Where are the doctors?"

Susannah nodded in the direction of the mob. "I think they're out *there*. The only man here is Mr. Davis, the owner."

Anna turned to Gavin. "We'll get the children. You and that gate-keeper have to do what you can."

"*You* should go down there," said Gavin. "You saw how those other people reacted to you. You'll scare the hell out of them."

Anna wanted to object, but how could she? She *had* seen how
the other people had reacted. She had told them not to hurt Gavin
Clarke and they, even in their madness, had obeyed. Reluctantly,
she followed him back down to the gates, where the mob surged
and swelled: they were mindless like the ocean and just as fierce.
Several men were trying to form a human ladder. The gatekeeper
yelled into the thunder, his ugly revolver forgotten at his side. The
ocean was just a vague mass of torn clothes and ugly faces.

"*Children!*" the guard was saying. "We're talking about *children.*"

"Why should we care about your children?" said a voice. "Lincoln
doesn't care about ours!"

"It's no use," said the gatekeeper, backing away. "Devil has them
now." And he turned and ran, leaving Gavin and Anna, a lone giant
and a single one-armed man, to stand against the mob.

"Please!" said Gavin. "You don't want to do this! You'll regret this,
all of you. This isn't who you are. Do what you want to this building. Just let us take the children to safety."

"The children are why we're here!" said someone.

But even as they spoke, something suddenly shifted in the crowd.
Common sense? A moment of reason? No. It was the sixteen-year-
old girl thought to be the only lady giant in the world. Eight feet
tall and with a face locked in rage. The gates to the asylum were
shorter than she was: she was almost a head taller, and the men
who had been trying to clamber over the bars now leapt back to
the earth.

"You didn't come here to burn *children!*" she said. "You came here
to make a statement, but what sort of statement is it going to be?
You're so worried about your sons and your brothers—are they
going to fight and die for people who spill the blood of *orphans?*"

A shift in the crowd. Still the ocean rolled. But it was drawing
back from the shore.

"Take your orphans!" hissed a woman at the front of the crowd.

"Yeah, take 'em!" shouted someone else. "But each one of them owe us their lives! You tell them that. You make sure they know."

The mob roared in agreement.

Anna turned to Gavin. "Get the children," she said. "I'll stay here until they're safe."

And so Anna Swan stood statuesque by the asylum gates while the others ushered two hundred and thirty-three orphans to safety. Arms folded, her great silhouette dark against the iron gates, she was as immovable as the Great Sphinx. The mob boiled and surged but never quite dared to make a move. She was astonished by her own power. She had stopped the mob in their tracks; the ocean had lost its way.

They're scared of me, she thought. *They're actually* afraid.

The rioters had not thought to surround the whole asylum, so Gavin, Susannah, and Mr. Davis, the asylum owner, were able to lead the children out by the back gate. When they were safe, Gavin called to Anna from across the grounds. She gave the crowd one final glare before bounding away. By the time she reached the others, the mob was once again crashing against the gates.

"We have to get them off the street," said Gavin.

"Where can we take them?" said Susannah. "Where will they be safe?"

The answer was clear to no one but Anna herself. There was only one place in the world she wanted to go; one place where she wanted to bury herself; one place where she truly felt safe.

"Follow me," she said. "No one will touch them."

And no one did. Who would have dared? The Nova Scotia Giantess, the sole female member of Barnum's thunder of giants, marched that ragged army of orphans through the wild streets of New York, and the mere sight of her kept even the boldest of rioters away. Behind them, the sky became filled with a fiery haze. The orphans' asylum was burning—by nightfall, it would be nothing but a shell.

In a daze, she finally led them through the doors of that great building at the corner of Broadway and Ann. The colors and wonders of the American Museum made the rescued orphans believe they had come to a paradise. Inside, they tried to swarm the enormous general who had led them, but Anna retreated in silence, somber, gasping for breath. She felt no pride in her heroism; she was not even sure heroism was what it was. Bravery involved risk. How much risk is there when your mere existence frightens a mob into submission? Colonel Goshen had said the world would never see her as anything other than a piece of amusement. But he was wrong. She could also be a weapon. All those early childhood fears returned in a flood, and she understood why Gavin believed it would take courage to be with her: like the ogres of myth, she provoked the fear that she might swallow the world whole.

Leaving the rescued orphans—leaving Gavin and his lovely Susannah—Anna lumbered her way back to the Top of the World. In the days that followed, the riot ended and order was restored, but Anna remained shuttered inside her room. If she had been told she would spend many more years there, she would not have been surprised. She suddenly had no interest in the rest of the world. She wanted only to hide, to sit in her cocoon and fight the hard thing that had twisted itself into her heart.

ELEVEN

The Hostile Witness

Detroit, 1915–1916

The war that sprawled across Europe was no longer a faint echo, the whisper of a raucous song playing thousands of miles away. The sinking of the *Lusitania*—the death of those 128 Americans—had turned the whisper into a trumpet's blare. That summer, Andorra was waking to her daydreams of Nicholas Kelsey; the rest of America, however, woke to the realization that when a world is at war, everyone is dragged through the mud.

In July, the Widow, who had rarely voiced a single political thought, announced she was organizing a talent night to raise funds for the families of those who had drowned. She pleaded for permission to place the Giant of Elsa Street on the bill. The thought of performing gave Andorra a startling case of anxiety; the mere idea made her stomach roll. She forced herself to reconsider. How could she expect people to see something other than an empty mountain if she didn't give them something else to see? And so she reluctantly agreed and spent a full week screwing her courage to the sticking place as she learned another Shakespearian speech—one that was *about* screwing your courage to the sticking place.

"I don't know if you should do something from *Macbeth*," said the Widow. "That show is notorious for being bad luck."

But Andorra liked Lady Macbeth's speech in Act I, Scene VII, the one where she convinces her husband to murder a king. Andorra enjoyed the fierceness of the words; she believed they would make her bold.

The very next week, the Detroit Temperance Hall overflowed with people from across the neighborhood. The Widow's various friends prepared various acts of skill: one man would perform amazing feats of memory while another would use ventriloquism to hold a conversation with his hat. No stranger to the dramatic, the Widow made Andorra the final act, forcing the girl to quiver in agony as the show played itself out. The tremble in her hands became acute: she might have had palsy. Her head ached. Now she couldn't breathe. Her mind went blank, and, in desperation, she tried to remember Lady Macbeth's opening words. *Was the hope drunk wherein you dress'd yourself?*

Yes, she thought. I must *have been drunk when I dressed myself—when I thought I could ever perform.*

At last the moment came. Onstage, the Widow, acting as emcee, stepped forward to give an introduction. "And now," she exclaimed, "I'd like to introduce a magnificent girl who is going to recite some Shakespeare. Three years ago, she did not speak a word of English, and now it flows from her like, well, like ink from Shakespeare's pen! This war is more personal to her than the rest of us, for she comes from Europe, where her own home is now in the grip of war. My friends, I'm pleased to introduce Ms. Andorra del Alandra."

Andorra's blood throbbed as she walked onto the stage. Her stomach churned as she claimed center stage. The hall had gone quiet. Andorra barely noticed the crowd. She had slipped into a void. For a moment she could not recall a single word of English; she would have been hard-pressed to recite her own name. Her stomach was a storm. She would either be sick or burst into tears—or she would do *both.*

The Widow, sensing trouble, spoke up from the wings. "Was the hope drunk . . . ," she prompted.

"W-w-was the hope d-d-d-drunk . . . ," sputtered Andorra. She made the mistake of looking into the crowd. There, not far from the front of the stage, she spied a familiar face. Or rather a familiar *logo*. It was the emblem of the Detroit Tigers; below it sat the devastatingly handsome face of Nicholas Kelsey. Their eyes locked: his were a magnificent blue. He seemed to sense her distress and, in encouragement, he shot her the same sly wink he had given her only a few weeks before. The effect of this was like an electric charge. Never before had such a small gesture had such a large effect (and on such a large person!). That it was the *opposite* effect of what he had intended probably couldn't be helped. In 1915, Andorra wasn't done growing; she also wasn't ready to perform.

"Was the hope drunk wherein you dress'd yourself?" she asked. Then she fainted; all seventy-eight inches of her crashed into the stage.

("You see?" said the Widow later. "I *told* you *Macbeth* would bring bad luck!")

Andorra left the hall humiliated. Never again, she vowed, would she allow the Widow to talk her into performing for anyone. The oppressive heat of that summer night only added to her melancholy. Her father, who had missed the performance, returned from the factory to find his daughter weeping in their rooms. "What's happened, *mi amor?*" he asked, cradling her large head against his chest. She told him the story, but she did not tell him *all* of it: the part about seeing Nicholas she kept to herself. There was too much shame. She had daydreamed of seeing both Nicholas and that magnificent wink—and when it had finally happened, look what it had done! Surely he was laughing at her; surely he was mocking her from beneath that insipid ball cap! Better she give up her fantasies. Better she stay alone and bury herself away.

How greatly it would shock Andorra when she learned what Nicholas's *actual* reaction had been. She could not have known this at the time, but the son of the Irish Queen of Burlesque knew all about stage fright. Since his earliest days, he had hoped to honor his mother's ghost by making a life on the wicked stage. But his hopes were threatened by nausea and blank void that comes with stepping in front of a crowd. That was why he had sensed her distress when she had stepped onto stage. Other people looked at Andorra and saw a giant; but on that night in the summer of 1915, Nicholas Kelsey had looked at her and seen himself.

Nicholas had eventually found a way to deal with his stage fright, but that was not the end of his struggle. Despite being devastatingly handsome—no, Andorra was *not* the only one who thought of him that way—Nicholas found the exciting roles were given to other men. If he auditioned for Hamlet, he was asked to play Fortinbras; if he wanted the romantic lead, he was asked to die in the first scene. By 1915, he had played nearly a dozen roles, but not one had made him proud. He craved the spotlight, and each time he was passed over a tiny part of his spirit was crushed.

"This was why I didn't try to see you for so long," he would tell her after they had married. "Fortinbras can never win a girl's heart."

It would be more than a year before Nicholas finally returned to Elsa Street. He never quite forgot the Giant of Elsa Street—who could?—and for much of that year he had quietly conspired to meet her again. Stage fright may have ruined Andorra's performance at Detroit Temperance Hall, but it had done a remarkable thing: it had wooed Nicholas Kelsey.

At last, on a muggy August morning in 1916, Nicholas made his way to the parlor of the Widow Holt. The armies of Europe were mired in the Battle of the Somme, but Andorra's future husband was preparing for a battle of his own. At long last, he had received a *bigger* role; at long last, the son of the Irish Queen of Burlesque would get to play a king. He had been cast in the title role in *The Life of Henry the Fifth*. Bursting with pride, he prepared to meet Andorra again with their parts reversed. Now he would be the one onstage; now he, in the role of his life, would woo her.

At least that was the plan. But stage fright had conquered Andorra; her future husband would be conquered by something worse.

The air was thick with humidity the day Nicholas returned to Elsa Street. Andorra was suffering running cold towels over her face as she attempted to read *Jane Eyre*—it was a book the Widow adored but that Andorra had always found dull. The heat conspired with the book to steal her energy, and she had fallen asleep when Nicholas Kelsey rang the front bell. She woke to the sound of his voice drifting up from the hall; thick with sleep, she wondered if he was part of a dream.

Given what had happened the *last* time Nicholas had come to Elsa Street, the Widow was initially suspicious of his motives. But Nicholas explained the he had not spoken to his father in almost a year; he had moved out of the family home shortly after that afternoon when he had allowed Geoffrey del Alandra to put the Ambassador of Goodwill in a headlock. This seemed to satisfy the Widow, and she brought him into the parlor. It didn't take her long to see that this was a defining moment; a man had come to the house with romance on his mind—but it wasn't to see *her*.

"I was hoping to see Miss del Alandra," said Nicholas. He had removed his Detroit Tigers ball cap, and it spun nervously in his hands.

"I didn't know the two of you were friends," said the Widow.

"We're not," said Nicholas. "Not *yet* anyway."

By the time the Widow came upstairs, Andorra was already in front of a mirror trying to rub the sleep from her eyes. Over seven feet tall, she still had the heart of a sixteen-year-old girl. She fussed with her clothes even as she tried to calm her nerves.

"But why is he here?" she asked as she smoothed out the folds in her dress.

"He says he wants the two of you to be friends." The Widow grinned.

"*Friends.*" The word held no meaning and every meaning: it could mean nothing and everything.

The moment she came into the parlor, Nicholas remembered why he had been remembering her. Perfectly proportioned, Andorra would always seem like she was in a movie, forever trapped in a single close-up. Having no time to arrange her hair, it swept around her like a spiral of stairs. Her shoes looked like they could crush a small dog; her dress looked like it could swallow the world. "You just aroused my instinct," he would tell Andorra after they were married. "Like a Shakespearian speech." Their courtship might have gone much faster if he had dared to say such a thing on that afternoon in 1916. Who had ever thought to compare her to a Shakespearian speech? Men had spoken of her size before. But never like *that.*

But on that muggy afternoon in 1916, with the humidity sitting on them like a brace, Nicholas would never have dared to tell Andorra how much her size aroused his instinct (or the other parts of him, too). They sat apart, separated by the Widow, he on the piano bench and Andorra on the ottoman. There was talk of the weather and the war, and then, at last, Nicholas looked right at Andorra and announced his news. (He definitely had the soul of an actor— only an actor would think that being cast in the lead role would be enough to impress a girl he barely knew.)

"Well!" the Widow exclaimed. "Henry! That's not an easy part. I was in *Henry IV, Part II,* you know." (The Widow had the soul of an actor, too; she could twist any conversation until it led back to herself.) "Women never fare very well in Shakespeare's histories. But I played Lady Percy, and she fares better than most. She doesn't get seduced or killed. She just gets forgotten."

Andorra shifted on the ottoman and fought for something clever
to say. "How many lines do you have?" she said.

"A true actor *never* counts their lines," instructed the Widow.
"Although we may, in a pinch, count the number of scenes."

"How many *scenes* do you have?" Andorra asked.

"Eleven," said Nicholas.

"I only had one scene in *Henry IV, Part II*," sighed the Widow.

"I'm in the whole play," said Nicholas.

"Shakespeare has no patience for us widows," remarked the
Widow.

Nicholas looked at Andorra. "Do you like Shakespeare?"

"Of course I like Shakespeare," said Andorra. "He taught me how
to speak."

"*I* taught you how to speak," said the Widow. "I used *Henry V.*
Act III, Scene IV to be precise. *D'hand, d'fingres, de nailès.*"

"'I shall never move thee in French, unless it be to laugh at me,'"
quoted Nicholas.

It was a line from the final scene of *The Life of Henry the Fifth*,
the moment when Henry attempts to seduce Katharine, the French
princess. Picking up on the cue, Andorra gave the appropriate reply. "'*Sauf votre honneur,*'" she said. "'*Le Français que vous parlez, il
est meilleur que l'Anglais lequel je parle.*'"

"Oh, wonderful!" The Widow began to clap. "Keep going!"

"I don't know all my lines yet," confessed Nicholas.

"I have the play on my shelf!" said the Widow.

There are three roles in this final scene: Henry V, the Princess
Katharine, and Katharine's maid. No doubt the Widow hoped to
play Katharine herself, but when Nicholas opened with the first
words—"Fair Katherine, and most fair"—he addressed himself
to the tallest girl in the room. Relegated to the role of the maid,
the Widow muttered her two lines before retreating to the background.

"I love thee cruelly," Nicholas proclaimed. "Put off your maiden blushes; avouch the thoughts of your heart with the looks of an empress; take me by the hand, and say 'Harry of England, I am thine.'"

Andorra gave him her giant hand. She would have said "I am thine"—if only it had been in the script!

They soon reached the moment when Henry kisses the young princess, only to accuse her of having "witchcraft" in her lips. He was every inch the man, but he was not yet every inch the king. At the appropriate moment, he merely went to kiss Andorra's hand—and even then he was so nervous that he accidentally kissed her wrist.

"I hope you'll come to opening night," he said when they were through.

"I've never been to the theater," Andorra confessed. "The seats are always too small."

"There are benches at *this* theater," said Nicholas. "They're along the back wall. Promise me you'll come."

Andorra did not have it in her to say no; she kept thinking of Nicholas Kelsey's magnificent wink and how terrible it would be if she never saw it again.

After he fled, she went to the window and watched him leave, exactly as she had the first time he had come to Elsa Street. It was starting to rain, and a cool breeze was sweeping in with the promise of carrying away the heat. As the rain fell harder, Nicholas created a canopy by pulling his coat up over his head. He turned back only once to look at the house; if he winked, she was too far away to tell.

The last time Andorra had seen Nicholas, her father had come home to find her weeping in her room. Now he returned home to find her full of smiles and jokes—and Shakespeare, for she was rereading the complete works . "What's happened, *mi amor?*" he asked, as he had before. But, as before, Andorra said nothing. She just smiled enigmatically and kept her heart to herself.

· · ·

THE LIFE OF HENRY THE FIFTH, starring Nicholas Kelsey, opened at the end of November, just after the end of the Battle of the Somme. America would be in the war within a year, but on that night in 1916, the only war was on the stage of the Goodwin Theatre. The Widow watched from the front row while Andorra, who found the benches too small, stood at the back wall, grinning as her future husband brandished a tin sword and ordered his men to go once more unto the breech. When that final scene came and he wooed the princess, Andorra shut her eyes and listened only to the voice. This let her pretend he was once again speaking to her.

"Wasn't he *wonderful?*" Andorra said after the show.

"That's not the word *I* would use," said the Widow. "That poor dear! He was a lot better when he played the scene with you."

"What does it matter who he plays the scene with? He's an actor."

"That boy is no actor," said the Widow. "An actor would have been able to act like he was *in love.*"

The critics agreed—Nicholas Kelsey was raked across the coals. He was accused of being "more prince than king"; specific mention was made of his unbelievable performance in the final scene. "He proclaims love like he's testifying in court," wrote the *Detroit Free Press.* "And he's a hostile witness!" No one was surprised when the production closed just four short days after it had opened. To be sure, it had other problems—but any production of *The Life of Henry the Fifth* rests on Henry the Fifth. Nicholas Kelsey's shoulders were not strong enough to bear the load.

To soften the blow, Andorra invited him to Elsa Street. It was just before Christmas now, and Andorra had taken time to decorate the house with wreaths. She dressed in red and took the rare step of adorning herself with some of the Widow's jewels. Nicholas barely noticed. He blew into the house like a snowstorm, untidy and unkempt, bearing the unhappy smell of a wet dog. His ears were as red as Andorra's dress, for, despite the cold, he was still wearing his Detroit Tigers ball cap. The brim almost entirely obscured his eyes; he was afraid of being recognized.

The Widow stayed only to greet him and then discreetly exited stage left, leaving Andorra to drag him toward the fire that roared in the hearth. The old armchair creaked as he slumped into it and sunk low in the seat.

"*Bon Nadal*," she said.

"What?"

"It means Happy Christmas."

"Great."

Silence.

"Are you going to try to see your father?" she asked.

"All he'll do is gloat!" he moaned. "He always said I was a terrible actor. God, what am I to do? If I can't make it in Detroit, what's going to happen to me once I move to New York?"

Her weak heart trembled. "I didn't know you wanted to go to New York."

"*Everyone* wants to go to New York. Especially artists."

"The Widow says that New York is very decadent."

"It is. *That's* why everyone wants to go."

"I think I might like to see New York. It might be fun to go."

"I should have kept playing baseball. I could have been a great shortstop. A scout once gave me his card. I threw it away."

"Oh, enough!" she snapped. All this talk of leaving town. He wasn't listening to her. And he hadn't even complimented her dress! "Even Shakespeare wrote *Two Noble Kinsmen*, and that's a terrible play. You ask me, a bad artist is someone who whines about their failures. If you're going to complain, then all those critics were right: you really *are* a hostile witness."

Nicholas blinked. Andorra turned and impulsively downed a glass of claret.

"He wrote *Two Noble Kinsmen* with John Fletcher," muttered Nicholas.

"What does *that* have to do with anything?"

"I'm just saying—Shakespeare needed *help* to write a bad play."

The armchair creaked again as Nicholas rose from his seat. She braced herself for the sound of the front door shutting behind him. But for a woman of her size, she still underestimated her own greatness. Nicholas could survive a bad critique from the *Detroit Free Press*; he could not take one from his future wife.

"Fair Katharine, and most fair," he said. "Will you vouchsafe to teach a soldier terms, such as will enter at a lady's ear, and plead his love-suit to her gentle heart?"

She shut her eyes. "Your majesty shall mock at me. I cannot speak your England."

Princess Katharine doesn't speak much as Henry seduces her. Henry does all the talking, allowing Andorra to once again be in the audience even though she was technically onstage. At first, Nicholas was stiff and unimpressive—out of habit, he was giving the same performance that had so underwhelmed the people of Detroit. Then something changed. A passion came into his voice, and it seemed as if he were speaking the words for the very first time. This was no hostile witness; this was a man who was cruelly in love.

How wonderful, she thought. *He really* is *a terrible actor.*

When it came time for Henry to kiss his princess, Andorra turned and stuck out her hand. But Nicholas was lost in the moment—or perhaps he was finally seized by it. He leapt onto the ottoman so that they could finally stand eye to eye. "You have witchcraft in your lips," he declared. He said this *before* he kissed her; perhaps he knew that once he did, they would never finish the scene.

TWELVE

The Monster's Bride

Hollywood, 1937

THE DEATH OF CHESTER SMITH, famed producer, was a tiny item on page 8 of the *Los Angeles Times*; meanwhile, the arrival of a woman who was seven-eleven (and three hundred and twenty-two pounds) enjoyed a prominent place on the front page. In the accompanying photo, Andorra towered over Grove Wilson. The caption seemed to say it all:

HOLLYWOOD GIANT FINALLY MEETS HIS MATCH!

She was stricken by this photo of herself. Thirty-seven years old, yet the colorless tones made her seem closer to fifty. Still, she clipped the article to send to the children. They might be interested; if nothing else, they always needed something to stuff in their shoes.

For two days she wandered New Annan while Jessica and Rutherford managed the chaos of death. Her needs were tended to by a small Japanese maid and an even smaller Japanese cook. Her room was luxurious. Two beds had been placed side by side with one enormous sheet stretching over them to create a single mattress. In the ensuite bathroom, the stunning shower, whether by chance or design, was almost large enough to contain her. Each time she used it, she stayed until the water turned her lobster red. Hot water was a luxury—she was accustomed to both a crowded house and a water heater that worked only when it was least convenient.

Left to herself, she spent her time rummaging through the library. New Annan boasted a rare collection, and she thought she had struck gold when she discovered a small chapbook penned by Anna Swan's husband. But it was mostly about him; Anna herself was rarely mentioned. *There's something in that*, thought Andorra. *In any history, the things we leave out are as important as the things we put in.* On another shelf, she came across various histories of Civil War New York, each dog-eared and bookmarked. Then she chanced upon an old ledger with a half-torn cover and a decayed spine. Inside was a series of columns and numbers. The columns were labeled: WAIST, NECK, ARM, INSEAM. Each entry was dated. Andorra frowned in wonder. They must belong to Anna—who else could it be? The measurements painted a stark picture. No wonder Chester Smith had dreamed of making a movie about Anna Swan! To anyone watching a film, the characters are twenty feet high—precisely how this world of measurements made Anna seem. Maybe this was why the doomed producer had never wanted there to be a book, play, or radio drama about the life of Anna Swan; he had probably known that a movie was the only way to capture what it was like to stand in her presence.

Now he would never see the film—assuming it ever got made. This fear sat with her throughout the day and kept her awake for most of the night. She had been brought to Hollywood to appear in a single movie. If the movie was canceled, she would be sent home. Back to the poverty of Detroit. Back to the family she had helped to destroy. Empty-handed. She didn't even have her husband's shirt.

Better to stay here, she decided in her insomniac's haze. *I came here to find money to save them, and I will. Any way I can.*

At last, Chester Smith was laid to rest at Forest Lawn Memorial Park. He was buried under his Hollywood name; he had buried his real name, Gavin Clarke Junior, years before. Standing in the cemetery, Andorra had the startling realization that this was her first funeral. Both her mother and Noria Blanco had died in another land; at Zachariah Kelsey's request, he had been cremated without ceremony. As for Nicholas, he had been buried without her. Her father had taken care of the arrangements while Andorra had sat in the bedroom, cradling a blue shirt. She was now a virgin to burials, and she stood behind the parade of mourners acutely aware that she didn't know how to behave. A pestilential breeze, heavy with some awful smell, swept across the cemetery as Chester Smith was placed in the ground. The funeral was, according to Rutherford Simone, a star-studded event, but Andorra was unable to separate the stars from the stardust. She was as ignorant of Hollywood stars as she was of funerals. Fred Astaire and Douglas Fairbanks were both in the crowd, but how could she tell one from the other? She had the unnerving sensation of being the agnostic on Mount Olympus. Stepping into the hall of gods, she was unmoved by any religious fervor. The cavalcade of stars displayed somber faces, but there was a marked absence of actual tears. Rutherford had described Chester Smith as a tyrant. Perhaps he was one of those men who had been feared but never loved. Excepting Jessica, of course. Jessica Simone wept from behind her veil.

Even here, it was Andorra's sad fate to never be inconspicuous. Aside from being the largest mourner, she was also the only one not wearing black—who runs away from home with their mourner's weeds? She seemed to demand attention. Step right up! See how a Hollywood giant mourns a man she never knew! There was the pop of flashbulbs and hushed whispers throughout the minister's sermon. None of it had to do with Astaire or Fairbanks; once again, the thunder of Hollywood giants had met their match. Jessica was tucked behind her veil, but Andorra imagined only cold fury in the woman's eyes. The doomed producer had been relegated to the middle of the paper while Andorra had made the front page; now she was stealing the spotlight again.

When the service ended, Andorra tried to move away with the other mourners, only to find herself surrounded by newshounds. How long had she known the deceased? Was she a relation? Had she been brought to Hollywood to star in a film? The journalists were a swamp, and she sluggishly pushed through them as, in the distance, she heard the sudden roar of the Duesenberg's engine. Rutherford! Over the heads of the crowd, Andorra saw the car take off and vanish down the road. She scowled. She was stranded, surrounded by reporters and spectators, with very little money in her purse.

Not knowing what else to do, she was about to endear herself to the reporters in the hopes they would help. But as she opened her mouth, she felt someone pull on her arm. It was Rutherford Simone. He had not left, after all. "Not now!" he barked at the newshounds. "For God's sake, show some *respect*." He guided Andorra down a row of gravestones, breaking free of the reporters so they could move swiftly to the western gate. The newshounds called after them and gave chase. At last, they found their way to the street. Unable to find a taxi, they leapt aboard a passing streetcar, whose sleepy driver rubbed his eyes in disbelief as Andorra dropped her fare into the box.

"I thought you left," said Andorra. "I saw the car drive away."

"It was Jessica. She left without me, too."

"She must be upset with me. I was such a distraction."

"Those people should be ashamed," Rutherford grumbled. "Not everything in this town has to become a show."

A few stray passengers studied her as she plodded toward the last row of seats. The streetcar wasn't exactly an iron tiger, but she still had to take care not to bang her head.

"What a lousy day," said Rutherford. "Let's put it behind us. We'll go to the Brown Derby tonight and paint the town."

"Isn't that the place shaped like a hat?"

"We'll go to the other one. It's on North Vine. We can watch the fashionable world, and I can tell you more about Anna Swan."

"I wish you would tell me more about her *movie*," said Andorra. "Is it still happening? Do I still have a job?"

Rutherford's face twitched as he removed his glasses and ran the lenses across his tie. "That's up to Jessica now. We'll have to give her a bit of time."

"How much time? My family's depending on me."

"I'll talk to her. But not today. She and Gavin were very close. We both need to give her some space."

He sighed and slipped the glasses back on his face. She decided to drop the subject. The poor man. While she had been upstaging Chester Smith's death, death had been upstaging Rutherford. The great reunion with his wife had probably been put on hold.

By suppertime neither Jessica nor the Duesenberg had returned, so Rutherford summoned a taxi to take them to the Brown Derby (the one that wasn't shaped like a hat). Situated near most of the major studios, the diner had become the rendezvous of choice for the Hollywood elite. Andorra, who had feared she'd find herself woefully underdressed, was relieved to see nothing but slacks and candy-colored skirts. The celebrities were there, yes, but somewhere in the shadowy corners were members of the quiet multitude who truly ran this celluloid world. Agents and producers and union men, almost invisible, plotted the future of the movies over Cobb salads and pastrami on rye.

As always, she still drew the eye, but the attention was of a much different sort than it had been at Forest Lawn. In a world of famous and important people, the denizens of the Brown Derby were more than accustomed to watching people out of the corner of their eyes.

They ordered salads, and Rutherford, who assured her he was picking up the bill, ordered them each a pair of highballs so they could raise a toast to Chester Smith. "And to you," Rutherford added. "For enduring a pretty crazy couple of days."

Andorra clinked her glass and put the edge to her lips. She could count the number of times she had drank alcohol on a single hand. One glass of claret on that Christmas in 1916, when Nicholas had come to Elsa Street; a glass of champagne in the summer of 1919, right after their wedding; a shot of whiskey in the twenty-four hours that had followed Nicholas's death. Alcohol had always been connected to her husband. Until now. Sure enough, the taste was different. Smoother. It went down like cream.

She told Rutherford about the book of measurements she had found in the library.

"I've seen it." Rutherford nodded. "Jessica's grandfather was Anna's tailor. He kept a record of everything."

"I also found her husband's autobiography. It's interesting that he hardly mentions her."

"An autobiography would be *his* story, not hers."

"True. But would you tell your life story without Jessica?"

He smirked. "It definitely wouldn't be half as interesting."

"Exactly. Nicholas is part of my story, too." She drank more of the highball, sucking an ice cube and letting it melt on her tongue. "You said Jessica thinks Anna might be her mother. A scandal like that would make someone want to edit you out of their autobiography, wouldn't you say?"

"I'd say it's dangerous to fill in the blanks with assumptions. Shakespeare doesn't mention his plays in his will. Does that mean he didn't care about them?"

"Tell me more about how they met."

"After the war, Martin Bates came to New York. He was giving lectures about the war and his time as a prisoner of war."

"Someone actually captured him?"

Rutherford grinned. "I think it's harder to believe that they *kept* him there as long as they did. He was there for eight months before he escaped. Apparently he hid in the mountains until the end of the war."

"And Anna met him during one of these lectures?"

"No. They didn't meet until later. There was a fire at Barnum's museum and the place was burned to the ground. Anna went home until it was rebuilt."

"Did she meet Martin then?"

Rutherford shook his head. "He was doing his own tours. They might have met when he came back if not for the fact that P. T. Barnum had the worst sort of luck. There was another fire. He lost everything."

"You're kidding. Did he rebuild?"

"Never again. He probably decided God didn't want him having any more museums. Anna went back to Nova Scotia but eventually agreed to a European tour. *That's* when she finally met Martin. Both of them sailed on the same boat. They must have fallen in love pretty fast because by the time they reached London, they were engaged."

"It sounds remarkable." Andorra sighed. "Was it that fast for you and Jessica?"

Rutherford grinned. "I loved her right away. For her, it was love at tenth sight. What about you and your husband? I'm sorry—I shouldn't have asked."

"No, it's all right. With us, things were more or less instantaneous. But it was still four years before we married."

"Why so long?"

"The war got in the way. He promised he would marry me when he returned."

"It must have been a hard thing to wait."

"Second hardest thing I've ever done."

Rutherford didn't ask for the *first* hardest thing. *He probably thinks it's burying my husband,* thought Andorra. *Little does he know. Burying your husband is nothing compared to killing him. Or having to survive the days that follow.*

They turned the conversation to lesser things and lost themselves in food and dessert—and another pair of highballs. Andorra became delightfully tipsy and lost herself in the atmosphere. There was a tranquility to the night that thrilled her, and she left the Brown Derby feeling soft and pliant, as if she was now made of foam. She dozed off in the taxi as it ushered them back to New Annan, and her dreams were playful, such that when Rutherford shook her awake she came back to the life with a grin, almost happy to return to the world.

Stepping from the taxi, she saw the Duesenberg had returned: it was a dark silhouette framed against the house. Jessica Simone sat on the front steps, still in her mourning dress. Her peroxide-dyed hair was wrapped in a white kerchief, giving her the somber air of Whistler's mother. But Whistler's mother never had this much to drink: there were two empty wine bottles nearby, and she was clearly enjoying the third. Yet what struck Andorra the strongest was not the prevalence of wine. The blousy blonde was reading a certain old issue of the *North American Review*—Andorra recognized the cover at once.

"Hello, Elionor Nicholas!" crowed Jessica Simone.

Andorra flinched. Her story had been published under an assumed name, but it wasn't something she liked to remember.

Turning the magazine toward them, Jessica waved the first page of "A Spanish Reunion." The first sentence, printed in a font so large it would grab the reader's eye, danced before her. "In the days just after the war, Katharine moved through the plague-ridden city just to give her future husband a shave . . ."

"How did you find that?" asked Andorra.

"Rowena gave it to me before we left," Rutherford confessed. "She seemed to think it was something you might have forgotten to pack."

A magnificent lump rose in her magnificent throat; only magnificent willpower could push it back down.

"I thought it was very good," added Rutherford.

"It was *good*," corrected his wife. "But you're not without potential."

Rutherford examined one of the empty wine bottles. "You shouldn't have left us at the cemetery."

"I had to take an important meeting."

"What was so important that it couldn't wait?"

Jessica looked at Andorra. "We had to talk about your future."

It seemed that the chaos at the funeral had not angered Jessica Simone at all; instead, it had provided the spark of inspiration. Even at the funeral, Andorra was someone who easily drew the public eye. She had already been mentioned in the papers twice—yes, said Jessica, the Giant of Forest Lawn Memorial Park had made the evening edition. "You've attracted interest," said Jessica. "We should capitalize on it."

"In order to promote the Anna Swan film?"

"In order to make you a *star*."

The Anna Swan film, explained Jessica, had always been a pet project. Chester Smith had been the driving creative force and without him, the Studio wasn't half as excited about the picture's potential. What they *were* excited about, though, was Andorra herself. With the right marketing, they thought they could turn a woman who was seven-eleven (and three hundred and twenty-two pounds) into box-office gold.

"You're unique," said Jessica. "People will always pay to see the unique."

"I didn't come out here to be a celebrity," said Andorra.

"Would you rather go home? Because that's what will happen. Here's the deal: the Studio is willing to offer a one-year contract. They'll provide training and publicity. By this time next year, you could be one of the great stars of the silver screen."

The idea astonished her, and, still in her haze of highballs and food, Andorra found it hard to speak. It was Rutherford who spoke next, speaking up from where he had planted himself at the bottom of the stairs.

"What sort roles are they going to give her?"

"Does it really matter?" asked Jessica.

"I'm just wondering what sort of movies they see her starring in."

"They have a lot of . . . *interesting* ideas."

"Such as?"

"I don't think this really concerns you, Rutherford."

"I'm just asking a question."

Jessica sighed. "They want her to be the bride of Frankenstein. It would be a remake of the one they did in '35. She'd even get second billing."

"So they want her to be a monster," said Rutherford. "Or rather, a monster's bride."

"They want to give her roles that she's best suited for."

"Monsters and villains."

"And what's wrong with that? We both know there are only certain roles a girl like her will ever get to play."

Rutherford glanced at Andorra and then back at his wife. "Don't you think it's all going to come across as being a little crass? Exploiting her just because of her size?"

"We're not exploiting her," said Jessica. "We're singling her out because she's extraordinary. It's why we pick pretty girls out of the chorus line and handsome men out of the crowd. And it's why you picked Andorra out of Detroit. If that suddenly bothers you, get another line of work. Because this has always been your job."

Rutherford shrank back and fell still. He busied himself by cleaning his glasses on his tie.

"If I do this, I'll have to stay for a year," said Andorra, slowly finding her voice.

"Hopefully longer," said Jessica. "Hopefully this works and your contract is renewed."

"And I'll have money?"

"It's a very reasonable contract."

"You'll have to play whatever parts they want," said Rutherford. "You'll have to *do* anything they ask. You didn't come all the way here for that."

"No," said Andorra. "I came to help my family." She looked from Jessica to Rutherford to that copy of the *North American Review*. "Elionor Nicholas," she said. "I want that to be my stage name."

Jessica shrugged. For her, an enormous actress by any other name still smelled like potential. For Andorra, it was something more. When the story in the *North American Review* had been published, the pseudonym had been a charming joke. Now it had weight. Elionor Nicholas. Her mother's name and her husband's. Both were ghosts now; but both could be revived even as she herself was transformed into a monster's bride.

Jessica raised the bottle of wine. "Hello, Elionor Nicholas!" she crowed again. She took a swig and passed the bottle, and the woman formerly known as Andorra Kelsey drank deep. Her sixth taste of alcohol was sharp, like a net of thorns sliding down her throat.

PART FOUR

Marriage

THIRTEEN

No Rank or Profession

London, 1871

IN JUNE, two weeks before her wedding, Anna Swan spread her legs and revealed herself to a man for the first time in her twenty-four years. To her great surprise, the young British doctor barely reacted at all. As wondrous as she was, she was nothing compared to the *other* giant the doctor had examined less than twenty minutes before. Anna's future husband weighed nearly 450 pounds, an impressive percentage of which was taken up by the grand appendage that hung between his legs. The memory of this had stunned the young doctor into silence; he would feel wholly inadequate for the rest of his days.

Having completed the exam, Anna returned to the security of her petticoat and high-collared dress. She slunk to the adjoining anteroom as if exiting a den of iniquity. She felt vile; she wanted a bath.

Miss Eaton dozed softly in a chair. Behind her, beyond the tall oblong window, the skies of England were charcoal gray. It had taken Anna almost eight years to keep her promise to take her chaperone away from New York—but that's only because it had taken almost eight years to actually leave New York herself. In the fog of London, which seemed to seep into the doctor's offices, Miss Eaton seemed even plainer than usual. She had become dour and skeletal, like a poplar that continues to grow but can't be bothered to bear any leaves.

Not far from here, standing against the wall, Captain Martin van

Buren Bates studied *The London Times*. If Miss Eaton was a dull poplar, then the Captain might have been a cherry tree—or rather, a *forest* of cherry trees, all in full bloom. At twenty-five, he was immense and full of color. This was despite the fact that he still wore his gray Confederate uniform, for he had adorned himself with medals and pins that caught the eye like so many flowering blossoms. No wonder the rumors of his wartime prowess had reached the ears of Gavin Clarke; the man known as the Kentucky Giant was a brawny beast with a fifty-inch chest. Anna had scared mobs, but the Captain had scared entire *armies* during the Civil War. As that humbled young doctor had learned, nothing about the man was unimpressive: even his moustache inspired awe.

As she entered the room, he let the newspaper drop away. He had Southern breeding and was adept at giving her his full attention whenever she walked into the room.

"How was it, Annie?"

"Humiliating."

"Doctors," sighed the Captain. "Every one of them is a brute. Does he seem concerned?"

"I really couldn't tell."

He patted her hand. "It'll be fine. You just wait."

The door to the street opened and H. P. Ingalls entered, idly smoking a cigarette and wearing a dark bowler pressed low over his ears. The New Yorker had gone white in the years since he had first appeared in Tatamagouche, but he had also become wilier, if such a thing was possible. He had practically hired himself to manage her European tour and proudly admitted it had been his idea to put Anna and the Captain on the same boat. It was hard to imagine he hadn't hoped a marriage would result; the quest to pair Anna off had never quite stopped, even after each member of Barnum's thunder of giants had disappeared. Angus MacAskill was dead now, while Jean Bihin had returned to Belgium. As for Colonel Goshen, he had completed his American tour and had retired to New Jersey. So when the Captain had appeared in New York delivering his lectures on his wartime adventures, Anna was certain that both Ingalls and Barnum had begun to scheme. For them, love and marriage were just great publicity stunts waiting to be arranged.

The proof of this was in the whirlwind of events Ingalls had arranged ever since she and her future husband had stepped off the boat. He had wasted no time informing the press that Anna Swan and the Kentucky Giant were engaged. The report had caught so much attention that within a week they had secured an audience with none other than the Queen. There, in the splendor of Buckingham Palace, Her Majesty had offered her own parish as a wedding site. She had even insisted on providing both jewelry and a dress. Anna was so overwhelmed by the speed of events that, even now, it still barely registered that she had stood in a *palace* and met a true bonafide *queen*. It felt like another of Barnum's humbugs, an illusion whose truth would soon be revealed.

H. P. Ingalls snuffed out his cigarette as he glanced at the sleeping Miss Eaton. "God, is she asleep again?"

"Don't be cruel," said Anna. "I don't think London agrees with her."

The New Yorker gave a small belch. "I know this food doesn't agree with *me*. Next time you visit Her Majesty, tell her to teach her subjects how to cook."

"The Brits aren't known for their cuisine," said the Captain. "But I'll tell you, it's still better than anything I ate in the war."

There you go again, thought Anna. The war had been over for just over six years, but the Captain still brought it up every chance he could. *Gavin Clarke lost an arm*, she thought. *But even* he *managed to talk of other things.*

No. Don't be negative. And don't *compare him to Gavin Clarke.
Why would you? You haven't talked to Gavin in years. Look forward.
Forward!*

She squeezed the Captain's hand and then, for good measure,
brought it to her mouth. She wanted to stay optimistic. Marriage
was a publicity stunt for H. P. Ingalls. But for her it was tomorrow
and the next day and all the years to come.

A few minutes later, the young doctor called for them. Leaving
Ingalls and the snoring Miss Eaton, Anna and the Captain returned
to the doctor's office. Anna cringed at the sight of his sofa. Since
arriving in London, they had caused couches to crack, bed frames to
buckle, and a dining room chair to break in two. She made a small
prayer to God that the sofa would hold: the examination had been
embarrassing enough.

"The good news," said the doctor, "is that there's nothing but good
news."

"We can have children?" said the Captain.

"I don't see why not. Everything indicates you and you wife are
in perfect condition."

"But what would they be *like?*" asked Anna.

"They?"

"The *children.*"

"I imagine they'd be like any children," stammered the doctor.
"Half you and half him."

"That's what I'm afraid of," said Anna. "Two halves of two giants
still make another giant."

"Is that what's troubling you?"

"That's what's troubling *her,*" said the Captain.

"Two giants might make an even *bigger* giant," Anna continued.
"Can you imagine someone bigger than us? How they might suffer?"
Like her, the Captain endured constant pain in his back that often
made him hunch; she envisioned it getting so bad that one day his

knuckles would touch the ground. She wasn't any better. What right had she to bring a child into the world who might have the same troubled existence? Almost eight years ago, Colonel Goshen had warned her that giants would only ever be seen as pieces of amusement. Did she really want to birth another bauble for Barnum to play with?

"You just wait," said the Captain. "We'll have us a dozen little ones, just like our mothers did. God made sure that we met, Annie. You have to be content to keep letting Him do as He will."

Anna shrugged and forced a smile. Although she had a great faith in God, she did not feel as confident about His intentions.

Still troubled, she trailed the Captain into the other room—and there, in a sudden moment, her confidence in God's intentions was shaken even more. Eight years ago, she had looked out into Barnum's Great Lecture Hall and seen Gavin Clarke staring back at her; now, to her great surprise, he was staring at her once again. There he was, in the flesh, striking and strong in a well-tailored suit. Susannah was next to him, and Miss Eaton, now awake, appeared to be making introductions to H. P. Ingalls; but for Anna they were background players, costumed extras populating the fringes of the stage.

"Annie!"

How his voice came at her, like a blare from a bassoon! As he came toward her, she saw that his gait had improved. He had found his balance. He had also, it seemed, found some measure of success. His beard was trimmed and his shoe tips shone. As he kissed her hand, the light caught his watch chain, thick as her own finger. Gold? She hadn't seen him since the day he had married Susannah at the hospital in Fort Schuyler. The next day, he had taken his new wife to Nova Scotia to meet his father. After that, there had been nothing. She had sent letters, but there had never been any reply. Now here he was, tall and prosperous, standing before her in a foreign land.

"We're here on holiday!" chirped Susannah Clarke. She giggled a little and then stared past Anna at the Captain, who was watching the reunion in silence. "Look at him, Gavin! It's like staring at the moon!"

The skin above the edges of Gavin's beard flushed red. "Why don't you have a seat, Susannah?"

"We're here to see a doctor-man," Susannah whispered. "It's a holiday—but it's *not* a holiday, too."

Gavin looked at Anna. "We've come to London for a bit of a break. I'm in munitions now. I have a few factories out in Boston."

"Congratulations," said Anna. She was distracted by Susannah. Her memory of the girl had always been a beautiful bride with a veil as long as her hair; this girl here looked wild and unkempt. There had been an attempt to fit her into a proper dress, but everything was slightly askew. Her pins were fighting a losing battle to keep her hair in place.

"Susannah's a little under the weather," Gavin said. "Someone recommended that we come here."

The Captain coughed, probably annoyed that he had not yet been introduced.

"This is Captain Bates," said Anna. And as an afterthought, "My fiancé."

The handshake redefined the meaning of awkward. The Kentucky Giant, still in his Confederate colors, was meeting a sergeant who had lost his arm to a pair of Confederate bullets. It was a wonder the meeting was as peaceful as it was.

Gavin turned back to Anna. "I heard you were here. It's all over the paper."

"Yes, we're a bit of front-page news," said the Captain. "We even met the Queen."

"The Queen!" repeated Susannah, and she suddenly did a little twirl.

"Sit down!" said Gavin.

"The Queen, the Queen!" said Susannah again.

"We should go," said the Captain.

Definitely, thought Anna. "It was good seeing you," she said out loud.

"We're here until the end of the week," said Gavin quickly. "May I call on you?"

"If you like," she said after a pause.

"We've taken a house on Craven Street," said H. P. Ingalls, who smoothly appeared and slipped a card into Gavin's hand. The card was probably still warm from the press; the New Yorker had picked them up from the printer earlier that day.

There was a flurry of farewells, and then the sudden reunion was done. Susannah's high-pitched voice chased after them as they fled into the street. "After the doctor-man, I want to see the Queen . . . ," she was saying. Then her giggle was drowned by the noise of a London afternoon.

"Well," said Miss Eaton to Anna. "I certainly didn't expect to see *him* ever again."

"I wonder what's wrong with his wife," said the Captain.

"She seemed a little daft to me," snorted H. P. Ingalls. "I know you both are large. But what sort of lunatic would compare you to the *moon?*"

THE WEDDING, which would be held at St. Martin in the Fields Church in Trafalgar Square, was destined to be a great public event. Every day, Anna and the Captain were discussed in the columns that detailed the lives of high society —in this case, the *very* high society, as one reporter cheekily wrote. In those last days before their marriage, the two members of Very High Society appeared at the theater, the opera houses, and countless parties. This was in addition to their public performances—a variation of what Anna had done back in New York—and each day they arrived at the rented hall to find the auditorium sold out.

Time spun past her, but Anna barely noticed. Each morning she went into the world with her future husband at her side; each evening she returned home, wondering if Gavin Clarke had come to her door. It angered her that he had not yet appeared and angered her more that she cared. Why could she not let these daydreams go? Here she was, obsessed with yesterday's desires, when at long last, after all those years hiding in the American Museum, tomorrow held something new. So long, Anna Swan. Welcome, Anna Bates. As she whirled from one engagement to the next, she fought to remember the mantra she had invented that day in the doctor's office. Forward! Forward!

She could not deny that the Captain had romantic appeal. He had an incongruous mix of both an aristocrat and a brute: he was an educated man who held nothing back. He had shown this at their very first encounter on the deck of the *City of Brussels*, the ship that had taken them away from New York. She recalled that first afternoon when she had stepped into the cold mist and found him already on deck with an umbrella, as if he had been waiting for her to appear. He had offered his arm and led her gallantly along the deck, even as it started to rain, leaving poor Miss Eaton to follow like a forgotten pet. There had been some small talk about the weather and even smaller talk about their health. Then he had launched into his favorite topic: the war.

"I was a prisoner for seven months," he remarked.

"I heard," she said. "You lectured on it in New York."

"That's right. They had to carry me to the camp in chains. Yoked me like I was an ox."

"You're joking."

"I wish I was. They made me walk for miles like that. Sometimes the other prisoners saw someone they knew and could get things like blankets and food and money. But everyone I knew was back in Kentucky. Still, folks took pity on me and gave me what they could. And I was such a wonder that even federal boys kept finding excuses to talk to me. I never lacked for company on that march, I can tell you that. That's the way it is when you're as big as we are, darling. You're never alone."

No, we're never alone, thought Anna. *But that doesn't mean we aren't lonely.*

She noticed him looking at her. He had mistaken her silence for disinterest. "Perhaps these things disturb you," he said.

"It's nothing I can't handle. I volunteered at a hospital during the war."

"Do you want to know more?"

She was surprised that she did. She asked him about life in the prison camp itself.

He looked off into the Atlantic, wiping the spray from his face as he gathered his thoughts.

"The camp itself was just the outside world surrounded by a high board fence. There were cabins, but they'd all been built for twenty men, and some of them were holding more than sixty. Lord, they stank! The other prisoners were all scared of me when I arrived: they saw that I would need more food, more water, more space. They thought I would just take what I needed. Men went in there as gentlemen, but not all of them stayed that way, if you know what I mean. I had already determined I wouldn't resort to such behavior: our war was with the federals, I thought, not with each other. So to show my good faith, that first night I slept on a pile of sawdust on the floor. I stayed there all winter and into the following spring. Believe it or not, I was lucky. I know a few men who were there after I left, and they told me horror stories of crowds and sickness, and men eating rats and birds. But when I was there, it was still early enough that there was still some sense of order. We were given food rations and soap, allowed to read, even sent letters home. They let us receive letters, too, and that was how I learned that some Union sympathizers had kidnapped one of my brothers and tortured him to death."

"My God. Is that why you escaped?"

The Captain looked around and then leaned forward. "I'll tell you a secret, if you like. I just tell folk I escaped 'cause it makes for a better tale. I was definitely *planning* to escape. But the truth is, I cost too much to keep alive, and the federal boys were all scared of me. So the first chance they had for a prisoner exchange, I was sent on my way. I spent the rest of the war with the militia, fighting in the mountains."

"It's an astonishing story," said Anna.

"We're astonishing folk, you and I," he said. "We deserve as many astonishing stories as we can get."

He told her more of these astonishing stories as they sailed across the Atlantic. She supposed it was this that had seduced her. He had been open to her in a way that no one else had. When he finally revealed his heart, shortly after they crossed into the English Channel, he did it in a way that defied the business-like manner of Colonel Goshen. He appeared with an umbrella, just as he had the day of their first encounter, and pleaded his case in simple and elegant terms. He did not seem to consider it a matter of course that she would accept him. He wooed her like she was a regular girl; and he, for all his bravado, came across like a nervous youth.

It wouldn't be such a terrible fate to be his wife. She liked him well enough, though she had the sense to know she wasn't yet in love. But that didn't matter so much. Gone was that young girl who had told Colonel Goshen that a couple needed passion before they wed; at last she understood what he had meant about practicality. *Passion will come later*, he had said. She had agreed to marry the Captain, hoping that this was true. Who knows? One day her marriage might even involve a degree of love.

On June 16, her last day as an unmarried woman, Anna and her future husband went to the Office of the Registrar to sign the marriage license. Journalists had been dogging them for days, but even the British media found little value in following the tallest couple in the world to a government office. They traveled there alone, and inside, with only H. P. Ingalls and Miss Eaton as witnesses, Anna prepared to sign the license without a moment's thought. But she drew back her quill when she saw what the bucktoothed clerk had written on the page. In the column marked "Occupation," the clerk had written a single, peculiar phrase: *No rank or profession.*

"No profession!" she repeated. "What have I been doing all this time?"

"What *have* you been doing all this time?" asked the clerk.

Anna saw then that she did not have a word to describe herself. She performed in sketches and sang religious hymns. She lectured on Nova Scotia and quoted from *Macbeth.* What did you call such a profession? Was she a performer? Or was she just a human curiosity who did curious things?

Was "human curiosity" a profession?

"I think I'm an actress," she decided at last.

"Bite your tongue," said the Captain. "Actors are scoundrels."

"We perform in front of crowds. I think that makes us actors."

"It doesn't matter what you are," said the clerk. "For our purposes, acting is not a profession. You need to be a doctor or a lawyer or have a military rank."

"I was a captain in the Confederate Army," said the Captain.

The clerk nodded and went to write this down. Anna grabbed his hand. "The Confederacy isn't even a country anymore. His rank is meaningless."

"My rank is *not* meaningless," thundered the Captain. "The Confederacy may return. Write. It. Down."

The clerk obeyed—how could he not? Anna obeyed, too, despite her misgivings. The bemused clerk recorded the Captain as a member of the *American* army and the ink was dry before the Captain noticed the mistake. And so they were recorded for posterity: he as a captain in an army in which he had never served, and she as an unemployed spinster without rank or profession. Was this another encounter with revisionist history? Or was it just one more thing designed to never let her forget what she was?

Distracted by the incident, she returned to Craven Street without doing the one thing she had been doing for almost two weeks— she forgot to wonder if Gavin Clarke had finally called on her, as he had promised to do. Naturally, this was the one afternoon she would have had her answer. Gavin *had* called on her; in fact, the hired maid had left him sitting in the parlor. He had been waiting for almost an hour.

"Why the devil does he want to see you so bad?" grumbled the Captain.

"How should I know?" said Anna. "We grew up together. It's possible he has news for me about home."

She doubted this was true, but she suddenly wanted to meet with Gavin alone. There was something auspicious in his appearing less then twenty-four hours before she wed. The moment, whatever it would be, needed to be her own.

A few moments later, she was facing Gavin inside the small parlor, curtains drawn across the door. The Captain had gone to take a nap while Miss Eaton had reluctantly agreed to help the maid with their supper. Miss Eaton had not discussed Gavin since that day in the doctor's office; but the hesitant way she slipped away told Anna that the chaperone had no small interest in the reason for Gavin's return.

"I'm sorry it's taken me so long," he said. "I understand the timing isn't very ideal."

"We've all been busy," said Anna.

"I left Susannah at the hotel. It took some effort. She doesn't like to be left alone."

"Perhaps you shouldn't have left her then."

"I wanted to speak with you alone. As a friend."

"Are we friends? Because I seem to remember you vanishing for eight years. I sent letters to your father. Did you ever get them?"

"Of course I did."

"And you decided that instead of writing back, like a *friend*, you would simply show up in England."

"I couldn't write. I tried. I'm sorry."

"There's nothing to be sorry about. We're both living happily ever after. We don't have to think about the past anymore."

"But I do, Annie. That's why I couldn't write. I'm ashamed of myself. That's what I came here to tell you. I made such a lousy mistake."

There it was. What spurned lover has not dreamed of this moment? She felt glorious and terrible all at once. It was thrilling to hear him finally show remorse. But it was all coming too late. He had a wife. And she had a marriage license.

Gavin collapsed into a chair. He fumbled with a cigarette, but it fell from his hands and rolled across the floor. Anna sighed and plucked it from the carpet. She dropped it in his hand like it was alms for the poor. She purposely did not offer to light it, but she didn't need to. He had learned the art of lighting a match with one hand.

"Do you ever think of those days?" he asked.

"It doesn't matter anymore."

"Tell me anyway."

"I did for a time," she confessed.

"Then I'm not alone. I can't help it. I'm in such misery. Susannah's sick. That's the real reason we came to England."

"What's wrong with her?"

"You saw her. She's not right. She has these nervous fits. Sometimes she talks to people who aren't there. I've tried everything, and

I'm at my wit's end. Especially since now . . . well, the thing is she's going to have a baby."

"Gavin, that's wonderful."

"No, it's not. What if the baby's like her? These things can be passed along, you know. That's why I brought her to that doctor. Can you imagine if my child's like Susannah? How it might suffer?"

It was a perfect echo of what she herself had asked the doctor two weeks before. How could she not give an echo of the Captain's reply? "We can't control these things," she said. "You have to be content to keep letting God do as He will."

"That's good and well for some," he said. "As for me, I just want to escape. I have a good mind to take a boat to France and never return."

"You can't do that."

"Why not? Why should I have to live like this? The cripple with the crazy wife. It's not fair."

"Are you really going to talk to *me* about what's fair?"

"Oh, it's not the same. Look at you, with your great success and enormous husband. I think God's been pretty damn fair to you. Better than He's been to most." Gavin took a final draw of his cigarette and threw it into the hearth. "I don't know why I came. What good is apologizing? We make our mistakes and we live with them. Goodbye and good luck. Enjoy your blessed life."

She stepped forward, a barricade of woman blocking his escape. "Gavin, promise me you'll go back to Susannah."

"What do you care what I do?"

"If you abandon your wife and child, you are going to regret it more than you ever regretted not being with me. What did you say to me back then? Something about not ever having the right sort of courage. Force yourself to have it now. You fought in a war. You lay there while they sawed off your arm. You can learn to live with this. You can learn to live with anything."

He stared up at her, his face solemn and blank. It was impossible to know if her words had any effect. "I have to go," was all he said.

She stepped aside and listened to him leave. From the window, she watched as he staggered down the street. Was he going toward the hotel or away from it? There was no way to know.

Am I supposed to do something now? she wondered. *Follow him? Send word to Susannah?*

The answer swelled up from some dark place in her heart.

Don't do anything. He's no longer your concern.

It was a liberating thought, and she clung to it as she climbed the steps of the house. For the sake of propriety, she and her future husband had been staying in separate rooms. The Captain was sleeping on a bed of straw, just as he had done his first night as a prisoner of war. As for her, she had been using an enormous bed that had been built for Chang the Chinese Giant who had toured through London several years before. Somehow the Captain had obtained it and presented it to her as an early wedding gift. But now Anna forgot her giant bed and chose the Captain's room instead.

He was still awake, his boots removed, his hands laced behind his head. "So?" he asked. "What did he want?"

"He wanted to wish us luck," she said. "He told me to enjoy my blessed life."

She lay down beside him on the straw and curled onto her side. Her head came to rest on his magnificent chest, and he draped his arm around her. He smelled of musk and salt. He stroked her hair. If she had seen a glimpse of her bittersweet future, in that singular moment she might not have cared. Gavin was right. God had been fair to her, at least to a point. Lost in that bed of straw, it no longer seemed to her as if she was floating alone. *This might not be so bad. Who needs a rank or profession?* Anna shut her eyes and fell towards hope. She had, for once, a companion in the giant sea.

FOURTEEN

A Spanish Reunion

Detroit, 1917–1929

ISAPPOINTED BY HIS ARTISTIC CAREER, Nicholas was easily caught in the promise of adventure that came after America entered the war. The speed of his decision matched that of his romance with the Giant of Elsa Street: less then six months had passed since their first Christmas kiss. They were only starting to understand how they could love one another, and now he was disappearing into the heart of the European storm.

Before leaving for Fort Custer, he gave her his Detroit Tigers ball cap. Andorra promised to care for it; it barely fit, but she forced it over her head.

In August, they sent him overseas, and from then on the mailbox became a beast with claws. She dreaded receiving mail; she dreaded *not* receiving mail, too. There was little mention of romance in the letters. Instead, they were an assortment of complaints mixed with memories of Detroit. But it was almost worse when there wasn't a letter. When there wasn't a letter, she lost sleep; when there wasn't a letter, she read every newspaper in fear.

Autumn became winter. Winter brought her eighteenth birthday. It was an icy February, but she refused to take that ball cap from her head. Desperate for activity—*any* activity—she began to work for the Widow's friends. Many of them needed letters typed; some were writers who needed clean drafts of their stories or plays. Andorra found her large fingers were still well suited to a typewriter's keys and before long, she had become the unofficial typist for Detroit's artistic community. She found the work so pleasant that she quietly began writing pieces of her own, each one a fictional story whose plot was stolen from her life. It was autumn again when she began to write a short story about a boy, a girl, and their mutual love of Shakespearian kings. She often wrote before dawn, struggling to hold a pen since the typewriter would only wake those who were asleep. She guarded them as she would a diary, for the stories revealed too much of her heart. Geoffrey and the Widow knew that Nicholas Kelsey was, to use the Widow's word, Andorra's *fella*. Exactly what that meant, though, was something Andorra was still trying to determine for herself.

All throughout the year she continued to read the lists of the dead, a depressing habit which was now adopted by everyone in the house. The Widow read out of morbid curiosity while Geoffrey combed every page in search of news about Andorra—the *other* Andorra. All these years, Geoffrey had been religiously writing to Manuela Noguerra, and by the fall of 1918, it had been almost a year and a half since the last reply. The postal routes had been ruined.

Each time he found the mailbox empty, Geoffrey smacked it hard with his greasy fist.

"Your wife was very sick," said the Widow. "Do you really think she's still alive?"

"Until Manuela writes, I won't ever know for sure."

"What if she *never* writes?" asked the Widow. She reminded them there was a sickness going through Europe—something called the Spanish flu. "Do you really think your wife can survive both a fistula *and* the flu?"

"I will always be married," said Geoffrey. "Until I have reason to believe I'm not."

Andorra was touched by this loyalty. She also envied it. Recalling the sickly sight of Elionor as she stood by the Valira River, Andorra had long since considered her father a widower.

She was wrestling with a pen one gray November morning when church bells suddenly began to ring. Andorra frowned. It was hardly four o'clock. Some wayward bell ringer must have lost track of the time. When the bells woke her father, Andorra quickly stuffed her writing under dress.

"What's happening?" he growled. "Why are they ringing that damn bell!"

"Peace!" came a voice from outside.

"Peace!" came a voice from the hall. It was the Widow; *she* had been woken by the sounds of the neighborhood springing to life.

Peace! That bell ringer had not been wayward at all. The armistice had finally come. Signed just after five in the morning halfway across the world, the news had finally trickled through the time zones. Now, just as the sun was rising, people were bellowing into the coming dawn. It was November 11, but their friends and neighbors were basking in the sort of freedom that comes with the first day of spring.

The day became a holiday. Shops were shut down. Factory workers were given the day off. Geoffrey and the Widow fled to watch the celebrations unfold, but Andorra stayed behind. Returning to her work, she lost herself in the romance of her not-quite-fictional boy and girl. "You're like a Shakespearian speech," she had the boy say to the girl. "You're immense and daunting—but I'll conquer you just the same." She reread the words, nodded in approval, and adjusted the ball cap on her head. She had never shown anyone her writing, but she knew she would show it to Nicholas. She also knew she had to work fast; he'd be coming home soon.

At first, the men returned a handful at a time. Then the clouds burst and the city overflowed. Some of the veterans bore visible scars, but the eerie ones were those who bounced through the streets, whistling as if they'd never been gone.

Andorra wrote and waited.

Some men discussed the war, but most preferred to act like it had never occurred. These were the men who stalwartly went about their day, swinging their lunch pails, spitting on the sidewalks, stooping to shine their boots. These were the men who married their sweethearts or picked up new ones. They played pool. They rebuilt their homes.

Andorra wrote and waited.

Now these men sped through the streets, racing in their jalopies as they crowed at the women and howled at the moon. They played their new music: their trumpets made jazzy honks, their harmonica's blared, their ragtime shot from player pianos like a bullet from a gun.

Andorra stopped writing. But she continued to wait.

Soon the men were grumbling at the women who wanted the vote. They cursed the people who wanted prohibition. They went to Communist rallies. They went to anti-Communist rallies. They argued about the future. They continued to forget the past.

Andorra forgot the past, too. There was no avoiding it; she had become a casualty of war. She had reached her final, magnificent height: ninety-four and a half inches, just a few breaths shy of eight feet. She knew she was memorable; she did not think she could be unforgettable, too. In sorrow, she threw the ball cap into the sewer. As for that short story, she buried it along with Nicholas's letters, just as Jews do with books that contain the word of God.

Winter came, and the music died down. Snowfalls were ignored, and sidewalks went unshoveled. Garbage bags grew into hills. Gone was the noisy city, but that didn't mean it had fallen still. On Andorra's nineteenth birthday, the hacking coughs were making the snowy streets tremble like strings on a guitar. People began to disappear. Funeral bells became a daily sound. The Widow's Russian cook was seen spilling buckets of disinfectant across the ground.

"Is plague!" she told Andorra. "Is Spanish flu!"

"This is *Detroit*," said Andorra.

"Then is Detroit flu," said the Russian. "Whatever is called, is killing us dead."

The words were prophetic; three days later, the Russian cook disappeared from the world. Her death was so swift that Andorra was left winded, as if the death had come at the end of a marathon run. There was no funeral; out of fear of the disease, the body was burnt many miles away.

"I'd be grateful your Nicholas still hasn't returned," the Widow said. Her voice was muffled because she was now wearing a mask.

"He's not *my* Nicholas," Andorra said, blushing beneath her mask.

The Widow dabbed her eyes. "Time is such a monster. Why didn't I marry any of those men who asked? Now I won't have anyone in my old age."

"You're only twenty-nine!" said Andorra.

"For an unmarried woman, that's old!" said the Widow.

"Andorra and I aren't going anywhere," Geoffrey assured her.

"Some company!" snapped the Widow. "You're married to a ghost. And Andorra will leave as soon as her Nicholas returns."

"He's not *my* Nicholas," Andorra said again.

"You just wait," said the Widow. "He'll come back and marry you and I'll be left eternally alone."

The Widow's sorrow was so great that Andorra wondered if the woman would marry the next man who asked. But the pandemic was keeping most of her boars away, and the ones who did come were so full of caution that they often tried to seduce the Widow from the porch. The Widow ignored them, leading Andorra to assume she was not as desperate as she pretended to be. (Of course, the

Widow *was* desperate—but only for Geoffrey to finally start repaying her years of kindness *in other ways.*)

It was a lousy March afternoon when a knock came from the window rather than the door. Andorra, who was playing whist with her father, drew back the curtain. A man stood in the spring rain. One half of his face was obscured by the old sign that warned pilgrims would be shot; the other half was covered by a mask. Almost four years had passed since this visitor had battled Geoffrey in the front hall, but Andorra recognized him all the same. His eyes were the same as his son's.

"Uh-oh," said Andorra.

"Uh-oh?" said Geoffrey.

"The Ambassador's returned," said Andorra.

"Uh-oh," said Geoffrey. He was already making a fist.

But Zachariah was no longer an Ambassador of Goodwill. He had long since left the entertainment world and was now a stray cat with a face of matted fur. He entered with his hat in his hand, holding a single white envelope, which he delivered with an apologetic air.

"It's from Nicholas," he said.

"Uh-oh," said Andorra. She snatched the letter from his hand. Years before, Manuela had been able to trick her with those letters from her mother, because Andorra had not known to look for stamps and postmarks. But she knew to look for them now. "There's no postmark," she said.

"He gave it to me today," said Zachariah.

That was when she learned the truth: Nicholas was in seclusion at his father's house. Zachariah couldn't say exactly when his son had contracted the Spanish flu—he suspected it had been that crowded military transport that had carried Nicholas home. He had a fever when he returned to Detroit and had collapsed in a delirium at the door of his father's house. ("He *had* to have been delirious," said Zachariah. "We haven't spoken in *months.*") Zachariah immediately put his son in quarantine. He placed him in the attic and fed him through an old dumbwaiter.

"He sent that letter with the dishes," said the former ambassador.

"How long has he been here?"

"Almost three weeks."

Three weeks! Andorra tore opened the letter and began to read. Almost at once, the blood ran to her cheeks.

Geoffrey touched his daughter's arm. "Forget him, *mi amor*. There's no good in a man who breaks your heart with a note."

"Oh no," whispered Andorra. "He hasn't broken my heart at all." She turned to her future father-in-law—already suspecting that he *was* her future father-in-law. The future was as clear as a stain. "Take me to him."

"You can't see him if he's sick."

"Why? So he can die alone?"

"He won't be alone," said Zachariah.

"Right, he has the *dumbwaiter*. How could I forget?"

Zachariah still refused to lead her to his house. But the precaution was useless: there were several Kelseys in the phonebook, but only one with the initial Z.

The next morning, she crept from the house, and a terrible chill shook her as she moved through the coughing streets. Even in a frightened city, she could not help but attract attention. People ran to their windows. An old woman paused with her bucket of disinfectant hanging in midair. Andorra imagined the sick calling to their nurses to report a giant walking through the streets. ("Poor things!" the nurses would think. "They must be nearing the end!") The Kelseys lived on the outskirts of her usual six-block radius. It was a three-story townhouse with a red door that she ignored. If Zachariah was home, he might not let her inside. Instead, she explored the perimeter and soon found a side entrance whose lock broke easily against her weight.

She had to stoop to conquer the narrow halls, and this made her a poor intruder: she banged into furniture and tore her skirt as she pushed through the rooms. She was saved by the loud music coming from the attic: something in the latest style, a rag with a furious beat. As she turned to the foot of the stairs, she came upon the Kelsey's maid, a dark little scarecrow with a broom in her hand. She froze in midsweep.

"There's some antiques in the den," she sputtered. "Please don't hurt me."

"Why would I *hurt* you?" snapped Andorra. Was she truly so frightening that people could only expect the worst of her?

"Mr. Kelsey's not here," said the maid. "You're best to just take the antiques and go."

Andorra made a note to tell Nicholas how little he could depend on the maid: she may have been built like a scarecrow, but she wasn't much in the way of security. "I'm here to see Nicholas," she said, and she pushed her way to the second floor.

"He's very sick," said the scarecrow.

Andorra drew Nicholas's letter from her pocket. "He wants to see me," she said. "I have proof."

NICHOLAS HAD BEEN AVOIDING their reunion for much longer than three weeks. Had he emerged from the war as a hero, he might have headed straight for his future wife with a lion's conceit. But no one could lionize Nicholas David Kelsey. Onstage he had failed to inspire; in battle, things had proved much the same. "Once more unto the breech, dear friends!" he had bellowed at the Battle of St. Quentin Canal; the reaction was just as stifled as it had been

at the Goodwin Theatre several months before. He escaped the war
without a wound of any kind. Bitterly, he imagined that every bullet he ever fired had also gone astray. Other men entered peacetime
shell-shocked, but Nicholas entered with a survivor's secret shame.
In the story of the war, other men had played heroes, while he, as
always, had been given a minor role.

Now he lay wrecked in his father's house. Convinced of his im-
minent death, he had written Andorra a letter more inflamed than
anything he had dared to write during the war. He had known his
letters would be read by the censors—this was why they had always
been restrained. Now he was uninhibited. The letter was so charged
that it read like pages from a dirty book (one of which Nicholas had
read; a man has to do *something* while dying of plague). It was this
purple prose that had made Andorra blush; it was this that gave her
the proof that Nicholas had not broken her heart at all.

The attic was at the top of another narrow flight of stairs, but Andorra squeezed through by walking parallel to the wall. Beyond the
door, ragtime played from a phonograph. A ball glove lay beneath a
collage of photos of the Detroit Tigers. Each photograph had been
pinned to the wall and the various pitchers, shortstops, and outfield-
ers gazed down on the sick like grieving relations. In a cot, Nicholas lay swaddled in bedclothes. He was no longer devastatingly
handsome; he was just devastating. Unshaven and gaunt, his bones
seemed to creep from the depths of his torn clothes. The stench struck
her hard. For three weeks he had lived in this room; for three weeks
he had shit in this room, too. A makeshift bedpan sat by the bed,
consumed by flies.

He appeared to be sleeping until the floorboards creaked under
her weight. Then his bloodshot eyes went wide. "Go away."

"Hello to you, too."

"I don't want you to see me like this."

"I can see why."

He fell into a rough cough; he hadn't been shaving, and phlegm dripped into his beard. She refused to be revolted. Shaking the flies away, she took the bedpan and returned to the second-floor bathroom. She flushed the contents away. Then she found an empty basin and filled it with hot water. She soaked a facecloth. From the medicine chest she collected a razor, shaving mug, and soap.

When she returned to the attic, Nicholas tried to burrow deeper into the cot. "Will you please go home?"

"Don't be difficult." She dug him out of the sheets and laid the hot towel over his face.

"I have a fever!"

"You're being difficult."

"Why are you doing this?"

"I'm not kissing you with that beard."

"I don't want you to kiss me!"

"Yes you do. And I have the letter to prove it."

He took her hand—the one that was *not* holding the razor. "This isn't a joke. This isn't just about you. You could infect your father. And the Widow."

"Then I guess I can't leave until we're both all right."

"You can't stay here! It would be improper."

"I don't exactly have a choice. I'm in quarantine now."

She put the edge of the razor to his cheeks and he lay still, now frightened to move. Andorra was suddenly frightened, too. The blade was too small in her hands. She managed to shave his left cheek, but terror gripped her as she reached his neck. Nicholas sighed. "Well, I can't leave it like *that*," he said. He told her to bring the mirror from the wall so he could finish the job himself.

He winced when he saw his reflection.

"I gave up on you," she said.

"Quiet," he said. "I have to concentrate."

"I threw away your hat."

"You did?"

"And I buried your letters."

"Ow! I cut my chin."

A spot of blood appeared, and she pressed the towel to the wound. His skin was scruffy, but it was clean enough; in any case, she could no longer resist. She leaned down and kissed him. She was still wearing her surgical mask, so it wasn't a *true* kiss. Their lips never touched. Yet it might have sealed a marriage vow: if at that moment a minister had appeared to pronounce them man and wife, Andorra wouldn't have been completely surprised.

Nicholas remained in her care. Geoffrey was scandalized by the arrangement, but there was little he could do—as Andorra had said, she was in quarantine, too. It was easier to wait for the sickness to run its course. She almost never left the attic, except to use the bathroom (Nicholas *still* did not use the bathroom; Andorra continued to clean away his shit). She slept on a pile of old clothes. She played his records and burned his phlegm-soaked handkerchiefs and learned to shave his face with care. And she kissed him—how she kissed him! Always through her surgical mask, yes, but always with the full force of her weak heart. She finally told him about *that*, too. "A doctor told me that, scientifically speaking, the larger the animal, the shorter the life," she told Nicholas.

He tried to laugh, though it came out more like a croak. "I know all about it. Your father told me before I left for the war."

She frowned. "He did?"

"We were talking, and he mentioned something about your heart, thinking I already knew. He was mortified when he realized I didn't know a thing about it. Made me swear not to let on that I knew until you told me yourself."

"I'm sorry," she said. "I should have told you sooner."

"There's nothing to tell. Have you been to a doctor lately?"

She shook her head. That terrible doctor who had examined her when she was a girl had left her with an indelible dislike of the entire profession. She had not see a physician in all her years in Detroit.

Nicholas shook his head in wonder. "So you're basing your fears on a diagnosis you received when you were a girl? Not to mention, I'm pretty sure that doctor was a quack. Large animals can live an awful long time. Elephants live for seventy years. And the blue whale can live for eighty."

"Are you a zoologist now?"

He blushed and looked away. "I may have done some reading on the subject."

"You did some reading about elephants and blue whales?"

"I was *worried*," he said. "The point is, you don't have a weak heart. At best, it's *possibly weak*. You'll probably outlive us all."

She adored the prophecy and adored him more for making it. It gained credence as she continued to survive the days without developing so much as a cough. She was strong enough to defeat the Spanish flu; perhaps her heart was tough after all.

At long last, Nicholas's health returned. The coughing stopped, and the color returned to his cheeks. It was then that the inevitable occurred; it was then that they worked to bring Nicholas's lurid letter to life. Though alone in the attic, they had never been alone in the house. But one sultry August afternoon, when the gorgeous weather had driven Zachariah Kelsey to the park of Belle Isle, Andorra and Nicholas collided like comets in space. Nothing separated them now, not disease or surgical masks or war. Amazingly, he was more self-conscious about his body than she was. Weakened by illness, Nicholas Kelsey had become a ravaged field. He lay on his back, half covered in sheets, while Andorra cascaded over him. She forced herself to be fearless; it was the challenge of her life to reveal the great glory of her body without a hint of shame.

But there is a cost to fearlessness. Like her mother before her,

Andorra enjoyed a single fearless afternoon and received a daughter in exchange. After that, there was no turning back. Not that Andorra tried. This was no time for caution or resolve. *This is a world of war and plague,* she thought. *How could anyone afford to wait?*

THEY MARRIED ON JUNE 17 in the parlor of the Widow's house (the day was chosen out of convenience; Geoffrey del Alandra had Tuesdays off). Less than six months later, during a frosty December night, Rowena Kelsey was drawn into the world. The moment was a great relief for Andorra and even more so for her father, who had fallen into fits of paranoia the moment he learned of the pregnancy. Twenty years earlier, he had married a pregnant woman, and the result had been both a fistula and a daughter with a peculiar talent for growth. Noria Blanco had called it a curse, and he now worried that she had been right. Throughout the pregnancy, he became convinced that some terrible calamity would strike Andorra or Rowena—or both. But each of them survived the birth intact. Rowena was practically perfect, and no fistulas appeared in the depths of Andorra's magnificent frame. They never even needed to search for a wet nurse—her monstrous breasts produced so much milk that Rowena became sausage-plump.

Geoffrey's euphoria was so complete that he decided to bring a bottle of champagne over to the house of Zachariah Kelsey. The two men had barely spoken at their children's wedding; now that they were grandfathers, Geoffrey was determined to make peace. It would never come. He arrived to find the front door standing open. In the front hall, the former ambassador was splayed out on the ground, surrounded by rotting fruit. He had suffered a stroke: he had left the world with the speed of a passing train on the same night that Rowena was born.

It was 1919. Revolutions were happening across the world, but the death of Zachariah was a revolution, too. That the former ambassador had money was almost as surprising as the fact that he had left it all—and the house—to his son.

"Are we rich?" asked Andorra.

"We're certainly not poor." Nicholas grinned.

"We should take a honeymoon," she said.

But Nicholas was already thinking about the shape of his father's house. "What we should do is knock down a few walls. And we need arches in those doors so you can stop banging you head."

"You don't have to do that."

"I think I promised to take care of you. It was in the wedding vows or something."

"It's your legacy. We should do something that's for you."

"Oh, we are." He grinned. "I'm pretty sure we're going to see every ballgame we can."

In the spring of 1920, they moved away from Elsa Street. They spent the following summer alternating between cheering for the Tigers and building a world Andorra could call her own. She was a great sight at the ballpark. She loathed the attention but endured it for her husband's sake—they had, after all, made a deal. And he was more than honoring his part. In the heat of July he worked to enlarge rooms; in the depths of August, he widened halls. He had an undiscovered talent for carpentry—in September he surprised her with an enormous bed he built himself. All this work proved to be an inspiration. For months he had been trying to force a return to the stage; that summer, he started taking jobs behind the scenes. The same skill that had built a bed for his enormous wife soon also built Elsinore for a Danish prince. At long last, he had begun to accept what everyone else had known for years: he was not an actor.

"At least I learned how to put a nail in my own coffin," he joked.

"There's nothing wrong with being a carpenter," said Andorra. "Next to a tailor, it's the one thing I'll always need."

"Fair Katharine and most fair," he said and stretched to kiss her chin.

"That reminds me. I have something for you."

"Oh God. It's our anniversary."

"No. And it's not your birthday either."

From her desk she drew a short manuscript of paper. This had been another part of her summer; somehow, between baseball and renovations and the mewling Rowena, she had managed to write a short story of 4,894 words. She had not meant to give it to him to-day; she had hoped to do another draft. But perhaps it was better to give it to him in this rough, imperfect way.

Nicholas read the title. "A Spanish Reunion."

"It's a short story," she said.

"Is it *your* short story?" he asked.

"It's *ours*," she corrected. And indeed it was. "A Spanish Reunion" was based on those delirious days before children and marriage had turned them into adults.

"Read it to me," said Nicholas. "No. Wait." He ran from the room and returned with Rowena, not yet one and squirming in his arms. "Read it to *her*, too. If it's about what I think it's about, then she should hear it, too."

"A Spanish Reunion" was about *exactly* what Nicholas thought it was about. "In the days just after the war," it began. "Katharine moved through the plague-ridden city just to give her future husband a shave . . ." Of course, the future husband's name was Henry. Finding him racked with plague, Katharine became his foolish nurse. The narrative was a funhouse mirror: Andorra portrayed her alter ego as a woman of average height, while Nicholas was everything he had ever hoped to be. There was no plague of failures for Henry.

Henry played shortstop for the Detroit Tigers. Henry was a war hero adorned with success.

"It's wonderful," said Nicholas. "Isn't it wonderful, Rowena?"

Rowena gurgled and squirmed.

"We should try to get it published," said Nicholas.

"It's not ready," said Andorra.

"Will you let me try?" said Nicholas.

"Under no circumstances," said Andorra.

At that moment, Rowena began to cry.

"See what you've done?" said Nicholas.

"Oh, go ahead, you silly bug," said Andorra. "You can both try together."

At that exact moment, something welled inside her. She leaned over and vomited on the floor.

"Uh-oh," said Nicholas.

"Must have been something I ate," said Andorra.

But it was *not* something she ate; she did not suspect the truth because Rowena's arrival had not been heralded by the slightest touch of morning sickness.

This second pregnancy was almost completely dull until the afternoon it ended. It was seven months later, and the 1921 baseball season had just begun. The doctor who came to the house was not pleased at missing the game; the White Sox were playing the Tigers when Andorra's first son arrived. The Tigers had just rallied their way into a tie score when her second daughter began to crown. In the delirium of pain, Andorra thought this second baby was a dream. Almost at once, the baby boy began to cry; his sister followed, as if hearing her cue. These great wails helped Andorra and Nicholas settle on their names. The angel Gabriel was said to carry a trumpet whose blast would signal God's return. Gabriel's crying was like that trumpet; when joined by his sister, they were surely enough to be heard in heaven.

The Tigers had broken the tie when Geoffrey arrived with the Widow. He had come from the factory and he stained the swaddling blankets with his greasy hands. He was not as surprised as everyone else that there were two children instead of one. He reminded them that he himself was a twin.

"You couldn't have warned me of that before I married her?" asked Nicholas.

"You didn't give anyone a chance to warn you of *anything*," said Geoffrey.

He stuck out his tongue and cooed at the twins as if they were a pair of pigeons. Andorra couldn't take her eyes off him—or rather, she couldn't take her eyes off his *arm*. Over his coveralls, a black mourning band was wrapped tight around his arm. She understood, almost by instinct, what the mourning band meant.

"When did it happen?" she said.

"When did what happen?" stammered Geoffrey.

"Have you not told her?" hissed the Widow.

"She was with child. There are certain things you don't tell a woman with child."

"I'm a woman with *three* children now," said Andorra.

"What are we talking about?" said Nicholas.

"We're talking about my mother," said Andorra. "I think she's dead."

And indeed she was. Six weeks before the birth of the twins, Geoffrey had received a battered letter from the faithful Manuela: the fistula that had long ravaged Elionor Noguerra del Alandra had finally swallowed her whole. As for Manuela herself, she had married a local boy; at the time of writing, they were about to leave for parts unknown. The letter was almost a year and a half old; it had taken that long for it to travel across the world.

For a woman who had long since considered her mother dead, the news struck Andorra hard. Later, as the twins sucked at her teats, she broke into sobs for the mother who had shunned her by the Valira River. The next day, she began two new habits. She taught her children Catalan; she also began to write to her mother's ghost. The language lessons were a way of connecting the children to her past. As for the letters, they were a sorry attempt at capturing something that was already gone. She wrote as if her mother was still alive; she wrote as if the two of them had been exchanging letters for years. The letters became entries in a journal that she never kept. Each one was sent across the world without a return address. It pleased her to know they would disappear, forever unread.

The 1920s slipped by, and the old neighborhood began to change. 1922. Buildings fell. 1923. Geoffrey began appearing everywhere with the Widow on his arm. Another Christmas. Another New Year's. Geoffrey's arm continued to wear that mourning band, but the Widow still seemed happier than she had ever been. Andorra turned twenty-five; Andorra turned twenty-six. Trapped inside that house, dragging Rowena while the twins trod underfoot, she suddenly felt her only contact with the adult world was when showmen came to the door. Oh yes, they had continued to come—she was still the Giant of Elsa Street, even though she was no longer *on* Elsa Street. 1927, 1928. The years passed and new ambassadors of goodwill continued to appear.

Andorra knew something had shifted when 1929 dawned and, for the first time, she did not slam the door in the showman's face.

"Do you have a card?" she asked.

He gave it to her. "Whenever you're ready, ma'am, I'll be happy to show you the world."

She placed the card in the folds of her skirt and later tucked it into her hope chest. She thought of it as she ran the clothes along a washboard, cleaned the icebox, chased the twins, helped Rowena learn to spell. She thought of it when Nicholas snored; she thought of it as she massaged rubbing alcohol into her oh-so-tired muscles.

She was *still* thinking about it on the morning of their tenth anniversary. She didn't move after shutting the alarm clock. The twins had had nightmares; she had barely had five hours of sleep. *I'll be happy to show you the world*, that showman had said. *The world*, thought Andorra. What would it be like? And would it let her have some peace?

"Wake up," she said.

Nicholas rolled over. "Mmm-blurg," he said.

"It's our anniversary," she said.

"Mmm-blurg," grumbled Nicholas.

"Wake the children," she sighed. "I'll start on breakfast."

She staggered downstairs. Bleary-eyed, body tight and sore, she almost missed the magazine propped on the kitchen counter. Attached to it was a paper flower and a roughly cut card adorned with ink.

HAPPY ANNIVERSARY

Andorra had always assumed her husband's praise of "A Spanish Reunion" had been clouded by affection. It had been nearly nine years since she had first read it to him; she herself had almost forgotten it had ever been written. Now it sat before her again, this time printed inside a copy of the *North American Review*. A bookmark had been placed inside, allowing her to open instantly to page 34.

A Spanish Reunion

by

Elionor Nicholas

Nicholas appeared in the door. Gabriel was at his side, while Gabriella was perched on his arms. Rowena stood nearby, her notebook in hand—she was ready to record her mother's surprise.

"Happy anniversary!" said Nicholas.

"Happy anniversary, Mama!" said the children.

"Elionor Nicholas?" said Andorra.

"I was a part of the narrative," said Nicholas. "Why shouldn't I be part of the author?"

"But why Elionor? Why not *Andorra* Nicholas?"

"Rowena honors my mother. That story should honor yours."

She swallowed him in her arms; she swallowed them all. All her great exhaustion disappeared. Rowena squirmed, but Gabriel hugged her waist. Gabriella clutched at her leg. As for Nicholas, he found her arm and kissed her wrist. Andorra swelled. If she had known how close they were to chaos, she might not have let herself swell as much as she did. After all, it was the summer of 1929; Black Tuesday, the day of the crash that would herald the Great Depression, was only a few months away. Desperate times were coming, but Andorra would never have believed it. She felt only the thrill of the moment. How foolish she had been! What could the world ever give her? Out there, she was nothing but a lady giant. In here, she was something greater. A wife who was more than the sum of her measurements; a mother who just happened to be a little tall.

FIFTEEN

The Adventures of Elionor Nicholas

Hollywood, 1937

How glorious it was to be Elionor Nicholas! Having surrendered herself to the Studio, Hollywood's newest aspiring star found herself part of a great chaos of lessons and lunches and cocktails. In an acting class behind the Studio's walls, she was taught proper enunciation; in a tailor shop on Sunset Boulevard, she was measured for gowns and hats. Six days a week, she was shuttled through the city in that glorious Duesenberg by Rutherford the Chauffeur, who ensured she was punctual for her singing courses and dance teachers and costume fittings and her numerous appointments with important people whose important names should have meant more to her than they did. Gone was the life of Andorra the Reclusive Giant; Elionor Nicholas moved through Hollywood like a Cinderella for whom midnight would never come.

She quickly learned, to her surprise, that the Studio's first assignment was not for her to play the monster's bride. They wanted time to court some high-caliber director; in the meantime, a last-minute problem with another actress had led to an inspired solution: Elionor Nicholas's first role would be in an insipid bit of romantic fluff called *Bombshell Brunette*. A quick-witted screenwriter was all it took to rewrite the script to account for her great size. The role of the title character's sister was changed to that of a gigantic friend who was staying at the title character's home. ("I'm on holiday from the circus," the gigantic friend now explained; "With this family, you'll feel like you never left," was the brunette's caustic reply.)

"I hope that screenwriter isn't upset that he has to rewrite his movie just for me," Elionor Nicholas said to Rutherford.

"If they had any guts, they wouldn't rewrite the script at all," growled Rutherford. "Why do you have to be a character who's a giant? Why can't you just be a character who happens to be a little tall?"

They were in the Duesenberg, rocketing down the freeway and away from her latest tap dance class, where a poor choreographer had vainly tried to teach her to shuffle off to Buffalo with a little grace. "I hope I can do this," she called out, needing to be heard over the engine. "The last time I tried to perform, I fainted."

"When was this?" called Rutherford.

"1915!"

Rutherford laughed. "I'm sure things have changed since *then*!"

Andorra wasn't so sure. Just thinking about stepping onto the film set with its army of cameramen, technicians, riggers, assistants, caterers, security guards, other actors . . . a small bubble rose in her throat, came out like a belch, and was carried away on the wind.

She had time to screw her courage to the sticking place, for the first day of filming was still over a month away. In the meantime, she had a more immediate concern. The Duesenberg was headed to a small medical clinic. Elionor Nicholas needed to pass a physical so she could be insured. Without insurance, she could never appear in a film. Aside from her inherent dislike of doctors, she was terrified of what would happen when one examined her heart. It was supposed to be a weak little muscle. Nicholas had never believed this, but what if he had been wrong? She had survived a Spanish reunion, two pregnancies and a husband's death. None of those things could be very relaxing for a person's heart. She imagined it threadbare, a worn-out shoe, with newspapers plugging the holes.

She didn't dare tell Rutherford, and her nerves jangled as she followed him inside the clinic. From the way the staff reacted, they might have walked in nude. None of them had been warned about their two o'clock appointment that day, and, properly stunned, they became distracted as they tried to guess the size of her organs.

"I'll bet the liver weighs four or five pounds," said a nurse.

"I'll bet the brain is a behemoth!" said the doctor.

"How much do you think my heart weights?" asked Andorra.

"A normal heart is ten to twelve ounces," said the excited doctor. "Yours is probably twenty!"

Twenty ounces! She was desperate to hear what a twenty-ounce heart sounded like; she wanted to know if it sounded *weak* or *possibly weak*. But she didn't want to draw his attention to the stethoscope. Marveling at the weight of her brain and liver, he had forgotten all about her heart.

"You're the picture of health," said the doctor.

"Probably the biggest one we've ever seen!" added the nurse.

A hurdle had been passed, and in leaping over it, the actress known as Elionor Nicholas distanced herself from the enormous widow who had to worry about the strength of her heart. Now insured, Elionor Nicholas could spend the summer of 1937 in the thrall of her new existence. Even the arrival of a new dress became a cause for celebration. She had grown all too accustomed to stains and tears, to dirty elbows and bare earlobes and a face without a touch of blush. There was a crisp freshness to her now. She was something clean and new. Elionor Nicholas was truly another woman; after two and a half years of grief, Andorra Kelsey was beginning to disappear.

No wonder then that the world beyond Hollywood was melting away. Throughout that summer, she dutifully continued to send money home and only scanned the replies before tossing them onto her desk. She even stopped writing those letters to her mother, that *other* Elionor, for she no longer felt herself consumed by emotions that she needed to purge. Even her concerns about stage fright had been pushed away—it was *Andorra's* problem, after all. She day-dreamed about staying in Hollywood. Her father had taken her from the principality, and Nicholas had taken her from Elsa Street. Even Rutherford had taken her to Hollywood. All her journeys were on the whims of others. But maybe, as Elionor, she could finally choose to stay somewhere all on her own.

SEPTEMBER SLIPPED INTO OCTOBER. In addition to *Bombshell Brunette,* the Studio continued to talk about both the Frankenstein picture and a new idea of pairing her in a romantic comedy with an actor who was short (they mentioned Mickey Rooney, who was five foot two.) Rutherford continued to hate these ideas. Elionor Nicholas continued to tell herself she didn't care what she played as long as two things continued to happen: they let her stay in Hollywood, and they kept giving her money to send back to Detroit.

"I think I'm a terrible mother," she told Rutherford one day as they sat by the pool. It was terribly hot, and she lounged beneath an oversize parasol while Rutherford swam. In her hands was the paper announcing the end of the World Series, and she now tapped the article with a finger that obscured the entire column of print. "I promised my daughter I'd be home by now."

"You didn't know what would happen," said Rutherford. "You're taking care of them. You're not a terrible mother; you're just an absent one."

Elionor wasn't sure she understood the distinction. She put the newspaper aside and tried to read the latest draft of *Bombshell Brunette,* which had finally arrived by courier. Its latest incarnation detailed the frothy romance between the eponymous brunette, a wealthy heiress, and a young hero who was far beneath her station. As for the gigantic best friend, she appeared throughout the plot mostly so she could deliver pithy one-liners ("A husband and wife are just

Siamese twins joined at the wallet") or to engage in a more physical comic relief (to help the hero escape a humiliating predicament, she throws a pie into her own face). The film ended with the bombshell brunette's little cousin opening a closet to find Elionor's character in the arms of the hero's best friend. ("Sorry!" says the little cousin. "But could one of you pass me a broom?")

It wasn't explained just *how* the two characters end up in the broom closet, or even how they become lovers. Rutherford Simone, who had already read the script, grumbled that the moment was probably there because some executive had decreed the ending of movies had to be more romantic than anything in real life. These sour grumbles had been increasing in force for weeks. Today, as she lounged by the pool, she even thought she could hear him grumble as he performed a frustrated front crawl. *Everything* Rutherford did these days seemed to bear the touch of some inner frustration. He had no real occupation anymore, other than serving as Elionor's personal guard, chauffeur, and assistant. And his marriage to Jessica Simone appeared to be in name only. Somehow, through some backroom deal, Jessica had taken over managing the career of Grove Wilson, the handsome actor who had met them at the train station the day Elionor arrived. This seemed to take up all of Jessica's time. But it wasn't just her schedule that was keeping them apart. Elionor rarely saw her; Rutherford, it seemed, saw her even less and, although he didn't speak of it, Elionor knew the two had taken to sleeping in separate rooms.

"It seems like a good script," said Elionor as she read the final page.

"It's absurd," said Rutherford. "But it's better than watching you play Frankenstein's bride."

"I don't think that'll be so bad. It might be fun."

Rutherford stopped swimming and treaded water. "You need to make sure they give you more roles like the one you have now."

"This really bothers you, doesn't it?"

"I've sent actors to Hollywood before," he said. "But it was always to work for Gavin and Jessica. You're not working for them. You're working for the Studio, and that makes a world of difference."

Elionor dabbed her brow with the edge of the towel. She had a dull headache from the heat. "Tell me honestly: do you think they'll ever make the Anna Swan picture?"

Rutherford considered the question as he paddled to the pool's edge. His face was scorched—he had picked up too much sun and had burnt the edge of his nose. "In all honesty," he said, "I doubt it very much. It was Gavin's baby, and Jessica just doesn't have the right pull. But it's more than that. I've talked to a few of the boys at the Studio. The story itself just doesn't interest them. It's a good yarn at first. Small-town girl finds love and success after moving to the big city. Oldest plot in the book, but it works. The Studio would probably be delighted if we ended the movie there. But marriage isn't ever an ending, is it? Once married, Anna and her husband went on a tour of Europe. That's where she lost her first baby—it was stillborn. So they came home and moved to Seville, this small town in Ohio. They built their giant house, and then Anna got pregnant again. But that one was no better than the first."

Anna's first pregnancy had been fairly straightforward. Like her mother before her, it seemed she had swallowed a large stone, but she endured the discomfort with grace. The second pregnancy was worse. As it progressed, it had become clear to Anna that she had swallowed a stone that had swallowed a stone that had swallowed a stone.

"It must have been a wretched time," Rutherford said. "Though I don't know much about it. Jessica and Gavin only know these things from their father, but at the time of this second pregnancy, he still hadn't arrived in Seville."

The pregnancy itself may have been a mystery but Rutherford knew a few things about the birth. The attending doctors had written on the subject, and it was known that, though labor started on

January 15, 1878, the baby didn't arrive until just after midnight on the seventeenth. Anna's pain was so great that the doctors filled her with a combination of quinine, Squibs' ergot, and brandy. This sent her into a dreamy world as her son struggled to be born: his shoulders had become trapped by the narrow birth canal. The same thing had happened at Anna's own birth; the same thing had happened at the birth of the baby she had tried to have in Europe. Now it was happening again. It was God's irony: something about Anna Swan was actually too small.

"They used forceps to squeeze the skull," said Rutherford. "He only lived for a few hours after that. They went on tour to forget about what happened, but Anna was never the same. That's why Hollywood doesn't want to make this movie. It's just not a story with a happy end."

"Why? Because she never got to be a mother? She toured the world. She had money. A person is more than the sum of their tragedies. She experienced tragic things, but that doesn't make her life a disaster."

In the water, Rutherford shrugged. "It's just not light enough. There's a Depression, and tough stories won't fly. That's why I'm worried for you. The Studio doesn't just make movies to be artistic. They need to make a product the public wants. You're part of that product. And they will try to sell you any way they can."

"It sounds very cynical."

"Cynicism is just the truth with a sharper edge. You want to help your family, and that's noble, but would they really want you to just accept *any* job the Studio throws at you? Your family would want you to have your dignity."

"I have that now."

"Yes. *Now.* But later? A few years ago, a director named Tod Browning made a movie that featured Siamese twins and midgets and all sorts of folk they got from the circus. Do you know what they called it? *Freaks*. All those people in the film, they went along with it, probably for the same reasons you have for being here. Money. Obligations. And the final result was something grotesque. What did they think when they saw it? Did they think it was worth it? Or did they think the cost was too much?"

At last he started swimming again. She was touched that he was trying to protect her. Liked it even. He was sweet. Why was Jessica Simone so intent on casting him aside? Elionor mopped her forehead and reached for the pitcher of lemonade she had brought down to the pool. But it was empty, and she shifted in discomfort. She was overdressed for the day, despite being in little more than a robe. Beneath it was only a bathing suit that left little to the imagination. She felt naked inside it, but all at once she didn't care. She was overheating and tired of always sitting by the pool while others swam. True, she didn't know *how* to swim. But until five months ago she didn't know how to act or sing.

The next time Rutherford dove beneath the water, Elionor made her move. Slipping free of the robe, she stepped quickly into the shallow end and knelt on the bottom of the pool. By the time he emerged, she had crouched so far, he could only see her from the shoulders up.

Rutherford sidled up to the wall and slung his arms around the side. "You know, I taught my brothers to swim."

"He finds Hollywood giants *and* teaches people how to swim. You're really something of a Renaissance man."

"Renaissance men are good at many things. My talents are fairly limited."

"That's not much of a sales pitch, especially if you want to teach me to swim."

He laughed and she smiled and happily placed herself in his hands. He taught her to hold her breath. She closed her eyes and blew bubbles. All at once, she found herself wondering what it would be like to take Rutherford the Teacher into the house, to resurrect her younger self, her adventurous self, that young girl who once braved the Spanish flu. She had not had such thoughts of anyone since Nicholas died. She had abandoned all fantasies because she felt she did not deserve them. Yet here she was again, imagining Rutherford the Lover, Rutherford who would be endlessly fascinated by the brute strength of her arms. Would he be an echo of Nicholas? Or would he be something entirely new, a new abandonment to go with her new home, new face, new circumstance?

"Tomorrow I'll teach you how to float," he said.

Tomorrow, thought Elionor Nicholas. She was starting to adore the word.

But when tomorrow came, Rutherford the Teacher did not teach her how to float. At breakfast, Jessica made a rare appearance to announce an exciting bit of news: the role of the hero's best friend, the one who Elionor kisses in a broom closet in the final reel, would be played by Grove Wilson. Until now, the idea of the kiss had been a tiny speck in the brain but hearing Grove Wilson's name made it magnificent. She was unable to finish her morning croissants. Andorra's stage fright was rearing its head, turning Elionor's insides soft.

It didn't help when she was told she needed to learn how to kiss. It had not occurred to her that kissing was a talent she lacked. But this was 1937, and the Hollywood Production Code had long been regulating cinematic romance. Kisses that were too excessive or lustful were forbidden. Only closed dry mouths were allowed, and one foot had to stay on the floor at all times. And so, that afternoon, she found her closed dry mouth hovering over an enormous teddy bear that Rutherford had rescued from the attic. Rutherford himself stood back as she leaned over and kissed the teddy bear's plush little mouth.

"Too lustful!" he barked.

Elionor tried again.

"Too excessive!" snapped Rutherford.

"I feel ridiculous."

"All movie kisses are ridiculous. They're very neat and tidy. Real kisses are never neat and tidy."

Feeling foolish, she leaned over the teddy bear again. It was hopeless. One didn't prepare to kiss Grove Wilson by kissing a *bear*. Glancing past the toy at Rutherford Simone, she had the daring idea of asking him to take her in his arms and give her the exact sort of kiss the Hollywood censors would enjoy. She blushed at her own thoughts and swallowed hard. Here they were again, these shocking daydreams. Why not act on them? Why not take charge, as she had taken charge of Nicholas all those years ago?

Then she glanced up and saw that Jessica had appeared at the door, and she cringed, as if she and Rutherford had actually been doing what had only been in her head.

Jessica was holding the evening edition. She did not look pleased. Turning the front page toward them, Elionor saw why. A picture says a thousand words, and this one said even more: it was split into two photos, cropped so they were side by side. One was of Grove Wilson, looking sharp and smug as he stared into the camera. The other was of his swimming pool—and of the collection of somber police standing around the edge.

GIRL TAKES FINAL SWIM IN HOLLYWOOD GIANT'S POOL!

The girl in the caption was not anywhere in the picture; no newspaper would ever print the photo of a corpse—and certainly not a *colored* corpse. According to the article, the young girl—she was sixteen—had been found floating facedown in Grove Wilson's pool. The actor had found the body, but the newspaper remarked that he couldn't "exactly account for his whereabouts" in the four hours prior to the moment when he summoned the police.

"I'd say he's in trouble," said Rutherford.

"It's just scandal," said Jessica. "There's no such thing as bad publicity."

"What does *that* mean?" asked Elionor.

"It means you need to practice your kissing," said Jessica. "The show must go on." She was about to leave when she pulled a yellow envelope from the pocket of her dress. "Oh yes. This came for you. I almost forgot."

She tossed the envelope on a nearby end table and then disappeared into the house. Elionor was close enough that she could see the envelope had the logo of Western Union in the corner; she could also see that below the logo was her name—her *real* name. It was a telegram for Andorra Kelsey.

She forced herself to open it with a careless air. The breath fell out of her. It was short and concise but had a single world that stunned her. The name of the sender was at the bottom, and it struck her hard, like a boxer's punch.

"What is it?" said Rutherford.

"It's from my mother," said Elionor. She crumpled the paper in her fist and ran from the room. She did not have the courage to speak any more than she had the courage to ask Rutherford to demonstrate the art of the Hollywood kiss. Only a day ago she had been thinking of how much she adored the word *tomorrow*. Now tomorrow had come and brought yesterday in its wake. Locking herself in her room, she tore the telegram apart only to get small paper cuts on her enormous hands. That was when she broke down. Minor as they were, the slits felt like canyons. Or a series of fistulas. Her eyes burned and her fingers bled. She didn't think she would ever stop; she imagined that she, like her mother, would continue to bleed and cry for the next thirty-seven years.

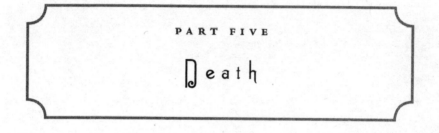

PART FIVE

Death

SIXTEEN

A Second Shame

Seville, 1883

OR ALMOST TWO YEARS after the death of their son, Anna and the Captain tripped across the United States as part of a traveling circus. Run by W. W. Cole (why do these promoters always go by their initials?), it required little of Anna other than repeating the routine she had perfected at the American Museum all those years before. Her performances lacked their usual energy, but this hardly mattered to the public; with sour certainty, she knew she could imitate a waxwork and obtain the same look of wonder from the crowds. It was a miserable time. She longed for her loyal Miss Eaton, who had stayed in Seville, Ohio, to care for their house; she longed for H. P. Ingalls, who had moved on to other adventures. Her family existed only in the occasional letters that came from Tatamagouche. She missed P. T. Barnum. She ached for New York. And, despite all effort to the contrary, she thought far too much about Gavin Clarke. Which direction had he walked that day in London? Toward Susannah or away from her?

Anna's gloom seized every corner of her life, including her sleep. In her dreams, she was giving birth again, and the babies were skeletal wraiths that clawed at the moon. She woke from these night terrors in a wild sweat and often burst into tears. A grouch when woken, the Captain would nonetheless hold her, and she would weep against his tremendous chest. This was the limit of their intimacy in bed;

in the months that followed their son's death, the tallest couple in the world was completely chaste.

She claimed she had grown too weak for intercourse, but the Captain wasn't fooled. "Babies are lost," he said. "Your mama lost some, and so did mine. It's a woman's burden, nothing more."

"Our mamas' children died in *infancy*. They had short lives, but they lived. Our children died at *birth*."

"Our son lived for eleven hours."

"Eleven hours is not a life."

She tried to sit up, only to hit her head on the Captain's elbow. They were in a hotel room in Cleveland, and nothing was the right size. He had become a fifth wall she kept crashing into.

"The Lord put you here to have children," he continued. "It does bad things to you when it can't happen. That's why you feel this way."

"So I just have some silly women's sickness, is that it?"

The Captain fumbled with his large hands. He was too large a bull for such a delicate conversation. "You have a woman's duty, Annie. You have a *wife's* duty, too."

A wife's duty. Sex. "Is that all you care about?"

"No, not *all*. But I think about it. That's the *man's* burden."

"Sex is a pleasure for a moment. There's a consequence to it. Every child we make is too large. If we know a baby won't survive and we still try to bring it into the world, what does that make us?"

"You're being melodramatic."

"Children aren't my problem, Martin."

"Then what is it?"

"I have no rank or profession."

"What the devil does that mean?"

"It means I'm not trained to do anything. Performing is all that's left, and I hate it. You say women were put in here to be mothers? Well, I can't *be* a mother, so what's left? Nothing except exhaustion.

I'm tired. I've been lugging this great big body around for years now, and it feels like I'm at the end of some long march."

Outside the hotel, the night had gone still. She slumped back into her pillow. The Captain was silent. *Now he'll skulk out of the room,* she thought. *The ape will lumber away to pout.*

But instead he wrapped a great arm around her and kissed her on the nose. "If you hate performing, then we'll stop performing."

"Do you mean it?"

"Of course I do. But in exchange, you have to stop pretending you're in this life alone. I know about exhaustion, too. It's exhausting living like this. We're in someone else's world."

They lay in silence, a pair of titans in the twilight of their age.

A few days later, while still in Cleveland, she glanced up from her battered copy of *Jane Eyre* to see the Captain standing in the door. By his side was an old birdcage covered with a brown cloth. "I have a surprise for you," he said, motioning to the cage.

She gave a weary sigh. "Let me guess: it's a bird."

"It's better than a bird."

"Is it a dog?"

"I'll give you a hint: a man in England says that it's one of our ancestors."

"Oh," said Anna. "Then it's a *big* dog."

Then she heard a chattering from inside the cage, and she knew at once that it wasn't a dog, big or small. With a flourish, the Captain pulled away the cloth, revealing a brown rhesus macaque whose simian face was pressed against the bars.

"I got him from the same man who sells animals to Mr. Cole," said the Captain. "He said that monkeys are better than dogs."

Anna knelt by the cage. The rhesus moped in the corner of the cage but came to life when she unlocked the cage door. All at once it scampered into her arms. For a moment it allowed itself to be held. Then it leapt to the bed, scaled the bedposts, jumped to the top of the bookcase, and released a stream of urine that dripped back to the floor.

"The fraud!" said the Captain. "He told me it was trained!"

"Maybe it was trained to do *this*," said Anna.

"I'll take it back. I'm sorry. I know you're lonely, Annie. I thought a pet would help."

Oh, Martin! Her husband, the ape, had bought her a *monkey*. She began to laugh. A *monkey* to replace lost children. A *monkey* as a reward for surviving the long march. It was all so absurd. Her laughter broke loose and became a storm.

"Lord, don't laugh at me. I only wanted to make you happier."

"I know," she said, wiping her eyes. "And I love you for it."

The Captain gave a queer smile. How long had it been since she had said she loved him? She felt, suddenly, that in her misery she had been exceptionally cruel.

"I'm taking him back," he said. "It was a dumb idea. Who has a pet monkey?"

"Who grows to be eight feet tall? We're just full of originality." From the top of the bookcase, the monkey released another stream of piss. "You'd better get me a towel. We're going to have to clean up this mess."

They named him Buttons, and despite his propensity for urinating in hotel rooms (or maybe because of it) she truly did feel a little cheered. They worked him into their performance, a clever success that allowed them to force W. W. Cole to pay for the monkey's food. He gave her some delight, but a monkey is no match for melancholy and soon Buttons soon became like all buttons: something only noticed when it was lost.

At last their contract expired, and the Captain, true to his word, announced their retirement. They bid farewell to the circus in Illinois and returned home by a rickety coach that rumbled and shook as they crossed into Ohio. She tried to think with pleasure of their giant house and the coming reunion with Miss Eaton. (What would that dour woman think of the pissing Buttons?!) When they reached Seville and she saw Mound Hill Cemetery through the window, the proximity to her son's grave plucked at her like she was a harp: her blood quivered in a minor key. She fought to swallow this new surge of grief. What was it she had told herself all those years ago in London? Forward! Forward! She was thirty-seven years old. There was life in her yet.

They turned down Main Street and she was still dabbing her eyes when she caught sight of Miss Eaton, standing outside a shop. Her companion looked plump and haggard, but it wasn't this that made Anna gasp. Miss Eaton wasn't alone.

"Driver! Stop the coach!"

The Captain glanced over. "What is it?"

"It's Gavin Clarke," said Anna, and she pointed into the street.

There he was again, making the latest in a long line of dramatic entrances. His hair had thinned enough to create a bald spot at the crown of his head. He was softer, with a paunch and plump cheeks that were guarded by a salt-and-pepper beard. And his left arm had returned, though it appeared to be due to craftsmanship rather than divine intervention. If the walnut-colored hand was any indication, his new arm was made entirely out of wood.

The greeting was awkward. They didn't embrace. She regarded him with alarm. She wanted to move forward. And the last time he had appeared, it had been to dredge up the past.

"I thought you were coming tomorrow," said Miss Eaton.

"What are you doing here?" said Anna to Gavin.

"Opening my shop." He grinned and motioned to the nearby storefront. A small sign hung in the window: THE ONE-ARMED TAILOR. TAILORING, HABERDASHERY AND SHOE REPAIR. He told her that after leaving London, he had gone back to Boston, but his fortunes had soured and he had been forced to sell his factories at a loss.

"I decided it was time for a change," he said. "I heard you were out here and thought Ohio seemed like a fine idea. And then you had the temerity to be somewhere else."

"You should have written," Anna muttered to Gavin. "*You* should have written, *too*," she said to Miss Eaton.

"I've been sick," Miss Eaton said, blowing her nose on a yellowed handkerchief. "This is the first time I've left the house in weeks."

The Captain called to her from the coach. "Lord, Annie, let's move on." He acknowledged Gavin only with a terse salute. He hadn't forgotten the one-armed former sergeant—any man who still wore his Confederate colors wasn't one to forget *anything*. *Maybe that's why we're ideal*, thought Anna. *We both keep our memories tucked in tight.*

"Come," she said to Miss Eaton. "We'll take you back."

"You'll come to the shop, I hope," said Gavin. "You'll probably need some new clothes. And you'll have to meet the children."

Children? She risked the delicate question. "Is Susannah there, too?"

The sudden crack in his expression revealed a touch of that morose face that had confronted her in London years before. "Yes, she's there," he said. "You can see her, too."

He scurried away and slipped into his shop.

"He has two children," said Miss Eaton, blowing her nose. "The boy belongs to them, but the girl's a foundling. They found her in an outhouse last month. Wait 'til you see Susannah. Remember how she was in London? Imagine that but ten times *worse*." She blew her nose again and wiped her eyes.

To CELEBRATE THEIR RETURN, the Captain arranged for a party to be held at the house. Lanterns were strung up, musicians were found, and neighbors helped supply platters of food. It was only with reluctance that Anna invited the one-armed tailor; they couldn't exactly exclude him when they had invited the whole town. She held out a vague hope that he would decide not to attend, but when the night came he appeared at the door with his unique family in tow. He had become a popular figure and was greeted amicably by everyone except his hosts. His sweet-faced son stood at his side, seven years old and already polite as a gentleman. He held his foundling sister tight in his arms as if protecting her from her adopted mother. Susannah Clarke was indeed ten times worse than ever before. In London, her peculiar nature was just starting to surface; now, almost nine years later, she wore it like a tattoo. A wild woman with frazzled hair, she immediately announced, without any provocation, the strange story of her daughter's discovery. "She was mewling in a puddle of shit," Susannah told Anna (and anyone else who listened). "Her parents' ghosts told me to name her Jessica—it comes from Shakespeare, you know." She added that the ghosts of Jessica's parents continued to advise her on a wide variety of things.

Anxious to avoid the Clarkes, Anna drifted through the party, as aimless as a lost ship. It had not escaped her notice that Gavin had a boy and a girl—exactly what she herself had lost. Odd as the family was, how could she not envy them? *Forward!* she told herself, but she knew she was fading like the moon after a long winter's night. The party roared around her. The Captain was loquacious, treating his guests as another audience whom he could amuse. Buttons was so startled by the attention that he broke from his silver leash and leapt onto the chandelier. The heat and clamor tightened around her until at last she slipped away. At the end of their wide halls, she ducked into the Captain's empty study with a glass of claret. From the bookcase, she took down *Jane Eyre*, only to have dog-eared pages fall into her hands—the binding had finally lost its worth. Given when she was young, when the notion of escape still held such promise, the familiar words still had the power to soothe. "What do I want?" young Jane and young Anna had both asked; old Anna could still quote the answer: "A new place, in a new house, amongst new faces, under new circumstances." She still wanted these things. She wanted another H. P. Ingalls. But it wasn't show business she craved. She just wanted someone, anyone, to offer her another escape.

Soft voices drifted toward her, and Anna quickly rose, book in hand. She didn't want to be found reading at her own party. The study was shaped like a crooked hairpin, and once she had squeezed herself against the wall, it became impossible for her to be seen from the hall. But the newcomers weren't interested in the study. They lurked in the entranceway; they wanted the shadows, too.

"Rebecca, listen to me." A man's voice. Gavin Clarke's.

"Don't be a fool!" It was Miss Eaton. There was a clatter and a crack: something had dropped to the floor. "You're drunk!" said Miss Eaton. "Go on now! Go back to the party!"

"I need to see you."

"You'll see me when you see Annie."

"I want to see you alone."

Miss Eaton blew her nose, and Anna imagined that yellowed handkerchief pressed to her unhappy face.

"Come to the shop next week," said Gavin.

"No. Never again. And don't stop me in the street anymore. I thought I was going to die when Annie saw us together."

"Should I ignore you? Pretend you aren't even there? You might as well ask me to stop breathing."

"Oh, you and your words." Her voice was broken. Was she in tears? "What sort of man are you? You've taken everything from me. And you still want more."

"I want only what I deserve. I've had a miserable life. Aren't I entitled to a little happiness?"

"What about what my happiness? You say you care for me, yet you left me to give birth in this house alone. What would people think if they knew what you had done?"

A sharp sound, flesh against skin, and Miss Eaton gave a small sob. He had struck her. Anna began to move but stopped when she heard the heavy footsteps: Gavin was stalking away. She held herself still as Miss Eaton took a few steps into the study. In one hand she carried a candle and the pieces of a broken plate. Her other hand was pressed against her cheek. She placed the candle and dish on the Captain's desk before taking out her handkerchief. She blew her nose again and again. Some women cry; Rebecca Eaton's sorrow had manifested itself in a flood of snot.

Unsure whether to reveal herself, Anna stayed in the shadows until Miss Eaton had gone. When she finally returned to the party, no one remarked on her absence; in the presence of a giant husband, a pissing monkey, and a tailor's peculiar wife, even Anna Swan could be forgotten. She found another glass of claret and drank deep. Gavin Clarke was dancing with baby Jessica in the crook of his good arm. He suddenly looked different. Shorter. Fatter. Balder. Here was something cruel, she thought. Here was a shame before God. What sort of bad decisions had led to those moments of intimacy between Gavin and Miss Eaton? Were they linked in loneliness or had it actually been love? If emotion was involved, it had been brief. Looking at Gavin with his family, she doubted the sincerity of his heart. *Why should I live as a cripple with a crazy wife?* he had asked her back in London. *It's not fair.* And now, because he felt his life was unfair, he was clawing for whatever happiness he could find. Nine years ago he had considered escape. Maybe it would have been better if he had. Maybe a man who is desperate for happiness at any cost is a greater danger than one who has the sense to leave his misery behind.

She wandered the party in search of Miss Eaton. In which of these many rooms had she given birth alone? Having been doped by the doctors, Anna barely remembered her own births, yet what she did recall was enough for her to consider the experience a terror. And the aftermath! Had Miss Eaton really been so distraught that she had abandoned the baby in the outhouse? Anna didn't doubt it, and it broke her giant heart. She thought she could understand Miss Eaton's mind. An unmarried spinster, a fatherless baby. Who would have accepted them? Oh, Rebecca. If only I had been here. We could have pretended the baby was *mine*.

She decided then she would never tell Miss Eaton what she knew. The woman had suffered enough; why also make her endure the knowledge that her shame had been discovered? So Anna did nothing with what she had learned, other than use her limited sewing skills to make Miss Eaton an assortment of monogrammed handkerchiefs. She presented them to the woman with a bittersweet grin. "If you're going to blow your nose all the time," she said, "you might as well do it in style."

SOME MONTHS LATER—it was winter now and the town was steeped in frost—Anna and Miss Eaton were on Main Street when a shivering horse limped into view. It carried a frozen rider who was clearly in need of directions. "I have important news for Gavin Clarke," he said. "Can you tell me where he might be?" He directed his question at the Lady Giant of Seville, which was for the best; Gavin's name tended to make Miss Eaton sneeze.

Anna pointed him toward the One-Armed Tailor. She was content to continue down the street but noticed the sharp way Miss Eaton stared after the man who was heading for Gavin's shop.

"Do you mind if we follow him?" said Anna, feigning curiosity. "I know what curiosity does to cats, but I'd like to chance it just the same."

They crossed the street and hovered nearby, busying themselves by helping some children build an army of snowmen. A half hour passed before the stranger emerged from the shop and led his horse by the reins toward Seville's only hotel. Miss Eaton watched the stranger. Anna watched Miss Eaton. Her dour eyes were wide and wet; it probably wasn't from the sting of the cold. It was hard not to pity her. Better than anyone, Anna knew what it was like to keep thinking about Gavin Clarke long after he no longer deserved the thoughts.

"Wait here, Rebecca. I'll only be a minute."

Inside the tailor shop, Anna found the Clarkes in a state of half celebration. Susannah was dancing with the children, but Gavin was somber and wiping his eyes with a cloth.

"I just needed a new dress." Anna improvised. "I'll come back if it's a bad time."

"It's a perfect time!" crowed Susannah, twirling around her. "We've had the most wonderful news!"

"It wasn't *wonderful* news," snapped Gavin. "My father is dead."

A sting in her eyes, a dip in her belly. Anna hadn't thought of Gavin's father for years. Yet she had always imagined that diminutive tailor to be like her copy of *Jane Eyre*: a book that may lose its binding but still find a way to stay on the shelf. "I'm so sorry," she said.

Gavin wiped his cheeks clean. "I haven't spoken to him in a while. We were just visited by a lawyer. It looks like he had some investments. If I sell everything, I could make a tidy sum."

"A tidy sum!" repeated Susannah. She lifted baby Jessica's face to her own. "Do you hear that, puppy? A tidy sum! We're going to California! We're going to see the ocean!"

"California?" said Anna.

"It was only a *thought*," said Gavin. "I'm not sure it's a good idea to stay here."

"Stay near Miss Eaton, you mean." An indecorous thing to say with Susannah nearby, but she didn't seem to notice. Gavin's face fell, and Anna made her glare hard, trying to turn it into a Medusa stare. She had loved him for such a long time. And he had done nothing but disappoint; he had failed her his entire life. "You should give some of that money to her," Anna said. "She deserves that, at least, wouldn't you say?"

She turned to leave and, as she did, stepped on his foot. This time it was no accident; this time, she relished the sound of his cry and of the bones cracking like fallen leaves.

"Well?" said Miss Eaton. "What was it all about?"

"He's going to California," said Anna, and she took her friend's hand. "He's a plague of failures. If we're lucky, we'll never see him again."

But Miss Eaton only blew her nose. "California," she said.

It was spring by the time Gavin Clarke hobbled out of town—this time, Anna really *had* broken his foot. He never once returned to the house, but he did have his nine-year-old son deliver a going-away gift in his place. If the boy cared that the Lady Giant of Seville had snapped his father's foot, he gave no notice. He lingered after delivering the package, if only so he could marvel at Anna one final time.

"Ma's right," he said. "It *is* like staring at the moon."

Anna weighed the small wrapped package in her hand. "Do you know what this is?"

"Pa just said it was a gift."

Anna wasn't sure if she wanted any mementos of Gavin Clarke. Given that she had broken his foot, she doubted it was anything pleasant. But she had misjudged him. When she unwrapped the parcel, she found only a decaying ledger with a half-torn cover and decaying spine.

"What is it?" asked Gavin Clarke Junior.

"This belonged to your grandfather," said Anna in wonder. "He used to take my measurements when I was a girl." She opened the old ledger with care. The list of numbers might have been photographs. They were her earliest measurements, a numeric history of her incredible growth. "Look," she said, "these are mine when I was your age."

"Damn and double damn." The boy whistled.

She found another page, one where the handwriting differed. It was Gavin Clarke's writing. From that day when he had touched her foot and she had decided she loved him? Anna shut the ledger. *Forward!* She didn't want any souvenirs.

"I don't really want this," she admitted.

"Can I have it?" asked the boy.

Anna handed it back and gave a magnificent wink. "Don't ever show it to your father."

Gavin Clarke did not give Miss Eaton any of his father's money; he fled Seville, leaving nothing of himself behind. The effect on Miss Eaton was immediate. She became a morose companion. Her cooking suffered while errands were left undone. And she blew her nose all the time: she washed her monogrammed handkerchiefs every day.

"Lord, I wish I knew what was wrong with her!" said the Captain. "Between the two of you, this house is becoming a mausoleum."

Anna knew he was right. It was hard to forget the past when her closest companion was also her partner in melancholy. Both had lost children; both were women unable to be what the world wanted them to be. How extraordinary! After all these years, she should see herself in a woman who happened to be a little small.

Gavin had been gone for two months when Anna summoned Miss Eaton into her room. "You're fired," she declared.

"I don't understand."

"I don't need a maid," said Anna. "I certainly don't need a chaperone. Twenty years of service is long enough." From her hope chest she removed a bag of money. She was, in many ways, still an ogre sitting atop a pile of gold. *What sort of good and decent person doesn't help people in need?* she had asked Gavin once upon a time in New York. Back then, she had given to charity. Well, this was charity, too.

"What am I to do?" said Miss Eaton. "I don't have anywhere to go."

"Go to California," said Anna.

"California," repeated Miss Eaton, and she blew her nose.

"The best cure for grief is hope," said Anna.

"And what exactly am I to hope for?"

"To be happy," said Anna. "Or, at least, *happier*."

THAT WAS IT for Anna Swan, the woman without rank or profession who toured America and Europe and once met a queen. She fought to be happy—*happier*—and maybe she was, but within a few years, she was gone just the same. She left without drama. While telling some visitors her anecdotes of the past, she lost feeling in her left arm just as she was trying to find an appropriate way of describing P. T. Barnum. "Not an all-together ill-looking man . . . ," she began. It was then that she fell apart. It took four strong men to carry her to the bed, while a fifth ran to find the Captain. She died without last words or a will. No one would ever find a letter or diary or anything that revealed a single personal thought. Her legacy was a rhesus monkey, a size 22 wedding ring, and a trunk of oversize clothes. And, of course, Miss Eaton. Miss Eaton, who was somewhere in California. Miss Eaton, who spiraled closer to Hollywood and her lost daughter and Andorra Kelsey with each passing year.

SEVENTEEN

The Perfect Event

Hollywood, 1937

THE STORY OF HER MOTHER'S RESURRECTION was relayed in a long-distance phone call, but Elionor—the *Hollywood* Elionor—was practically unmoved by this miracle of technology that connected her to the dead. Having told Rutherford everything about her mother, beginning with her terrible fistula and ending with her supposed death, Elionor Nicholas now asked him to be at her side when she placed the call. "I'm calling a ghost," she had told him. "It seems like an activity that demands supervision." But when the connection was finally made to Detroit, it wasn't a ghost who answered. Rowena sounded hoarse on the other end, and the Hollywood Elionor sunk into the sofa, burying the telephone between her hand and her face.

"If it's not true, then it's a terrible joke," she said.

"It's true," said her eldest daughter. "She's been here for almost a month."

Rowena, writer that she was, told the story in intimate detail—no doubt she had scrawled everything down in her elegant script. Elionor Noguerra del Alandra had appeared in Detroit the day after the last game of the World Series ("the day after you promised to return," Rowena reminded her mother). The Tigers had not been involved this year—the Yankees had fought the Giants—but that didn't matter to either Detroit or Gabriel and Gabriella. The city still had baseball fever, and so did the twins. For obvious reasons, they had felt obligated to root for the Giants, and when they lost, the twins elected to stage a rematch in the yard behind the house on Elsa Street. A makeshift diamond had been built while faux Yankees had been created out of the Widow and her newest borders; the faux Giants, of course, were the twins and Geoffrey. Rowena had *not* been playing. Future writer that she was, she had sat on the sidelines to report on the game. So it was Rowena who first heard the doorbell and Rowena who went through the house to answer the door.

From the living room window, she watched the porch. That famous sign warning agents away only partially blocked the shaggy gray women who were waiting outside. Rowena instantly mistook one of them for a mule. It was the same mistake that had been made thirty-seven years before when the same women had crossed into that prick between France and Spain; even after all this time, Manuela Noguerra still looked as if she carried a burden only God could see. As for Elionor—the *real* Elionor—she was so thin that she nearly vanished inside her coat. They had come to Elsa Street because it was the only address they had; the last time they had received a letter with a return address, it had come from Andorra's father. Not that Rowena knew this then. Rowena assumed they were potential tenants looking for a place to stay.

"No vacancy," she said when she opened the door. The words nearly died in her throat. Nearly eight years into the Depression, Rowena had become accustomed to bad smells. The sisters, though, carried with them a bona fide *stench*.

The women spoke in broken English.

"We are to look for Geoffrey del Alandra," said Manuela.

"*She* is to look for Geoffrey del Alandra," said Elionor. "*I* am to look for his daughter."

"She is to look for Geoffrey, too," growled Manuela. "She is just not to want to admit."

"Mama's not here," said Rowena. "And Avi's out back."

"Mama!" said Elionor.

"Avi!" said Manuela.

Now that they knew who they were dealing with, they studied Rowena with a great deal more care. Rowena, who still didn't know who *she* was dealing with, backed away.

"Thank the God you are not a giant!" said Elionor.

"Not yet," said Rowena.

"This, it is your house?" said Manuela.

"Our house is a few blocks away," Rowena said. "We're just visiting."

"We?" said Elionor. "There are more of you?"

"I have a brother and a sister."

"Are *they* giants?" asked Elionor.

"Not yet," said Rowena again.

"Are *they* looking like us?" asked Elionor. "*You* are not to look like us at all."

"Don't be rude," said Manuela.

"She is with red hair," Elionor muttered. "Who in our family is with red hair?"

"I look like my grandmother," said Rowena.

"*I* am your grandmother!" Elionor sniffed.

"My grandmother is dead," said Rowena.

"Not yet," said Elionor.

At last Rowena saw the resemblance, for beneath the grime and the stench, Elionor looked every bit like Andorra (except, naturally, for her height). Bewildered, Rowena led the two ghosts inside. Manuela begged her to lead them to the bathroom, and Rowena, overpowered by their smell, was more than happy to oblige. What Rowena didn't know—though she knew it by the time she reported the story to her mother—was that the terrible fistula that had plagued Elionor had never been cured. That bona fide stench was not because the shaggy sisters hadn't bathed. It was because her grandmother's waste bag needed to be changed; Manuela Noguerra had tried dousing her sister in rubbing alcohol in order to mask the smell.

In the bathroom on Elsa Street, the two women tried to wash themselves clean, but it was a rush job, and they emerged with the scent of soap mixing with all the rest. ("It was *awful*," Rowena reported to her mother. "All I thought was: how am I *ever* going to write about *this?*") At last, Rowena led the women into the backyard. The game was not going well for the faux Yankees. The score was tied, and Gabriella, who was hugging second base, represented the winning run. As Rowena stepped into the yard, she saw her grandfather standing at home plate. The Widow, pitching for the other team, lobbed the small ball in his direction. With a mighty swing, he smacked it hard, and all eyes watched as it sailed over the fence. No one cared about retrieving it. The home run meant the faux Giants had won. Gabriella crossed home plate and flew into her brother's arms. But Geoffrey never even scored. As he was rounding third, he was hit by a terrible smell—he smelled his wife's return before he saw it. When he caught sight of the shaggy sisters, he immediately tripped over his own feet and tumbled into the ground.

"Who is this?" asked the Widow.

"Apparently, this is our grandmother and great-aunt," said Rowena.

The Widow blanched and seemed to forget how to stand. She clawed her way to the porch step even as Geoffrey, chin bleeding, staggered toward his wife, one hand stretched before him. He later told Rowena he expected it to pass right through the ghosts.

Elionor took his hand and shoved it toward Manuela. "Embrace *her*," she said in Catalan. "I'm not sure yet if I'm happy to see you."

So Geoffrey hugged Manuela but did not touch the wife he hadn't seen in almost twenty-seven years.

"You told me she was dead," he said to Manuela, still in Catalan.
(They did not know the children understood the conversation.)

"Why would you tell him I was dead?" asked Elionor.

"I didn't!" said Manuela.

"You sent me a letter," said Geoffrey.

"Not me! I stopped writing as soon as we left for Spain."

"You went to Spain?" said Geoffrey.

"Years ago," said Elionor.

"Perhaps we'd all better sit," said Rowena.

"What's going on?" asked Gabriel, speaking in Catalan.

"They really *smell*," said Gabriella, speaking in Catalan, too.

"You speak Catalan!" said Elionor.

"Mama taught us," said Rowena.

"Mama!" said Elionor, and she shook her head in wonder.

The family collected around the ghosts. The Widow's tenants
drifted away, and the Widow escaped, hot on their heels. (Rowena
assumed she was annoyed with the language of choice; having found
a universal tongue, none of them had lapsed back into English.)

"After Noria died, we went to live in the house," Manuela began.

"Noria's dead," said Geoffrey.

"She died of a stroke," said Manuela.

"Is she *really* dead?" asked Geoffrey.

"I helped bury her myself," said Manuela.

"Who's Noria?" whispered Gabriel.

"Another aunt," whispered Rowena.

"Then we heard our father had died," said Manuela.

"Your father's dead," said Geoffrey.

"He died of a stroke, too," said Manuela.

"And he's also *really* dead?" asked Geoffrey.

"Are you going to ask that *every* time she tells you someone's dead?"
asked Elionor.

"With *this* family," said Geoffrey, "it clearly doesn't hurt to make sure."

Manuela continued. "We went home to Spain. Tata left everything to me. So we went to Madrid, and I sold the estate. Then we took the money and went to all the doctors we could find."

"Why?" asked Gabriel.

"Because I'm cursed," said Elionor.

The children were awed by the word. "What sort of curse do you have?" asked Gabriella.

"The worst in the world," said Elionor. "Every doctor I saw told me I can never be cured."

"After that, we went back to Andorra," Manuela said. "That's when we received the letters."

"What letters?" said Geoffrey.

"Andorra's letters," said Elionor. "They had been collecting for months."

"Andorra wrote you letters?" asked Geoffrey.

Elionor nodded. Andorra's letters were why they had come to Detroit.

"She wanted to find you," Manuela said to Geoffrey.

"I wanted to find *Andorra*," Elionor said, and at last she looked around the yard and asked when her magnificent daughter was coming home.

The family fell silent and looked away. "She's already a day late," Rowena explained. "We don't really know how much longer she'll be."

In Hollywood, the other Elionor listened to this entire story in silence. She might have been a painting on the apse of a church: all the while that Rowena spoke, Elionor Nicholas had barely moved. But now that Rowena had stopped talking, she realized she was expected to speak.

"Where's your grandmother now?" she asked.

"I'm here," said her mother's voice. The Elionor in Hollywood had not been the only Elionor listening to Rowena's story; the real one had been sitting on the extension and had somehow stayed silent. Now, at last, she spoke to her daughter for the first time since they had seen each other by the Valira River twenty-seven years before.

"Hello, Andorra," she said.

On hearing her real name, the false Elionor hung up the phone.

"Why did you do that?" asked Rutherford.

"Never mind," said the false Elionor.

"I'll get a new connection."

"Don't you dare."

"You haven't spoken to her in twenty years."

"Twenty-seven. What's another day?"

"If it were my dead mother, I'd want to talk to her."

"Well, it's not your dead mother. Your dead mother probably has the good sense to actually be dead." She collapsed into a nearby chair, or at least she tried to. It was not built for the likes of her, and she ended up crushed between the armrests.

"I've been writing to her for years," said the false Elionor. "I wrote her letters, and I put them in the mail. They were like a diary. Once you know there won't be a response, it becomes safe. Like when you put a prayer in a bottle and cast it out to sea. But she's not dead. She received my letters. Which means she read all the things I wrote."

"Were they that bad?"

"They were that *honest*. I wrote things I've never told anyone. I wrote things I never wanted *anyone* to know. Especially the children."

Rutherford came up beside her; because she was leaning against the chair, they were almost the same height. He took her great hand in his. "Whatever you told her can't be that bad. You're their mother. What could you have possibly done that was so wrong?"

"I killed their father," said the false Elionor. "Nicholas is gone because of me."

• • •

BY THE MORNING of October 3, 1934, enthusiasm for the Detroit Tigers had reached epic proportions: it was only the fourth time
they had made it to the World Series, and they had never won. "This
is the perfect event," said Nicholas. "Detroit has had too many dis-
appointments. We need this win as badly as we need work." Andorra
knew he was right. In terrible times, the desperation for symbolic
victories becomes magnified. On that morning in October, the Great
Depression had been crushing Detroit for nearly five years. Detroit
was enduring terrible times. Yet, for once, people weren't talking of
the economy or the unions; for once, the Kelsey family wasn't obsessed with soup kitchens or want ads or lice. *No one* was talking of
the shutdowns or the slowdowns or picket lines or typhus or the heat
or the dust storms or the New Deal or the Commies or the Nazis
or the tragic deaths of Dillinger and Bonnie and Clyde. Everything
had been exiled for however long it would take the Tigers to become
champions of the world.

Up and down Woodward Avenue, signs reading GO TIGERS! sat
in shop windows and in front of the destitute who lined the streets.
Supper clubs put roast tiger on the menu (it was chicken), while soup
kitchens promised bowls of tiger soup (really just squash). At the
Annex Theatre, Gabriel's Tigers hat earned him a free bar of candy,
while over at the Globe, Gabriella won a free lemonade because she
knew the name of pitcher Schoolboy Rowe's longtime sweetheart
(it was Edna). Down at Packers Grocery, Andorra had only to pres-
ent a ticket stub from any game in order to win a tenth of a pound
of beans. She used a ticket from the summer of 1921. She certainly
didn't have any ticket stubs for *that* summer; the Kelseys were far
too poor. They had been on the brink of survival for years. Whatever
money they had saved had been lost on that Black Tuesday in 1929
when the stock market crashed. Now Nicholas was stuck in a parade

of odd jobs while the children had been pulled from school. Rowena maintained a steady presence in the breadlines while the twins became scavengers who stripped discarded shoes of their laces and stole eggs by hiding them in their armpits. Bit by bit, they were pawning everything they owned. A skeletal existence was all that remained.

Their one luxury was their life insurance, bought some years before. Nicholas was fearful of accidents, and Andorra was concerned about her possibly weak little heart. They struggled to make their payments, anxious to know that, in the event of a tragedy, the children would be safe. At last, during the summer of 1934, Andorra had been forced to borrow money from the Widow, who, having never believed in banks, kept a small fortune beneath the floorboards of her room. When Nicholas found out (it was Geoffrey who let it slip), he flew into a rage. The loan had damaged his pride; he had wanted to solve their troubles himself.

"He was always trying to be the hero," she told Rutherford. "But he was never quite up to the role."

Poverty pushed them away from who they once were. They were no longer the sort to reenact Shakespeare; Nicholas was not going to surprise her with a story published in a magazine. How could he when she had no time to write? She had no *strength* to write either. They were living hand to mouth, but Andorra's mouth was far too large to ever be filled. Hunger left her weak and sad. Gone was the great hope that had once lifted her spirits. Nicholas was not immune. They slept at either end of their tremendous bed, and when a leg strayed over the gulf, the other party always moved it back into place.

At last came the autumn of 1934 and, with it, the World Series. The Tigers were facing the St. Louis Cardinals, and it was widely agreed that it would be a rout. She knew that over on Paradise Alley the bookies were giving impressive odds. The most notorious of these men was the barber, Hawk Mosley, a man Nicholas had once visited all the time. Now he had stopped shaving and conscripted

Gabriella to cut his hair—so Andorra knew there was little chance of running into him when she went down to visit the gambler/barber on the morning of October 3. Nicholas was known in Hawk Mosley's shop as the man who had married a giant—it had, he said, given him a certain amount of fame. When his wife stepped into the shop, then, Hawk Mosley knew exactly who she was. She was already a legend in his mind.

The bet was the work of a moment. In mere seconds, she pinned her family's hopes to those of every baseball fan in Detroit.

"And you really thought it would work?" asked Rutherford.

"Do you really think you'll win the lottery? Or win a fortune at cards?" She shrugged and shook her head. "Desperate times make for desperate hopes. I felt lousy because I had brought children into the world at such a terrible time. I kept thinking there had to be another way to live."

To take the Series, the Tigers needed to win four out of seven games; their quest would consume the city for the better part of a week. To Andorra, the smallest part of each game became as enormous as she was. Each strikeout was an epic battle in an epic war, and she became unruly as the rolling sea. By the end of Game 2, she had headaches and cramps; by the end of Game 4, she had insomnia and a terrible cough. By the time the Tigers had won Game 5, she felt she had had a stroke.

"We just have to win one more game!" hooted Gabriel.

"One more game!" cheered Gabriella.

Thank God, thought Andorra.

Now victory was in their sights. The Tigers had won three games. If they took Game 6, the championship was theirs. In Detroit, the police prepared for riots. The mayor prepared for a parade. That night in bed, Andorra drew her husband into her arms for the first time in months (or was it years?). Nicholas resisted at first and then he seemed to remember who he was and who she was and he clawed at her nightdress, hiking it up to her waist. He tore at her stains and bruises; she buried her mouth in his dirty beard. Their lovemaking was fierce, as desperate as everything else in their lives.

It was here, in the afterglow, that she was fooled by the glory of sex. She thought one act of lovemaking was enough to bridge the gap between them, and so, in the dark of their bedroom, she confessed what she had done.

Nicholas sat up. The heat of his body left hers, causing her bare breasts to be stung by the cold.

"You cashed in the life insurance?"

"I'll buy it back." She tried to pull him back, but he had gone stiff. "I needed to do something."

"How big *is* this bet?"

"Do you think I have it in me to do anything small?"

Nicholas didn't even favor her with a grin. *"How much?"*

Andorra had wanted to make the sort of bet that would end their troubles. She didn't just want to save them for *now*; she wanted to find a way to save them for as long as she could. The insurance money had been good—but only as collateral. "Hawk Mosley loaned me the rest," she said.

"Hawk Mosley is a crook."

"I really think they're going to win."

"That man is dangerous."

"Is he going to want a pound of flesh?" Again she tried for humor, not wanting him to probe too deep, not wanting to confess the enormous rate of interest she had agreed to pay.

Nicholas was already crawling out of bed. "Do you have any idea what you've done to us?"

"I've tried to save us."

"You had no right to do it *alone*."

"I'm sorry if I stepped on your precious pride."

"You think this is about pride?"

"You were a lousy actor and now you think you're a lousy husband. One of us had to do something, Nick. It might as well be me."

Nicholas gave her a hard look. He hated her in that moment and she could see it and she thought she might crack. "Yes, one of us had to do something. But *something* does not mean *anything*. There has to be a limit, or we're lost." He stalked out of the room, only to return a moment later. "And I was *never* a lousy actor," he said.

For the rest of the night she swam alone in that great big bed. She still had every reason to be optimistic. Nicholas would forgive her when the Tigers won tomorrow's game. She believed with the certainty of faith that she was ripe for a storybook ending, a success to carry them through all the coming days and nights and years.

But the Tigers didn't win. The next afternoon, in St. Louis, they lost Game 6, forcing the series into sudden death. In the house, something began to shift. Rowena brought up the *last* time Detroit had been in a World Series that had gone to seven games: it had been 1909, and the team's roster had included the legendary Ty Cobb. And they had *still* lost. The twins fought to keep the sporting blood running hot, as if their fever was enough to push the Tigers to victory. Nicholas merely stalked through the house in silence. And Andorra? Andorra moped with the terror of a jilted bride. The next day, as the Tigers played Game 7 in Detroit, the family gathered around the radio. Andorra maintained her composure only until the top of the third inning. That was when Schoolboy Rowe gave up seven runs; that was also when Andorra began to cry. She tried to put her hand on her husband's shoulder, but he shook her away. Then he took up his coat and disappeared into the street; they never saw him again.

Everything was changing—for Andorra *and* the Tigers. In the sixth inning, Joe "Ducky" Medwick, of the Cardinals, slid into Marv Owen as he took third. The fans, deciding he had done it on purpose, soon took their revenge. The next time Medwick took the field, he was pelted with garbage from the crowd. It started in the wildcat stands and spread to the box seats, where even society's cream had curdled. Ducky Medwick shielded himself from the assault of bottles and rancid fruit. The Tigers sat in their dugout and let the fans have their way. (Better him than us, they probably thought.) By the seventh-inning stretch, Detroit's victory parade was scrapped. The devastation lasted two hours and nineteen minutes; it would have been shorter, if not for the need to clean up all the trash that had been thrown on the field. The final score was 11-0.

No one would report on the sadness better than Rowena. "In the house, we backed away from the radio as if it had teeth," she wrote. "In taverns, men thanked God that Prohibition had been repealed. Outside Navin Field, a work crew gathered to tear the bleachers down. And in Paradise Alley, in a dark space between two buildings, my father was beaten to death by persons unknown."

Rowena would not be able to report on the *reason* for her father's death, at least not with any accuracy. She believed—as everyone believed—that Nicholas had simply stepped into the wrong scene, like an actor who ends up in the wrong play. Andorra knew better, especially after she went to see Hawk Mosley. What had Nicholas done? It would never be entirely clear. Hawk Mosley himself said only that Nicholas had agreed to do him a "favor" in exchange for wiping out the debt. This "favor" was probably why Nicholas had been in Paradise Alley. But something had gone wrong, and even Hawk Mosley didn't know what it was. The gambler seemed sincerely shaken. "You don't owe me a thing," he told Andorra in a somber tone. Then he handed her a wad of cash. It was everything she had given him; it was enough to buy her insurance back. And so she staggered out of Paradise Alley swallowed by a void. Nicholas had performed a great sacrifice; her burden was that she would never know exactly what it had been.

It was, she told Rutherford Simone, a terrible cruelty when the Tigers reached the World Series the following year; it was even crueler when they won. The twins' elation was hardly muted by the anniversary of their father's death. They didn't know he had died *because* of baseball; they thought it was *appropriate* that the Tigers had won. But for Nicholas's widow, who alone bore the truth, it seemed the universe was taunting her. If *this* had been the year she had sold the life insurance, if *this* had been the year when she had gone to Hawk Mosley . . . if she had waited one more season . . . if she had lasted one more year . . .

"How could I not become bitter?" she asked Rutherford Simone. "I knew I was living outside myself and that I was starting to degrade, and suddenly it wasn't a question of *if* I would leave but *when*. I just needed an excuse."

"And then I came along," he said.

"I suppose you're going to tell me it wasn't my fault."

"No," said Rutherford the Honest. "I'd say it was *definitely* your fault."

"So much for absolution."

"Absolution is a myth. We make mistakes and we either learn to live with them or we don't."

"I've been trying to live with it. I don't know if I can."

"Your mother has lived with a gaping hole for thirty-seven years. I think you can live with *this*."

"Mama has had to live with that hole because of me. Tata had to live without her because of me, too. Now my children have no father. Because of me. *Again*."

"You're just a plague of failures, is that it?" Rutherford shook his head. "Your mother *chose* to leave home. Your father *chose* to let her. Nicholas *chose* to go to Paradise Alley. You may have been the reason a choice had to be made, but you aren't the reason they chose the things they did. You can live with this. We can live with anything. We just have to want to."

He offered her the phone and she reached for it, but at the last second she shook her head. For days, there would be no further contact with either her resurrected mother or her family in Detroit. The silence terrified her. But the thought of breaking the silence terrified her even more.

A WEEK LATER, at ten o'clock in the morning on the hottest day of the year, the actress known as Elionor Nicholas finally made her Hollywood debut. Her first scene was also her last: she was scheduled to film the final scene of *Bombshell Brunette*, the one where she would enjoy an unexcessive and lustless kiss with Grove Wilson. They dressed her in an ivory gown with a butterfly pattern that they said was majestic, and, though she tried to be majestic as she moved, the butterflies left her feeling trussed, as if her twenty-ounce heart was bound and gagged. She was short of breath. Her raucous stage fright, dormant ever since that long-ago night in Detroit Temperance Hall, roared like an angry beast.

Grove Wilson was already on set, dressed in dark pants and a crisp dinner jacket the color of milk. No amount of effort could hide the terror in his eyes, for the scandal involving that corpse in his pool had still not floated away. He had not been seen in public for several weeks, and today the other actors were keeping their distance. He was the topic of hushed discussion for everyone except a single eight-year-old girl and her mother, who stood nearby having a conference that was entirely their own. The girl, named Jenny Tuck, had been hired to play the young innocent who discovers Elionor and Grove at the end of the film. Elionor immediately disliked everything about her, from her fat cheeks to her imitation Shirley Temple curls. Her mother, thin as a railway spike, was equally obnoxious, insisting that Jenny repeat her single line again and again.

"Sorry!" chirped Jenny Tuck. "But could *one* of you pass me a broom?"

"Could one of *you* pass me a broom!" prompted Mrs. Tuck.

"Could one of *you* pass me a broom!" parroted the girl.

"That's right," whispered Mrs. Tuck. "No matter what the director says, you say it just like that."

The makeup artist instructed Elionor to get down on her knees so that she could touch up her blush—at which point the costume designer instructed her to *crouch* so the butterflies would stay clean.

"The air conditioner is broken," said the makeup artist. "Try not to sweat."

Elionor knelt slowly, holding her lower back. She was sorer than usual. She squinted, for the lights were hot in her eyes. The soundstage was filled with noise. Someone yelled at someone else about the rigging. A man swore loudly as he spilled coffee on his shirt. Everything felt foreign and wild, and she suddenly felt as she hadn't in years: like an immigrant fresh off the boat.

At last, she and Grove Wilson were placed in the broom closet, or rather a clever imitation—it was wider than the usual closet, designed to accommodate both Elionor and the cameras. As she took her place, a wet gurgle rose from her stomach and echoed in her giant frame. She tried to brace herself against the wall, only to find it had no support. It was a set piece, after all. Thin as paper and just as frail.

"Lights!" called the director, and her twenty-ounce heart began to shake.

The shot involved young Jenny Tuck swinging open the closet door to reveal the lovers, which meant they had to be kissing once filming began. Grove was placed on a riser, so he and Elionor were now face-to-face.

"Camera!" called the director, and her legs trembled beneath her dress.

She was acutely aware of every member of the crew. The other actors. Jenny Tuck's mother. Rarely had her own monstrosity been more apparent. She was King Kong atop the Empire State Building. Once seen, it was impossible to look away.

"Action!" said the director, and Grove Wilson dove toward her lips first.

Emotion swelled from the deepest part of her core. For the first time since the 1934 World Series, she was kissing a man. Yes, this kiss was an illusion. Yes, this kiss was unexcessive and lustless. But her possibly weak heart still fell for the fiction. There was a hiccup inside her, and then something gave way. She began to cry.

"*Cut!*" screamed the director. "Why would you make your character *cry*? It's a happy ending!"

Oh, Hollywood! Accustomed to illusion, no one realized her tears were real. They thought they were a *choice*.

She dried her eyes. The makeup artist touched up her face. Lights, camera, action. Grove Wilson leaned in for the kiss. And a bubble of anxiety caused a great belch to rise out of her throat.

"*Cut!*" yelled the director.

"Are you all right?" said Grove Wilson.

"I have stage fright," whispered Elionor.

"How can you have stage fright? We're not onstage."

"Then it's *sound*stage fright," she snapped. She felt feverish. Had the heat become worse?

"Could one of *you* pass me a broom!" said little Jenny Tuck. She had a tendency to rehearse between takes.

"Let's try it again!" said the director.

"Could one of *you* pass me a broom!" said Jenny Tuck.

"You'll be fine," said Grove to Elionor. "Just breathe."

"I think I'm dizzy," she said.

"Could one of *you* pass me a broom!" said Jenny Tuck.

"Lights!" said the director.

"I really can't breathe," said Elionor.

"Camera!" said the director.

"Could one of *you* pass me a broom!" said Jenny Tuck.

"Will you *shut up?*" said Elionor.

She was towering over Jenny, and the sight was all it took for the girl to burst into tears.

"Make her stop!" screamed the makeup artist.

"Oh, for Heaven's sake!" said the director.

"She told me to *shut up!*" said Jenny Tuck.

Mrs. Tuck swooped in. "My poor baby!"

Elionor staggered. Her heart thundered in her chest. This was more than just stage fright—more than just *sound*stage fright, too. As she tried to steady herself, she glanced past the makeup artist and noticed something twinkling in the dark. Elionor frowned. In the shadows, at the back of the set, she saw an old woman. No. Not old. *Ancient.* She might have been a wizened peach. The top of her silver cane had caught the light.

"Can we please try to get this done?" pleaded the director.

"I don't think Ellie's feeling well," said Grove Wilson.

"Has anyone seen Jessica Simone?" called one of the gaffers. "This lady here says she's her ma."

They all turned to the gaffer who was standing amongst the cameras, guiding the woman with the silver cane. The cane might have been enough to hold her on any other day, but right now the woman was clinging to the gaffer for support. She was staring in wonder at the newest actress in the room.

"My God," said the woman, and she hobbled closer, dragging the gaffer with her. "Is it really you? Or do you just *look* like you?"

"I always look like me," said Elionor, holding her head.

The old woman released the gaffer and toppled a bit as she leaned forward to have a closer look. "You're not her. You're too big. Annie was never *that* big."

"Annie?" said Elionor.

"Annie was *pretty.* By no means an ill-looking girl."

All ninety-four and a half inches of Elionor sagged; all three hundred and twenty-two pounds trembled.

Then Jessica Simone appeared. (*Where had she come from?* wondered Elionor). "Excuse me," said Jessica. "This is a closed set. How did you get in here?"

"I told them I'm looking for Jessica Simone," said the woman. "I'm her mother."

"I'm Jessica Simone," said Jessica. "But you're not my mother."

The woman began to shake. She had been stunned by Elionor; amazingly, she was stunned by Jessica more. "I think I need to sit down," she said.

"I think I need to sit down, too," said Elionor, but no one was listening.

"Why are we letting crackpots on the set?" asked Jessica.

"I didn't know you had married!" said the old woman. "All these years, I've been looking for Jessica *Clarke*."

Jessica paused. Elionor held her head. The hot world was spinning fast.

"Can we discuss this later?" asked the director. "We really have to get this done."

"How did you know my name?" asked Jessica.

"I've been looking for you," said the old woman. "I hired detectives."

And just then, as if on cue, a graying man in a battered fedora stepped onto set. He was flanked by two policemen. Elionor did not realize they were *real* policemen. The graying man looked like a typical Hollywood detective: whether by accident or design, he appeared to have modeled himself on Sam Spade. As for his men, they seemed to be nothing but a couple of large and silent extras. She didn't understand the true menace that had just arrived: she simply thought one false reality had collided with another.

"*Now* what is it?" said the director.

"Grover Wilson," said the graying man. "We have a warrant for your arrest."

"I thought you hired detectives to find *me*," said Jessica.

"Those aren't *my* detectives," said the old woman.

"What's this all about?" said Grove Wilson.

"What do you *think* it's about?" whispered the detective.

"You can't possibly be my mother," said Jessica.

"I had nothing to do with that girl," said Grove Wilson.

"Are we *ever* going to get this done?" moaned the director.

"I'm your mother all right!" said the old woman. "I left you in an outhouse."

"I *really* need to sit down," said Elionor.

"I'm a very big fan," said the detective. "I'd rather not do this in public."

"I'm sorry, but we're trying to work," said the director.

"How do you know about the outhouse?" said Jessica to the old woman.

"We're trying to make a *movie*," said the director.

"Could you help me please?" said Grove to Jessica.

"Just keep your mouth shut," said Jessica to Grove. "I'm his manager," she said to the detective. "You can talk to me."

"*I'll* talk to you!" said the old woman. "I've been wanting to talk to you for *years*."

"There's nothing you can do," said the detective.

"I'm sure there's some mistake," said Jessica—to the detective or the old woman or both.

"There's no mistake," said the old woman.

"Oh, there's a mistake all right," said Grove.

"I told you to shut up," said Jessica.

Jenny Tuck pointed at Elionor. "*She* told me to shut up, too!"

"Could everyone just *stop*?" begged Elionor. She had been sucked into an eddy. Everything spiraled.

"If I could just get *one* shot," said the director.

"I think the shot's the least of your concerns," said the detective.

"*Water,*" said Elionor.

"You don't look well," said the old woman.

"I'm not," said Elionor. She was red, and her chest had gone tight. The butterfly gown might have been a cage.

"Lord am I sick of this!" said Grove. "For weeks I've put up with gossip and rumors. Now you come in here, and for what? I didn't kill that girl."

"We know," said the detective.

"If you know, then why are you here?"

"Because we found the girl's grandmother," said the detective. "We also found her son."

"The girl had a son?" said Jessica. "She was sixteen."

"That's right," said the detective. "She was sixteen. And he's under arrest for statutory rape."

At the word "rape," Mrs. Tuck covered her daughter's ears. There was little point: the world had exploded. The graying detective shouted at Grove. Grove shouted back. Jessica Simone shouted at everyone else. The ancient woman tottered on her silver cane. Elionor swayed. She lost control of her legs and reached out to catch herself against the walls of the set. She forgot how fragile they were. Never meant to support the weight of a regular actor, they could hardly withstand an actress like Elionor Nicholas. The wall tottered and fell back. Elionor fell with it.

Something caught her just in time. It was Rutherford Simone, making another dramatic arrival. He had come out of nowhere and, with some great mysterious strength, kept her from crashing down. The wall of the set, on the other hand, cracked as it hit the floor, and the sound caused everyone to turn toward them as every panicked conversation ground to a halt.

"Son of a bitch!" said the director.

"I've got you," said Rutherford. "You're all right."

Leaning against Rutherford, her gaze turned up toward the grid of overhead lights, Elionor noticed that one light seemed closer than the rest. The others were static, but this one was dancing; the light seemed to swing from left to right.

"Now look what you've done!" said the director.

"Everyone shut up!" said Rutherford. "Give her some space."

Because she was still looking up—because she was so much closer to the ceiling—Elionor saw what was happening an instant before everyone else. That light had *not* been dancing; it had been preparing to fall. The light was standard for a Hollywood set: a globular piece of metal, it was the size of a small bomb. With a clatter, it fell from the overhead grid and smacked against one of its neighbors before hurtling down—right toward Rutherford Simone. Elionor had always been lacking in speed; she was not exactly known for her grace. But she made up for everything in size. She flung herself over him. Her body was the perfect shield.

The falling light struck her squarely between the shoulder blades, yet when the pain came, it was in her chest; when the pain came, it was in her possibly weak heart. Down she went, pinning Rutherford beneath her. Her face was next to his. He was only a breath away. "Could one of you pass me a broom?" she whispered. It was the last thing Elionor the Actress would ever say—and it wasn't even her line.

PART SIX

Afterlife

EIGHTEEN

Rutherford the Hero

Hollywood, 1937

SHE STOOD in the Great Lecture Hall of Barnum's American Museum, trapped in a vast sea of New Yorkers, each as dirty and ripe as rotten flesh. As for the would-be actress, she was still in the costume she had been wearing on set; she was still dressed as the gigantic friend of a bombshell brunette.

Onstage, Anna Swan and her husband were in the midst of re-enacting the courtship scene from *The Life of Henry the Fifth*. "Fair Katharine and most fair," said the Captain. "Will you vouchsafe to teach a soldier terms, such as will enter a lady's ear and plead his love-suit to her gentle heart?"

"Your majesty shall mock at me," said Anna. "I cannot speak your England."

"O fair Katharine!" said the Captain.

Just then, Anna glanced into the crowd. "Oh!" she exclaimed and tugged at her husband's sleeve.

"Concentrate!" growled the Captain. "A true actor works with any distraction."

Anna ignored him and glided from the stage as if on skates. The dirty crowd parted to create a path.

Anna Swan is dead, thought the would-be actress. *If she's here, then I must be dead, too.*

She glanced around the lecture hall. Surely, if there was any justice in the afterlife, then Nicholas would have been sent to greet her.

Unless he *had* been given the chance and turned it down. Unless he wanted nothing to do with her.

Anna Swan reached her, and the two women stood face-to-face. They were a mirror and a reflection—but who was which?

"How did you like being an actress?" asked Anna.

"I don't know if I ever became one."

"If you go back, try getting married. If they say you have no rank or profession, you probably became an actress." Her gaze fell on something behind Andorra. "Well, he's certainly got an actor's blood. Look—he's making a dramatic entrance."

Andorra turned. Nicholas stood on the edge of the mezzanine, dressed in his costume from *The Life of Henry the Fifth*—and his Detroit Tigers ball cap. He held the end of a long rope and, with a Tarzan bellow, swung into the air and dropped into the audience. Those dirty New Yorkers swallowed him whole. Andorra tried to move in his direction, but the crowd closed in around her. They were viscous, like the thickest of soups. The crowd was like an ocean, and each time she thought she had broken through, another wave swelled. She tried to remember what Rutherford the Swimming Teacher had taught her. Rutherford! She had forgotten all about him. Poor Rutherford, pinned beneath her. Poor Rutherford, whom she had probably crushed to death.

Something heavy and rhythmic pounded the air. Footsteps? Her heart?

All at once, the crowd was gone; the Great Lecture Hall was gone, too. She was in her father's room in the west wing of the house in her principality, that forbidden section where she had dared to look for Geoffrey so many years ago. Her family stood at the far end, framed by a large window. Rowena held Gabriella against her chest. Gabriel stood at Geoffrey's side. The loyal Manuela sewed in the corner. And there was her mother, the real Elionor, as young and beautiful as she must have been before a fistula—before a daughter—changed the course of her life. Andorra stepped toward them, and then Nicholas appeared, blocking the way. He was still in costume, but his face was split. Nose broken, lips torn. Blue eyes shot with streaks of red. Andorra didn't have to look down at him: somehow in this moment they were exactly the same height.

He kissed her with his battered mouth. It was the sort of kiss that would have enraged the Hollywood censors: lustful and excessive and oh-so bittersweet.

"There's witchcraft in thy lips," he said.

SHE SPRANG AWAKE with a gasp, holding her mouth as if to keep that last kiss from flying away. It took a moment for the delirium to disappear. Fade out on Nicholas. Fade in on a hospital room, where she lay splayed across two beds that had been pushed together. A window, its curtains a faded red, gave way to an unhappy night. The glass was rain-streaked, and beyond it was the faint howl of wind. Nearby, on the nightstand, she noticed a bouquet of yellow flowers was keeping watch. She knew them at once. *Adonis vernalis*. Pheasant's-eyes, the official flower of the Principality of Andorra.

Rutherford Simone was keeping watch, too, though he was doing a lousy job: he had fallen asleep. Still in the clothes he had been wearing on set, his glasses were held together by tape while his left arm sat in both a cast and a sling. So that's what she had done to him. She tried to sit up. Her head was heavy with fog. She couldn't feel the bed against her body; she couldn't feel her *body* either. Everything should have been screaming in pain, but it was all a distant hum.

"Rutherford," she muttered. "Rutherford, wake up."

"Mmm-blurg," said Rutherford, and he opened his eyes. "You're up."

"I can't feel anything."

"They gave you something for the pain."

Drugs. She yawned. It was a struggle to stay awake. "The flowers . . ."

"What do you think?" he smiled. "I had to find a specialist."

"They're poison," she mumbled.

"What?"

"They're poisonous . . ." She trailed off, barely aware of the embarrassed look that had crossed his face. She wanted to take his hand. She wanted to tell him how pleased she was by the gesture. *I'll tell him*, she thought. *I just need to shut my eyes first.* Then things went licorice-black as she spiraled into the well of sleep. There were no more dreams; it was nothing but a void.

The next day, she woke to find the poisonous flowers were gone. She wondered if she had dreamed them until Rutherford appeared in her room. "Why would the official flower of your country be *poisonous?*" he asked.

"Why did you learn the official flower of my country?" she countered.

"A man's gotta do something. You've been asleep for two days."

With the help of mirrors, he was able to show her the damage done to her back: a great yellow bruise stretched from her neck down to the middle of her spine. Anyone else might have woken with a few vertebrae knocked out of place, but Elionor Nicholas's incredible network of sinews and muscles had borne the burden with surprising skill. Nothing was broken; the bruises would heal. Her collapse had nothing to do with that falling light. It had been her possibly weak heart, which had proved weak after all, at least under the strain of heat and stress. By the time the medics had reached her, that twenty-ounce muscle had practically stopped. Rutherford had been pinned beneath her for almost half an hour but had not let anyone move her. "If she's hurt her back, you'll make it worse!" he had warned. And so, with glasses snapped and a ruined arm, he had willingly stayed trapped beneath her, a breath away from her unconscious face.

"We sent a telegram to Detroit," he told her. "No one's replied."

"How long do I have to stay here?"

"Until the end of the week. The insurance is paying for everything. You just take it easy."

"What about the movie?"

"Under the circumstances, it's been indefinitely postponed."

She thought she knew what those "circumstances" were. They had arrested Grove Wilson. The dead girl—her name had been Ethel Faye had been survived by a grandmother who recalled Grove Wilson making several appearances at her house. "And they weren't cameos, if you get my meaning," Rutherford said. " Those reporters are suffering from an embarrassment of riches. Ethel Faye wasn't just sixteen, you know. She was sixteen *and* black *and* a mother. It isn't one scandal—it's three."

"And they think the child is his?"

"That's for the courts to decide."

"But what does *he* say?"

"He's talking through his lawyers now," said Rutherford. "They swear he knows nothing about it. But that's not the craziest part. That light you saved me from didn't fall by mistake. Someone did something to the rigging. And one of the riggers who worked that day was Thomas Faye, Ethel's brother. Who has since disappeared."

Her response was a great and powerful yawn—the drugs were muting both the pain and any ability she had to be surprised.

"I'll let you rest," said Rutherford.

"Wait. That old woman, the one with the silver cane. Who was she?"

He gave a small smile. "That was just another mother back from the dead."

Rutherford had never met Miss Rebecca Eaton, but he had known the name. Chester Smith had mentioned her, but always as a minor character, a bit player in the drama of how his parents had met.

Rutherford was only now starting to realize how important she really was. While waiting for Elionor to wake, he had learned the official flower of her country; he had also taken time to learn how Miss Rebecca Eaton had gone from a giant house in Seville to a Hollywood soundstage in fifty years.

With her pockets filled with Anna Swan's gold, Miss Eaton had gone to San Francisco, where she had hired detectives to help her find the Clarkes. She was working a string of odd jobs when the detectives told her Gavin had gone into mining and settled his family in the Cahuenga Valley, not far from a ranch that bore what was then considered a peculiar name: Hollywood. Miss Eaton moved there and found work raising the children of the Danforth family, a clan of bankers who invested her remaining money with such skill that she could afford to spend the next few years paying more detectives to keep track of the Clarkes. The peculiar Susannah Clarke had been hidden in a sanitarium, where she eventually died; as for Gavin, he was taken by pneumonia during the first year of the Great War. With the Clarkes dead, Miss Eaton finally decided it was time to tell Jessica the truth. She travelled to the funeral only to arrive too late: by the time she reached the cemetery, the mourners—including Jessica—were gone.

Rutherford and Jessica eloped not long after. With Jessica's name changed, Miss Eaton lost track of where her daughter had gone. Still, Miss Eaton stayed in California, searching for a Clarke instead of a Simone. The Danforths became the Pierces; the Pierces became the Blackmores. Had she ever followed the new world of motion pictures, Miss Eaton might have noticed Chester Smith's name flash across the screen. But so what? It would have meant nothing to her, for how was she to know that this Smith was really another Clarke? So she did not find him until after his death. She had missed the headline about the arrival of a woman who was seven-eleven (and three hundred and twenty-two pounds), but she had easily found the story that had been buried on page 8 of the *Los Angeles Times* of the dead producer. Why not? She was ninety-five years old. Obituaries were the only thing that interested her anymore. The notice had mentioned Chester Smith's real name; in the end, despite all the detectives and private investigations, Rebecca Eaton had found her daughter because some nameless reporter had done his job.

Thanks to the wise council of the Danforth family, she had survived the Depression with a portfolio that provided a healthy annuity, and, upon her arrival, she had taken a room at the Hollywood Roosevelt Hotel. Rutherford had visited her in her stylish room on the eleventh floor, but Jessica had refused to come along. "I don't care how rich she is," Jessica said. "She left me in a puddle of *shit*. They should bury her in one when she dies."

"I don't want to lie to this woman," Rutherford said to Elionor. "But I feel like I need tell her something. Technically, she's my mother-in-law."

Elionor, whose Aunt Manuela had lied to her about *her* mother so many years ago, thought she understood the value of stretching the truth. There is a danger in lying to children about their mothers. But lying to old women about their daughters is different. One is cruel, thought Elionor. The other is charity.

"Tell her Jessica is very busy," she said. "Tell her Jessica is one of the most important people in town."

THE NEXT DAY, a telegram came from Detroit. For a writer, Rowena had been all too terse:

ARE YOU OKAY? WHAT DO YOU NEED?

Elionor did not write back; she did not know how. *Was* she okay? What *did* she need? The telegram also didn't tell her what she *really* wanted to know: it didn't tell her whether Rowena—or anyone—knew the truth about the 1934 World Series.

Discharged a few days later, the would-be actress returned to New Annan just in time for Halloween. She celebrated the day by wandering the mansion like the resurrected dead, caught in a daze that was mistaken for a drug-induced fog. She had little choice but to obey her doctor's orders and convalesce. Movie studios are accustomed to a wide range of problems, but when an actor is charged with both miscegenation and statutory rape, even the most seasoned producer is forced to take a pause. *Bombshell Brunette* had been mentioned in the press, and what should have been a frothy comedy of errors was now linked in the public mind with scandal. Yes, they could always recast. But it seemed easier to scrap the film and move on. Only Jessica hoped to save it; only Jessica hoped to save Grove Wilson, too.

"He's been *framed*," she proclaimed. "I'd bet my life on it."

But Jessica, like Elionor, had no talent for placing bets. A week after Elionor returned to New Annan, Grove Wilson pled guilty to the charge of a sexual misdemeanor; in exchange, prosecutors agreed to overlook the rest. Not that it mattered. Grove Wilson should have cut a deal with Hollywood; *Hollywood* hadn't agreed to overlook a thing. And they never would. Grove Wilson was ruined; Rutherford predicted it would be a snowy day in California before the handsome actor ever worked again.

Jessica Simone had bet her life and lost. At long last, something inside her cracked. She had lost her brother, found a mother she didn't want, and publicly defended an actor who was now a disgrace. She began wandering New Annan, muttering to herself and swaying into walls. They suspected alcohol or drugs but found no evidence of either. Rutherford tried to summon a doctor, only to have Jessica lock herself in her room.

"People are telling me I need to put her in a sanitarium," Rutherford told Elionor Nicholas. "I laughed at them. Who am I to put her anywhere? She left me long ago." He shook his head. For months—maybe years—he had been Rutherford the Divorced. And he was only realizing it now.

They were sitting by the pool, bare legs dangling in the water. The pool was littered with debris. No one had cleaned it; Jessica had frightened many of the servants away.

"So what happens now?" said Elionor.

"Nothing's changed," said Rutherford. "I told you: you don't work for Jessica. You work for the Studio." He had taken over as Elionor's liaison with her employers, and it was clear he wasn't enjoying the task. His glasses had been fixed, but his broken arm had yet to heal. This, combined with a somber voice, gave him a morose air as he told her the Studio was finally charging ahead with the plan to have Elionor Nicholas play a monster's bride. "They should be ready to start filming by the first week of the new year," he said.

"You really hate this idea."

"You know I do."

"It's just one picture."

"You want to hear what you're doing next? They're making a new Flash Gordon serial. You'll be the wife of Ming the Merciless."

"And then?"

"The Green Hornet. You'll be his nemesis, Gigantica."

Rutherford scooped up some water to run through his hair. Elionor tried to imagine herself as Frankenstein's bride. Then as Mrs. Ming the Merciless. She couldn't do it. Whatever else had happened on the set of *Bombshell Brunette*, she knew that her weak heart wasn't entirely to blame. Whether it was stage fright or sound-stage fright, one thing had become clear: like Nicholas, she was a terrible actor.

"What if I said no?" she said. "Can they force me to be in these films?"

Rutherford glanced up, straining his neck so he could meet her eyes. "Are you changing your mind?"

"I think I'm changing my mind about everything."

"It might be too late for that."

"There must be something we can do."

He sighed. "I'll look over your contract. In the meantime, you'd better work at your recovery. They'll want their monster's bride at full strength."

She spent the following days avoiding her own mother in favor of someone else's. Along with Rutherford, she visited Miss Eaton and perpetuated the lie that Jessica Simone was the most important woman in town. Seeing that the old woman used a set of ratty monogrammed handkerchiefs, they bought her new ones and claimed Jessica had picked up the bill. They took her to museums and galleries. They bought her lunch and invented stories about Jessica's success. They even lied about the Anna Swan film, even though it was clear the movie would never occur. Jessica was the last person left who had wanted to see the picture made. But word of her condition was robbing her of what little influence she had left. Besides, she had hoped to make the film to honor her personal connection to Anna Swan; the story was no longer one the woman who had been found in a puddle of shit wanted to tell.

Decades earlier, Anna Swan had seen herself in Rebecca Eaton; now Elionor was seeing herself in Miss Eaton's not-so-little girl. Elionor had exiled herself to Hollywood and Jessica had exiled herself to oblivion; was there really a difference in the end? It was this question that led to her finally place a phone call one rainy November afternoon. Choosing to face the matter alone, she called the house on Elsa Street. If her mother had told the family the truth about the 1934 World Series, it was likely the Widow would know.

"You probably know I was in the hospital," said Elionor.

"Why would I know that?" snapped the Widow.

Elionor toyed with the phone cord. "Are you angry with me?"

"Why would I be angry with you?"

"Did my mother tell you anything about me?" she asked carefully.

"Don't talk to me about your *mother*," hissed the Widow. "Don't talk to me about your father either. I want nothing to do with them ever again. All these years! All those men offering to marry me, and I turned them all down! I lost my youth waiting for that father of yours!"

Elionor sat down on the bed. "What exactly was it you were waiting for Tata to do?"

"What do you *think*? He's a goddamn fool. Not that anyone knows it. That aunt of yours is a loyal dog. And your mother! I told him she was dead—and he *still* preferred her to me."

In Hollywood, the rain smacked hard on the roof.

"You didn't tell him Mama was dead," she said. "It was Manuela."

"*I* wrote that letter," spat the Widow. "I was tired of competing with someone who was five thousand miles away. Who knew that competing with a ghost could be *worse*?"

"You wrote the letter."

"I signed Manuela's name!"

"Does the family know?"

"They do *now*. Why do you think I haven't talked to them?"

"How could you have made me think my mama was dead?"

"How can he prefer her to me?" retorted the Widow. "I may be old, but at least I don't smell like a sewer! And as for you, you owe me some of the Hollywood cash for all those lessons I gave you. Your father was supposed to pay me back, and he never did."

Elionor knew she should be upset over the Widow's betrayal, but her mind kept tilting in another direction. Her parents were *together*. Never in her entire life had she seen such a thing. They had always been separated by something: rivers, curses, a shoddy postal system. And now, after thirty-seven years, could they actually be sitting, talking, taking a walk, eating dinner, speaking softly in Catalan? You can learn to live with anything; but why would she want to live without seeing her parents together?

"I have to go," said Elionor.

"You owe me!" screeched the Widow. "What do you have to say about that?"

"Thank you," said Elionor.

"*Thank you?* What am I supposed to do with '*thank you*'?"

"Good-bye, Marianne."

It was the only time she had ever called the Widow by her name. Dropping the phone, Elionor sprawled across the bed and daydreamed of this new incarnation of the family she had left behind. Her parents. The loyal Manuela. Her freckled Rowena, her precocious twins. It was a glorious photo, but of course something was missing: the biggest gap was the easiest to see.

MISS REBECCA EATON'S ANCIENT BODY finally quit a week before Christmas. Jessica Simone didn't come to the funeral, but she did reiterate her fondest wish: she wanted them to bury the woman in a puddle of shit. Neither Rutherford nor Elionor obliged. Miss Eaton had money, and so, after Rutherford pulled some strings, they were able to have her interred in Forest Lawn Memorial; she was not anywhere near Chester Smith, but she was near the celebrities, as if she were one, too. On that sunny Saturday morning, Rutherford and Elionor were the only mourners to stand over her grave. Elionor wore the solemn smock she had worn to Chester Smith's funeral. As for Rutherford, he lumbered awkwardly in his suit. The cast had come off, but he was still sore and was keeping his arm in a sling.

"I went thirty-seven years without a single funeral," said Elionor. "Now I've been to two."

"It's a lot quieter than the last one," said Rutherford.

"At long last, no one seems to care I'm here."

"That might change."

"Once I'm the bride of Frankenstein?"

"If that's what you want."

"I told you it wasn't."

"You changed your mind once. I've been waiting to see if you would change it again."

Again she considered it, and again her family appeared to her, her *whole* family, so nearly close to being complete. She shook her head. She wasn't an actress. She was a woman who wanted to go home.

"There is one option," Rutherford said. "There's a subclause in your contract. You can ask the Studio to release you on the condition that you buy yourself out. The price is everything they've already paid you plus thirty percent."

"That sounds like robbery."

"It's meant to. They invest a lot of money in their stars. They don't want to make it easy for them to get out and go to a rival studio."

"But I don't want to go to a rival studio."

"Yes, but they don't know that, do they?"

She sighed. "I imagine I can't afford to pay them."

"You probably can't. But never mind. It's already done."

"I'm sorry?"

"You just need to sign the paperwork."

"But who paid them?"

He coughed and removed his glasses and, as he always did, ran the lenses across the edge of his tie. But this time he fumbled, and they fell to the grass. She knelt and gingerly retrieved them with her giant hands.

"Was it you?" she asked.

"Technically, it was Miss Eaton. She gave me some money before she died. I was supposed to give it to Jessica."

A sound escaped her: a small laugh of disbelief. "What if I had

told you I *had* changed my mind? What if I had told you I wanted
to stay?"

He shrugged. "I suppose I could have gotten the money back and
gone on vacation. Norway, maybe. Or Iceland. I'm tired of all this
heat. I want somewhere cold."

"Jessica won't be happy about you taking her money."

"She wanted nothing to do with Miss Eaton—why would
she want her money?"

Elionor blew on his glasses and wiped them clear on her blouse
before placing them, ever so carefully, on Rutherford's tiny face. He
had an odd expression. No. Not odd. Just rare. He was Rutherford
the Proud. She had saved his life, and now he had saved hers. She
didn't know what to say. She had become accustomed to surround-
ing herself with men who were bad at playing the hero. It was be-
wildering to finally meet one who had, even with one arm, managed
to get it right.

"When does that sling come off?" she asked.

He frowned. "Monday."

"Good," she said. "I need you to drive me home."

"Me?"

"You want to go somewhere cold, don't you? Or do you have a
reason to stay?"

But she didn't really give him a chance to respond. Even if he *did*
have a reason to stay, she didn't want to hear it, at least not now. She
leaned down and took his face in her giant hands and brought his
mouth to hers and made sure the kiss was bold and brash, the very
thing that would enrage the censors. It was not Elionor's kiss but
Andorra's. When they finally left the cemetery, hand in hand,
Elionor Nicholas was gone. She had been left behind. Another dead
actress in Forest Lawn Memorial; another Hollywood giant forever
buried in the hills.

NINETEEN

Homecoming

Detroit, 1937

I T WAS RUTHERFORD who brought her back: Rutherford the Good, Rutherford the Happy, Rutherford the Man Who Said Good-bye to His Wife Through a Locked Door. Jessica Simone refused to come out of her room, and the last he heard of her was her husky voice telling him she was glad he was walking away. All the servants had left except a single loyal Japanese cook. It would be this cook who would deliver the epilogue to the story of Jessica Simone. She would emerge from her stupor by the time they reached Detroit and, not long after, she would send divorce papers, which Rutherford would duly sign. A year after that, he would hear that New Annan had been sold; three years later, the former Jessica Simone was found with a broken neck at the bottom of a hotel staircase in Mexico. He never learned why she was there.

All that was still to come. For now, Rutherford, Andorra, and the 1931 Duesenberg wound their way back across America, cutting through the ravaged farms and the fields of crops that had been left to rot. Everything seemed to be a signpost, purposely put there to remind Andorra of what she had hoped to escape. The best cure for grief is hope—but what happens when you run out of hope? Andorra didn't know what to expect when she came home. She had sent a telegram to Detroit informing them of her return, but she had sent it on the day she left. There was no way for the family to reply.

Night loomed, and they were forced to share a room at a roadside motel—it was all they could afford. Rutherford the Gentleman suggested they divide the room with a bedsheet, just as Clark Gable and Claudette Colbert did in *It Happened One Night*. But there was only one bed, and Andorra knew she would never fit and offered to sleep on the floor. It was difficult on her back, and she was still wide awake when she felt Rutherford nestle in behind her. He threw one of his small arms over her shoulders and rested his head in her hair.

"Technically, I'm still a married man," he said.

"I'm still getting used to being a widow," said Andorra. "But we can learn to live with anything."

Her possibly weak heart trembled, but she did not stop Rutherford the Lover from undressing her great body. She let him see it exactly as it was: immense and lumbering and wrecked from the years.

She wanted to be back in time for Christmas, but neither could resist stopping in a small cemetery in Seville, Ohio. Anna Swan's grave was easy to find: the Captain had erected a twenty-two-foot statue of a Greek goddess as a monument to her grave. She had been buried next to her enormous son, the one who had lived for eleven hours. The Captain was there, too, but he was a relatively recent arrival: he had died shortly after the end of the Great War. (Unlike Anna and Andorra, he had not suffered from a weak, or possibly weak, heart. It was his kidneys that failed him; they had waited until he was eighty-two.)

Andorra wandered up to the grave alone, bearing a handful of pheasant's-eyes—before leaving Hollywood, she had gone back to the same specialist who had provided Rutherford with her get-well bouquet. She had struggled to keep them alive; poisonous or not, she believed they were the only appropriate thing to leave behind. It was an unhappy day. The hard wind carried the scent of the coming snow, and Andorra trembled in her thin coat even as she stooped to arrange the flowers so they would lean against the monument's base. She noticed the biblical inscription that Anna had asked to be put on her grave. Andorra read it several times. It was, she knew, the closest thing she had to hearing Anna's voice.

AS FOR ME, I WILL BEHOLD THY FACE
IN RIGHTEOUSNESS
I SHALL BE SATISFIED WHEN I AWAKE
WITH THY LIKENESS

The snow began to fall, and Andorra raced down the hill. Why had Anna wanted that Psalm on her grave? Had she hoped to wake from death looking like something other than herself? Born again into a smaller body, reincarnated as something unremarkable? Maybe she had hoped to be forgotten; maybe she would have liked the idea that no one in Hollywood thought her story was worth being told. Maybe she would have been happy knowing that today she was no longer the famed Nova Scotia Giantess; today she was just another woman who had died.

From Seville they wound their way into Michigan. Near the outskirts of Detroit, they began to pass the snowy shantytowns filled with transients who had come to the city but had not been allowed inside. The Duesenberg was what got them into the city; that gorgeous car immediately set them apart from the usual set of weary travelers. Soon the dilapidated skyline rose before them, slightly crumbling yet stubborn in its resolve. The chill was relentless. People crouched in abandoned doorways. Wayward snowmen kept watch on the lawns. A cheap sort of Christmas sat in the frosted windows: newspaper angels, acorns, broken ornaments on scrawny trees.

Into the old neighborhood they went—her old island, her old cocoon. They passed Elsa Street and saw the Widow's house brightly lit with a handsome wreath hanging on the door. It did not seem to Andorra that Mrs. Marianne Holt deserved Christmas; anyone who fakes a woman's death should not be allowed to celebrate the holiday again. She wanted the place boarded up; she imagined a mob burning it to the ground. As for her own house, it was a sleeping dog, quiet but always ready to bite. There were no handsome wreaths here and no easy way to get to the door. A path had been beaten in the snow, but no one had taken the time to carve an easier route.

The Duesenberg came to a stop, and, after a shudder, the eight-cylinder engine went still. Neither of them moved. The cockpit filled with the fog of their breath.

"They may not know anything," Rutherford said.

"I'll have to tell them anyway."

"Do you want me to come with you?"

"I should go in alone."

"I'll find a hotel."

"Don't be an idiot. You aren't staying in a *hotel*."

Rutherford kissed her trembling hand. "In that case, you better hurry up. I don't want to freeze."

The driveway was entirely too short: all too soon, she reached the house she had abandoned in order to save. Her body ached from being folded in the car, and each shiver brought a second of pain. She realized she didn't have the key: it was inside some pocket of some skirt buried at the bottom of her trunk. She rang the bell twice before remembering that it was broken.

When she knocked, the door fell open at her touch. She peered inside. Nothing. All quiet on the western front. The family's coat hooks were bare, all except the one that had belonged to Nicholas: *that* one still wore his hat. It was likely no one was home; it was likely the door had simply been left open out of neglect. But her imagination went to the worst possible place. She imagined the family had picked up and left everything behind, everything except for Nicholas's hat, as if they had wanted no memorials in the days to come.

But just inside the front hall, she saw that the entrance to the living room was masked by a curtain of popcorn strings. The entire room was full of newspaper streamers and paper-bag balloons. The décor had nothing to do with Christmas; there wasn't even a tree. Instead, a banner had been posted over the mantel on which two words had been written in paint:

WELCOME HOME!

Her breath spilled out of her and hung in the frosty room. Floor-boards creaked above her. The sound of running water. Andorra left the living room and followed the sound to the foot of the stairs. The wood beneath her gave a groan, and the movement on the second floor stopped.

"Hello?" A creaky voice. Her *mother's* voice.

Andorra was already scaling the stairs. The voice had come from the bathroom—but the door was closed tight.

"Hello," she said in English.

"You to take what you want and leave!" said Elionor.

Andorra grimaced. Taken for a common thief. "Mama, it's me," she said in Catalan.

A moment's breath. "It's open," said Elionor.

As she pushed on the bathroom door, a pestilential stench fell upon her as if carried on a wayward breeze. Her mother, angular and gaunt, was knelt by the claw-foot tub, thin arms deep in a pool of soapy water. A washboard was propped against the faucet. A pile of clothes, dark and rank, lay piled by her knees.

Elionor still hadn't moved, so Andorra came to her and, hating the way the light made her great shadow fall over her mother's face, knelt by the claw-foot tub. The smell from the clothes brought sharp tears. She held her gaze. Mother and daughter were not quite eye to eye—but it was close enough.

"They think you're coming tomorrow," said Elionor. "They're at the movies."

"Good," said Andorra. "One reunion at a time."

Picking up one of her mother's soiled skirts, Andorra placed it in the water, and together they worked to wash the shit away.

The Giant's House

ANNA'S GIANT HOUSE had fallen into the hands of a family who maintained it throughout the Great Depression. At one point they decided to tear it down, but the morning before the wreckers began their work, two men burst into town with the astonishing claim that the ghost of Anna Swan had been seen towering over her grave.

The first man was the groundskeeper, who was known for his tall tales. But the second was Mr. Baum, the owner of the giant house and a respected member of the community. He had been paying his respects to a friend when he looked toward the immense monument the Captain had erected all those years before. There, Mr. Baum had spotted an enormous figure towering over Anna's grave, one whose silhouette could easily be seen against the sky. It was clearly a woman, said Mr. Baum, and she must have been nine feet tall—as tall, legend had it, as Anna herself. Both Mr. Baum and the groundskeeper had observed this startling specter without daring to approach. Then snow began to fall, and the men took shelter. When they looked toward the cemetery again, the thing that might have been the ghost of Anna Swan had disappeared.

A group agreed to investigate the grave. The sun was already setting when they reached the top of the hill and found the grave deserted. Yet coming out of the ground in front of the monument was a single flower. The monument had saved it from being buried completely by the storm, and its position made it seem as if it was sprouting out of the snow. The flower was so rare that none of them would have known it if not for one woman, who was an amateur botanist.

"It's called a pheasant's-eye," she said. "I think it may be poison."

So there they were with the hint of a ghostly visit and a poisonous flower that had grown during a blizzard. Who could blame Mr. Baum for delaying the demolition of Anna Swan's house? He put it off for a year and then another, until at last he knew the time had come. As a precaution, he returned to the cemetery and waited for Anna Swan's ghost. But her grave remained forlorn, and, giving up, he returned home to tell the wreckers it was safe to proceed. And so another piece of Anna Swan was erased from the earth. The house was carted away in bits and pieces, leaving Anna to be remembered through sales pitches, newspapers, distorted memories, showmen's hyperbole, half a dozen lies, and, hopefully, a tiny handful of truth.

AFTERWORD

NO WRITER IS AN ISLAND—although we may float away from time to time. I am indebted to an innumerable number of librarians and archivists who helped guide me through my research. Even my magnificent copyeditors helped point the way whenever I got lost in history's web. Their work was faultless. Any errors of history are entirely mine—and may be completely intentional. Needless to say, this is historical fiction, and, while many of the characters and events are real, liberties have been taken. I love history; but I guess I love novels more.

In every case, Anna's measurements conform with what was reported in the press. A good historian would take into account a reporter's tendency toward hyperbole; a good writer will always ignore it. Hyperbole, after all, is where most fiction lives.

Anna Swan's many siblings don't get mentioned in this book, but that's my fault, not theirs. Maggie, John, Mary, George, Eliza, James, Christina, David, Janet, and Margaret Swan were no doubt fascinating people; they probably deserve books of their own.

Some of the research indicates that Anna suffered from "consumption" for many years before her death. One should always be wary about any diagnosis that stems from nineteenth-century medical knowledge. This was the era when they tried to cure "female hysteria" with vibrators; it was also the time when sadness and grief were considered a disease.

A lot of delightful historical details were cut in order to keep the novel down to a reasonable length. There were conjoined twins at Anna's wedding; after retiring to Seville, Anna and the Captain played host to their many friends from the circus, including the diminutive Tom Thumb. Why did I dismiss these things but keep the story of Anna's pet monkey? I guess some facts are too much fun to ever dismiss.

Special thanks to:

Dale Swan, the great-grandnephew of Anna Swan and the curator of the Anna Swan Museum in Tatamagouche, Nova Scotia.

The Canada Council for the Arts, for providing me with financial support during the writing of this book.

My various editors, namely Kate Ottaviano, Nichole Argyres, and Laura Chasen, for their insightful editorial advice and for spending all those nights and weekends with Anna and Andorra (and with me, I suppose).

My stalwart agent, Wendy Schmalz, who kept pushing this book even as the rejection letters piled up.

A word on those rejection letters: I am grateful to everyone who wrote them. Many of the remarks found in those letters guided me toward the version of the novel that now exists. A stopped clock is right twice a day; a rejection letter is right just about as often.

My mother and Andorra's mother share the same name. My father loves baseball, which plays a key role in my novel's plot. My future biographer will probably make much of this; cynics, meanwhile, will call it a wild coincidence. Which is the truth? You know, I really don't remember. But I think I'd better thank my parents, just in case.